DRAWN TO THE MAFIA

EVELYN AND LEO ROMANTIC SUSPENSE SERIES
BOOK TWO

KAT SHEHATA

ANGEL BEA PUBLISHING

For Ash

PROLOGUE

*N*icoletta Vanzetti

I HAD three hours to get the job done.

As I drove across the border from Chicago into Wisconsin, I loosened my grip on the steering wheel. It was the middle of the night, and traffic was light. No phone calls from my husband, which meant he hadn't discovered I had left our hotel room.

If he happened to wake, he'd find my note explaining I couldn't sleep and went to the rooftop to enjoy some fresh air. He would be angered when I wasn't there, but my reason for lying would soon be clear.

Everything was going according to my plan—except the weather.

The windshield wipers slapped away a wintery mix of snow and icy rain. Not ideal conditions, but tonight gave me an opportunity to execute my plan, and there was no room for adjustments in my schedule.

Luckily, the lake had not frozen over yet.

Thank God for this small miracle.

No other drivers were in sight when I drove off the highway onto a rural road. At this hour, that was to be expected. The road to our lake house was lined by trees illuminated only by the moonlight and my car's headlights.

I checked the rearview mirror—still no other drivers in sight.

My hands trembled with a mix of nerves and excitement. Everything I had worked for was about to come to fruition. A few more steps. A few more strategic moves, and we would finally have our freedom.

My husband will be shocked at first. Then his Italian rage will settle over him from the betrayal. I had planned everything behind his back, and he had no idea what I was about to set into motion.

As I drove down the winding road, I checked the rearview mirror.

Headlights.

There hadn't been another car for miles. It seemed strange that another driver had caught up with me on the icy road.

Stay calm, Nicoletta.

I pressed my foot to the gas to put distance between us.

I rechecked the rearview mirror. The car was now a safe distance behind. No one had followed me. There was no way anyone could have known my plan. I covered my tracks.

Breathe.

Tonight, after my charity ball, was the only night I could make this work. The only night when I could sneak away. The only night to stop the terror. The only time to right the wrongs. The lies and deception end tonight.

Once I retrieved the briefcase and set everything into motion, the guilty will fall.

Headlights shined in the rearview mirror.

The car behind me was closing in.

The lake house was minutes away. One more turn, and I would cross the covered bridge that led to my family's private estate on the lake.

I pressed the gas pedal. My car skidded on the icy road, but I did not lose control. I was too close now to make a mistake. Freedom was within my grasp.

Focus on your future, Nicoletta.

The covered bridge was just ahead. I checked the mirror. The driver behind me flashed his headlights to get my attention.

My cell phone rang.

Fear chilled my blood when I saw his name on the screen.

No, no, no. He knows. Is he the driver behind me, flashing his headlights?

"*Cazzo,*" I swore in my native tongue.

As I approached the bridge, there was a stop sign. The road across was one-way, and habit told me to slow down to check for oncoming cars, but that *pezzo di merda* was behind me.

With all the snow accumulating on the road, no one else would be stupid enough to be out here, so to hell with habit. I needed to get the job done. I kept my foot on the gas and sped toward the narrow opening.

A set of headlights appeared under the bridge as I was about to pass through—a car was parked under the bridge, blocking the road.

I slammed the brakes to avoid a head-on collision, but I lost control, and instead of slowing the car down, it skidded off the road and—

Crash! The impact into the tree left me stunned.

The car horn blasted as I pushed away the airbag. What was happening? I guessed the airbag had saved my life, but my head was throbbing, and I was having trouble concentrating.

I grasped the handle, pushed the door open, and crawled out of the car. My legs wobbled on the snow-covered grass as I stood. The road. I had to get to the road. Get to the lake house. To the briefcase.

The car was totaled—impossible to drive. No matter. The lake house was a mile away. I would walk there, get the briefcase, and drive one of the other cars parked in the garage to make my getaway.

After I managed to trek back to the road, headlights blinded me.

In my state of confusion, I had forgotten why I had driven off the road.

"Need a hand, Mrs. Vanzetti?" A burst of adrenaline pumped through my veins. Three shadows spread across the road before me. *Which one spoke my name?* No matter, I didn't recognize the voice. They knew me, and I knew who had sent them.

The adrenaline was clearing my head, so I considered my next move. There was no going back now. Failure was not an option.

Stick to the plan, Nicoletta. This is your only way out.

I checked the road behind me. The car that had been following me was still there. The driver had blocked me in. Even if I could start my car, I would never get past them.

A shadowy figure stepped out of the black Mercedes and stalked toward me. When the man stepped into the light, I saw his face.

Oh, God. It's him.

"You thought you could leave me?" He crossed his arms and narrowed his eyes as my betrayal seeped into his blood. "I know your every move, Nicoletta. You disappoint me. Get in the car, and I'll give you a second chance."

"Never." I spat on the ground at his feet as I backed away.

The only way to survive his retaliation was to run. The lake house was just beyond the bridge. If I cut through the woods, I could elude the men. Once I got the briefcase and retrieved the package inside, I would hide until I found a way to escape.

As I backed away, the shadows closed in on me.

Sensing my plan, the leader stepped forward. "No one wants to hurt you, Mrs. Vanzetti. Get in the car, tell us where you hid the package, and we'll take you home. Give us what we want, and we'll forget this ever happened."

Lies. My *famiglia* was unforgiving. The penalty for desertion was death. If I surrendered, I would not live to see the sunrise.

Run, Nicoletta!

I choked back my fear and ran down the hill toward the woods. Once I crossed the creek, I would break into a sprint. They knew my plan, but no one on this earth knew where I stashed the briefcase.

There were six houses on the estate. By the time the men were done searching the property to find me, I would already be gone.

The men yelled in Italian as they chased after me.

"You're only making this harder on yourself."

"You won't get away from us."

"Stop running now, and no harm will come to you."

As I neared the creek, I slipped on the icy embankment and lost my footing. I skidded down the hill on my back and crash-landed on the rocks that lined the water.

I crawled toward the bank as blood and ice dripped down my forehead. I tried to stand so I could run, but my body was not strong enough. As I lay there, stunned, a mob of shadows surrounded me.

The moonlight illuminated the faces of my killers. Of the

four men, I only recognized one of them—the man hovering over me with a jagged rock in his hand.

"Tell us where the package is, and we'll let you live," the shadow leader said.

I clamped my mouth shut. No more would I cave to their demands. I had been controlled and manipulated since I married into the family, and my last act against them would be defiance.

No more would I do their bidding. No more would I bow at their feet. No more would I turn a blind eye to their illegal activities.

In this life, I have no power over these men...but in the next, they will fear my wrath.

"We could've been happy, Nicoletta. This is all your fault." The man I once trusted lifted the rock above my head. His face held no remorse as he prepared to take my life.

Finally, I saw him for what he was—a soulless monster.

As I took my last breath, I screamed an Italian curse:

"Fantasma!"

FREEDOM—EVELYN

I placed the tip of my pencil on a clean sheet of paper and began to draw. My subject was seated by the window a few tables away, gazing at the steady flow of commuters cruising in and out of the coffee shop.

Regulars greeted him by name, but this cool customer acted aloof and uninterested in the attention.

Out of the corner of my eye, I noticed my boyfriend, Leo, stealing glances at me as he checked his phone. Dating a detective had its advantages, but never being able to keep a secret from him was not one of them.

Nothing gets past him.

His gaze shifted between my untouched cappuccino and half-eaten pastry to the sketchbook on my lap. On a typical day, I drank my coffee steaming hot and never let a crumb of my breakfast go to waste.

Although it was normal for me to draw and for him to check his phone as he prepared for work, my subtle change in routine had not gone unnoticed.

I was hiding something—and Detective Ricci knew it.

The tension between us was palpable. Something important was weighing on my mind, but I had been reluctant to talk to him about it because he wouldn't like what I had to say. Instead of opening up and starting a conversation, I was being evasive.

Not something I could get away with in our relationship.

I was quiet. Too quiet. My silence had officially piqued the detective's interest.

Leo placed his phone on the table next to his healthy green smoothie cup, crossed his muscular arms, and focused all his attention on me. I bit my lip to suppress a smile at my incoming interrogation.

His body rocked, and his big arms, tight abs, and broad chest distracted me as I tried to think of something to say to thwart his suspicions. What I had to talk to him about wasn't a bad thing. It was good for me. But knowing how overprotective my sexy boyfriend was, he would not share my enthusiasm.

"Something you want to say, Evelyn?" Detective Ricci's piercing dark eyes were locked and loaded on mine. He knew I found his domineering persona incredibly attractive and was pouring on his alpha male energy to intimidate me.

"You must've read my mind." I peeked through my curtain of sandy brown hair and smiled at him. "I have some good news to share." I put my sketchpad face down on the table and gave him all my attention. Maybe if I breached the subject with an optimistic spin, I might soften the blow.

"I'm going on an adventure today. Something I've been wanting to do for a while, but when I woke up this morning, I felt today was the day to move forward."

"Forward with what?" Leo eyed me skeptically.

"Life. I'm not afraid anymore."

Since my abduction, Leo and I had never spent more than a workday away from each other. He had introduced me to every cop in the city and never let me go anywhere or meet with potential new clients until he had thoroughly run a background check.

In the months after the attack, I craved his attention, and our relationship blossomed from friendship into a deep and passionate love for one another. But now that I was healing from my trauma, Leo and I needed to work toward a new normal.

A life where I wasn't under his surveillance twenty-four-seven, and I was free to walk the city streets of Chicago without Leo serving as my bodyguard. I wanted my boyfriend to walk me to work because we loved each other and enjoyed our morning coffee routine—not because he was afraid someone would abduct me and steal me away from him again.

Leo processed my news silently. Part of him was probably relieved I was healing, but the street-smart homicide detective side of him never wanted me to let my guard down in the Windy City ever again.

I reached across the table and touched his hand. "I'm going out today. I don't know where or what I'll do, and I don't know who I will meet along the way." I inhaled a cleansing breath.

"But whatever happens, I'll be grateful to the universe for leading me into a new adventure."

Leo's expression sharpened. The two of us were on opposite ends of the personality scale. I was a free-spirited artist who let the will of the universe guide me, while Leo was a calculated, no-nonsense alpha male who controlled every situation based on facts.

As I waited for his response, I imagined Leo was mentally tallying all the things that could happen to me as I headed out alone into the city without a weapon, a plan, or the training necessary to get myself out of a dangerous situation.

Today was a milestone moment in our relationship. I was

excited to move forward, but the worried expression on Leo's face suggested we were not in agreement.

"If there's a dead person on that page, the deal is off," Leo finally broke his silence.

I shot my gaze back to Leo and smirked at his dark humor. He was right, and that was one thing we wholeheartedly agreed on. I didn't want to break free so that I could run out and get myself into trouble again.

All I wanted was the freedom to make my own decisions.

"Well, Detective. What do you think about this?" I flipped over my sketchbook and revealed my latest masterpiece. Leo narrowed his eyes as he scrutinized my drawing. It was a sketch of Mr. Jones—the coffee shop cat basking in the early morning sunshine, ignoring his adoring fans.

I had taken some liberties and given the King of the Coffee Shop a royal makeover. I penciled in a crown adorned with jewels, some devil horns, and a leopard print cape. The sketched version of Mr. Jones licked his razor-sharp paws as his loyal subjects bowed before the dark lord.

"I can take a couple of personal days starting tomorrow. I'm glad you feel confident and want to enjoy the city, but please, do it with me."

I squeezed his hand in support of his assessment. I knew he would be happy for me—he loved me—now I just needed to convince him to let me go. "I would love to spend time with you, babe, but today, I need to do this alone."

Leo's internal alarm system was flashing the red-alert sign. Still, I needed him to see me through the eyes of Leo—my loving boyfriend—instead of the homicide detective who dealt with death, danger, and dirtbags for a living.

I tugged on his hand and pulled him over to my side of the table. I was seated on a bench and snuggled into his arms. I laid my hand across his lap and slid my finger into his belt loop, giving the leather a tug.

Leo and I had a secret language, and my naughty gesture made me smile. "You didn't get enough this morning?" he growled in my ear.

I blushed at the memory of our early morning quickie. I buried my head on his chest and gave him a loving squeeze. We were getting some looks for our public display of affection, so I got back on track with our conversation.

"Tell me how I can ease your mind?" I couldn't live under his strict umbrella of protection indefinitely. My abductor was dead. I was no longer in danger. It was time I made a fresh start.

"Have you had any dreams I should be concerned about? Ghosts contacting you for help?"

"No."

"Any automatic drawings of crime scenes or restless spirits?"

"No."

"Any clairaudient messages from beyond the grave pop into your head?"

"No."

Leo tapped his fingers on the table. "What if something happens and I'm not around? We're still trying to figure out what triggers your premonitions."

"If something comes up, I'll use my best judgment."

"Is your phone charged? Do you have your personal protection device?"

"Yes."

Leo's phone buzzed with an incoming text. "Parker's here. I need to go." He leaned down and kissed me on the lips. "Be careful. Don't do anything reckless. No ghost hunting. Stay away from dark alleys. No visiting any of my crime scenes—"

"Deal." Most couples kiss and say "goodbye" or "love you" or "I'll miss you" when they part. Leo and I were not a typical couple, and when a psychic/medium and a homicide detective formed a relationship, it wasn't without complications.

I tracked Leo as he left the coffee shop and entered his partner's car. I would always be grateful to have my strong, protective man, but now, I was ready for my first taste of freedom since my abduction.

Time to come back to life—*again*.

GHOSTS IN THE
GRAVEYARD—EVELYN

A warm summer breeze blew through my hair as I passed through the castle façade and toured the scenic final resting place in search of the perfect spot to draw.

Welcome to Rosehaven Memorial Gardens
Many Hopes Lie Buried Here

The famous cemetery had been on my bucket list since I moved to Chicago, and today was the perfect time to scratch this allegedly haunted landmark off my list.

The cemetery was lightly populated with tourists snapping photos in the historical section, couples holding hands, families strolling the pathways, and a few mourners paying their respects to loved ones in the modern area of the grounds.

Pangs of guilt swirled in my gut, knowing that Leo would not approve of what I was about to do next. I had been honest about my desire to start living a normal life again, but

I had failed to mention that I knew exactly where I was going, what I would do, and who I wanted to connect with.

Since my abduction, Leo had supported me every step of the way as I recovered from my trauma. He held me when my nightmares woke me in the night, comforted me while I healed from my injuries, and encouraged me to return to my art.

I was eternally grateful for my loving boyfriend, but one important issue threatened to come between us—*ghosts*. The problem was, that restless spirits no longer visited me in my dreams. My paranormal gift had dried up.

At first, I was relieved when I got a reprieve from my gift. A ghost-free life seemed too good to be true, but as the weeks and months rolled on, I feared I had lost my ability to communicate with the dead forever.

I was the ghost girl. Evelyn Sinclair, the edgy artist of Halsted. The spooky lady who communicated with the dead through her art. My near-death experience as a teen led me to alter my career path, leave my family and small-town life behind, and even change my name to suit my new personality. I'd gotten used to the new me. I felt empowered on my own.

What if my gift never returned, and I wasn't *me* anymore?

Leo tried to keep me positive by telling me it would return to me when the time was right. He suggested that my paranormal abilities had gone dormant until I was prepared to receive them again.

What bothered me was that instead of communicating with the dead, I started having premonitions. While this new gift would be fantastic if it helped me save lives or alter a grim future, the information I received was just *meh*.

Instead of drawing corpses and crime scenes, I predicted what Leo's mother would make for dinner.

I had drawn flowers in a vase on our kitchen table just

before Leo had brought them home to surprise me. I predicted a new pair of shoes. Dogs I would meet at the park. A broken wine glass. A flat tire…

These lackluster premonitions came to pass ninety-nine percent of the time. On occasion, I got a tiny detail wrong, like when I had a premonition that one of my fellow artists would bring a box of bagels to share at the gallery, but she had brought cupcakes instead.

Not a major change, but enough of a difference that led me to understand that my premonitions were not set in stone. So why was I receiving this useless information?

I once could save lives by communicating with the dead. Now, my gift had been reduced to a paranormal card trick. Visiting the cemetery today was my way of inviting the spirit world back into my life. I was tired of pacing on the sidelines, hoping things would change.

If I wanted my gift back, I would have to work for it.

As I strolled deeper into the memorial gardens, I reached a fork in the path. If I chose to veer right, I would enter the cemetery's historic section. Left would take me to the modern area where the freshly dead were laid to rest.

I closed my eyes, mentally called out to the ghosts in the graveyard, and invited the spirit world to guide me.

I'm here. Let me help you. What is holding you back in this life that is keeping you from moving on to the next?

A clairaudient message popped into my head for the first time in months.

Lago.

HEAVENLY—EVELYN

I typed *lago* into my phone. It was an Italian word that translated to lake.

Excited I'd made a connection, I followed the trail deeper into the cemetery toward a body of water that seemed more like a pond than a lake, but there was no need to get technical.

As I strolled along the path, I noticed a black Mercedes roll up and park on the side of the road that curved around the cemetery. The car sat idle. No one got out. I couldn't make out anyone inside the vehicle because of the dark-tinted windows, but I felt I was being watched.

Now is not the time to be paranoid, Evelyn.

I shrugged off my uneasy feeling and continued toward the body of water. Along the way, I studied the headstones, hoping my sixth sense would give me a jolt when I found the grave of the ghost who made contact.

Many headstones in this modern section featured lifelike portraits of the dearly departed etched into the granite. I followed the faces of the dead until I reached a particular monument that stood out from the rest.

The headstone belonged to a young woman and was adorned with potted flowers and lush greenery. A low fence surrounded her gravesite to deter foot traffic from trampling over her final resting place.

Nicoletta Vanzetti

Twenty-eight years old

Died six months ago today.

It was heartbreaking to see her beautiful face on a gravestone. She died tragically young, and I wondered what had happened. I reached for my phone to research her name, then stopped myself. Why do research when I could get the scoop straight from the source?

I wasn't sure if Nicoletta was the ghost who had given me the *lago* message, but this was a perfect opportunity to use my gift to find out. I moved closer to her memorial and stared into her light-colored granite eyes.

What happened to you, Nicoletta?

In the distance, I heard a car door shut, then another and another. When I had taken the path, I turned around the bend and could no longer see the black car. I didn't want to be in the way of mourners, so I went off the path and found a bench where I could draw privately.

I was close enough to see Nicoletta's memorial but far enough away that I wouldn't disturb anyone visiting nearby graves. I lifted my sketchbook out of my purse, flipped to a fresh page, and placed the tip of my pencil on the paper.

My hand moved across the page as I meditated to relax my mind. I tuned in to the sounds of nature and imagined myself basking in a bright purple light. When my gift took over, I had no idea what I would find on the page when my automatic drawings were complete.

The graphite pencil scratched across the page as the information flowed from my fingertips to the paper. My hand moved quickly and furiously, which meant my communication with the dead was surely returning—then I suddenly stopped.

My concentration had been broken by the heavenly scent of a man's cologne.

I opened my eyes and found a handsome man in a suit, sitting beside me on the bench, admiring my art.

"You're talented." His big brown eyes held a hint of amusement. "How do you draw this masterpiece with your eyes closed, eh?" He held his hands out as he spoke, as if the weight of his heavy Italian accent required hand delivering.

A rush of panic snapped my attention back to center. I dropped my gaze to my sketchbook to find out what I had drawn in front of this stranger. To my shock, I had sketched Nicoletta, but not in my typical post-mortem, crime scene kind of way.

I had depicted her as an angel, soaring over the memorial garden with her wings spread and her long hair blowing in her wake. In the background, I added clouds and a flock of doves who doted on her as if Nicoletta were their heavenly queen.

I was relieved I hadn't drawn the ill-fated beauty as a corpse, but this on-the-nose, lovey-dovey cliché type of art was far from my normal macabre style.

"Uh, thanks. It's a new meditative drawing technique I was testing out." I smiled nervously, hoping the stranger accepted my explanation.

"Did you know my wife?" He nodded at her memorial.

When I followed his gaze, I noticed dozens of beautiful roses and vibrant exotic floral displays had been placed at her memorial while I was drawing. I remembered the date on her headstone and realized today was the six-month anniversary of her death.

"No, I never met her. I was just walking by and felt inspired."

"Fascinating." He eyed me curiously as if I looked familiar. "What is your name?"

I didn't want to lie, but people often recognized me. I had gained notoriety as an artist and made headlines when I helped Chicago P.D. end the reign of a serial killer.

I didn't want to turn our chance meeting into an awkward situation. If he associated my name with the fact that I was the spooky artist on Halsted who painted the dead, I didn't want to offend him by having the gall to sketch his late wife. "Hi, I'm Eve."

"It is lovely to meet you, Eve. I am Stefano Vanzetti." The introduction rolled off his tongue as if he had announced himself as royalty. He pushed his shoulder-length black hair away from his face and then extended his hand to initiate a formal greeting.

The guy had a raging, bossman energy packed with enough *oomph* to uproot a tree. He grinned confidently while waiting for me to snap out of my stupor and shake his expensive hand.

"Nice to meet you, too, Stefano. I'm very sorry for your loss. I hope I haven't disturbed you. I'll go—"

"Is your art for sale?" He pointed at the drawing. His fingers were loaded with gold rings and dark, precious gemstones, and his watch sparkled from all the diamonds.

Stefano's confident vibe outed him as a man accustomed to getting what he wanted. Unfortunately for him, my automatic drawings were not for sale. "I can't take your money for a sketch."

"Of course, you can. Name your price." I sensed Stefano was the kind of businessman who wouldn't take no for an answer. He had that king of the jungle arrogance and considered me his easily manipulated prey.

"I'm sorry, Stefano. My drawings are not for sale—at any

price." I closed my sketchbook and slid it back into my purse, ending the negotiation.

"Ah, I understand. What about solid gold bricks? A generous donation to your favorite cause? Maybe an exotic sports car mysteriously shows up in your garage tomorrow?"

I laughed at his negotiation technique, feeling grateful he wasn't taking my refusal personally. However, the awkwardness had reached the tipping point, and I needed to leave.

I wished Stefano a pleasant afternoon and was about to bolt, but as I stood from the bench, I gasped when I realized a muscular man in a tight black suit was standing directly behind us.

The big guy had a short, military-style haircut and a clean-shaven face. He held his position and didn't react to me nearly jumping out of my skin when I noticed him. I had the impression of a secret service guy turned evil henchman.

Damn, this was one weird encounter.

"Allow me to walk you back to your car, Eve. We were leaving as well." Stefano motioned to the big guy with dark shades, whom I decided was a member of his personal security team. Billionaires were high-value targets and often had around-the-clock protection.

Stefano introduced his guard, Dino, then placed his hand on my back and nodded for me to lead the way. My mind scrambled for a way to separate myself from this duo. Stefano was intriguing, I'd admit, but Dino—yikes.

The good news: I got what I came for—an encounter with a ghost.

The bad news: I had drawn the attention of a powerful man who wanted something from me that I was unwilling to give. Alpha men like Stefano were not accustomed to being denied. With money came power, and the fact that I had refused to cave to his desires made the chase more exciting for him.

Ditch him before he figures out who you are, Evelyn.

As we neared the parking area, an annoying car alarm went off. It was so loud that I covered my ears to block the sound. But as we approached my Audi, I realized the noise was coming from my car.

"Oh, crap." I pointed at my car's busted-out window. "That's mine." I fished my key fob out of my purse and pressed it repeatedly to cancel the alarm. As we approached the vehicle, I saw my driver's window was broken and my steering wheel busted, making the car undrivable.

"Someone broke into my car?" I turned in a circle, looking around for I don't know what. The thief? Bystanders who may have witnessed the crime?

Stefano crossed his arms and clicked his tongue in disgust. "Can you believe these criminals? Don't worry, Eve. I will take care of this for you." He barked orders to his guard, then lifted his hand and snapped.

While Dino made a call on his phone, a black Mercedes rolled up in front of my car. I exhaled a deep breath to calm my nerves. Everything was happening so quickly. I needed a moment to process what was happening.

Before I could devise my own plan, Stefano had already come to my rescue. "The tow truck will arrive shortly, and my driver will take you anywhere you need to go."

Wait. What?

Yes, I needed a tow truck. Yes, I needed a ride. But there was no way I was getting into a car with a stranger. "Thank you for the offer, but I don't need a ride. I'm going to call my boyfriend. He's a detective."

"A detective? What's his name?"

"Leo Ricci."

Stefano stared at me in disbelief. "You're Leo's girl?"

"You know him?"

He grinned as he tapped his phone, seemingly to search for evidence.

My jaw dropped to see a photo of a young Stefano Vanzetti with his arm around an adorable pre-teen Leo. "You grew up together?"

As if I needed more proof, he swiped through a timeline of photos with the entire Ricci Family. "Leo and I are like brothers."

Before I could process the connection, Stefano made a call and began speaking in Italian. He seemed to be having a lively conversation with someone, then, a moment later, Stefano handed the phone to me.

"Babe? Are you okay?"

"Leo?" I was shocked to hear his voice. "Yeah, I'm fine. Apparently, I've run into your old buddy."

After Leo made sure I was okay, he told me to wait for a tow truck, then informed me Stefano would give me a ride back to the gallery—where I had a dozen or so of my graphic, gory, and macabre paintings of ghosts on display.

Sheesh. So much for protecting my identity.

MEMORY—EVELYN

When the limo rolled up to the gallery, I thanked Stefano for the ride and hoped he would drop me off and be on his way.

No such luck.

Mira, his lovely brunette chauffeur, opened his door, stood dutifully as her boss exited the vehicle, and then cruised to my side to help me out of the car.

As Stefano escorted me to the door, I thanked him for his help. It was Friday morning. He must have business meetings or something more important to do than babysit me until Leo arrives.

When we reached the door, I pulled out my keys and spotted the steely-eyed bodyguard Dino taking a position at the door as if readying himself for guard duty. "You don't need to go to any more trouble for me. I'm sure you have a busy day planned."

Stefano's big brown eyes fixated on mine. "I promised my friend to make certain you arrived at your gallery. I will wait with you until Leo arrives. There is nothing more important to me today than your safety."

I slid the key into the lock and noticed Stefano eyeing my portrait in the gallery window. It was a painting of me—as a ghost—aiming my finger straight ahead as if blaming the viewer for my death.

He studied the details of my art. My blue-tinted skin and horrified expression, my breasts spilling out over my gown, the harbinger of death with his black-tipped wings and talons for feet swooping down on my tortured soul...

His gaze drifted from the painting then up to the sign above the door:

The Death of Me
An Evelyn Sinclair Gallery

"My style isn't for everyone," I said apologetically as I opened the door.

Once inside, Stefano cruised around the gallery and studied my collection of paintings. On one side of the room, my ghost paintings were on display.

On the other side, I featured my edgy collection of guardian angels charged with protecting the good citizens of the Windy City.

These not-so-heavenly beings were nothing like the peaceful rendition of Nicoletta I had sketched at the cemetery. I only designed *"nice"* paintings for my commissioned projects, like when clients asked me to memorialize their loved ones.

"Evelyn, your talent is immeasurable." Stefano studied one of my latest paintings of a shifty-eyed guardian on duty outside one of the city's iconic churches. The angel lounged on the stairs with her raggedy gray wings spread out behind her like a dirty blanket.

While her body appeared relaxed, her gaze was set on an

elderly couple heading up the stairs toward the entrance of the church. The man had a cane, and the woman clutched his arm as she helped him up the last step until they reached the landing.

When I imagined this scene, I gave the angel one mission: Don't let him fall. I titled the painting, One Last Step.

"Thank you. I love what I do."

"Have you been an artist all your life?"

The question was simple enough, but explaining how I survived a near-death experience and came back to life with an artistic gift was not easy. "I started painting my senior year of high school. Something happened that changed my career path."

"What?"

"I died."

Stefano shook his head, not understanding what I meant.

"I drowned in Lake Cumberland. I was dead for more than five minutes. First responders were able to resuscitate me, but I was in a coma for several days after that."

I continued my story of coming back to life as a different person and how I'd given up my dream of a career in finance and ditched college to become a fine artist.

Stefano listened intently, especially when I explained how ghosts visited me in my dreams. He remained silent when I spoke of the restless spirits that inspired my art and how it was my calling to share their stories through my art.

"What do ghosts want from you? Do they ask for help? Do they frighten you?"

I had to be careful. I kept certain details of my dreams and the entirety of my gift private. Yes, ghosts wanted something from me. Yes, I did everything I could to help them, but I never revealed the nature of my automatic drawings or the extent of my communication with the dead.

"I don't know what they want, but as an artist, I feel compelled to share their stories." A canned answer, but it was partially the truth. Not the whole truth, but that was all I was comfortable sharing.

"What about the angels? Do they visit your dreams?"

"No. The guardians all come from my imagination."

"How long does it take you to paint one like this?" He pointed to the angel painting he had just been admiring.

"A few days. Once I start a project, I go all in until it's complete."

Stefano gave me a sad smile. "Nicoletta would've loved your art. If she had visited your gallery, all your paintings would be displayed in our home right now. She would've adored you too, Evelyn. She was brave. Fearless. Never let obstacles stop her from achieving her goals—*like you.*"

I rubbed my arms to chase away the goosebumps prickling my skin. His comment made me uneasy. True. I was brave, maybe not fearless, but I had plowed over many obstacles and self-doubts when I decided to open my gallery.

Stefano's observation of my character was spot on, but how had he come to this assessment after only meeting me about an hour ago?

"I am certain Nicoletta and I would've become fast friends."

A chime sounded, signaling Leo had arrived at the gallery. "Hey, sweetheart. Everything okay?"

"All good here, babe. You didn't need to leave work to check on me." I knew Leo wanted to grill me about why I had gone to the cemetery and how I had met his friend there, but he would wait until we were alone.

"Thankfully, Stefano was there to help."

Stefano placed his hand over his heart. "I would give my life for this man." He opened his arms and embraced Leo as the two conversed in Italian. Stefano had an accent, but Leo was a native Chicagoan and sounded like the other guys born and raised in the city.

"I've known Leo since I moved here from Sicily when I was a kid," Stefano said. "His mother gave me English lessons at the kitchen table while she stuffed me with chicken parm."

Stefano grinned at the memory. "I spent more time at Leo's house than my own. I can still taste Silvia's Sunday gravy and your father's Pabst Blue Ribbons."

Stefano was doing all the talking while Leo listened and gave him a half-hearted smile. "Nicoletta passed away six months ago today, right? Is that why you were at the cemetery?"

"The accident. It's a tragedy I'll never get over." He paused to collect himself. "The flowers and notes of sympathy from your family meant the world to me. I'm sorry I've been out of touch over the years. I have no excuse—"

"Hey, you don't need one," Leo said. "You'll always have a place at my mother's table."

My heart swelled with compassion as Stefano's expression lit up as if a heavy burden had been lifted from his shoulders.

A round of guilt washed over me as I played back our meeting at the cemetery. He was there to honor Nicoletta's memory, and I had disturbed his somber day by sketching her portrait. Then I denied him when he asked if he could have the drawing.

Damn. Stefano must think I'm a horrible person. I never gave away my automatic drawings, but I hadn't sketched anything disturbing and should've just handed it over.

"Thank you for taking care of Evelyn today," Leo said. "I don't want to keep you from your work. Give me a call if you're ever in the neighborhood."

Leo was in a rush to get Stefano out of the gallery. If I had to guess why, I was sure it had to do with my art. There were paintings of dead people everywhere. *Ugh.* I couldn't think of a more uncomfortable setting for a grieving man.

My simple yet uplifting sketch had brought him joy, and I crammed it back into my purse like a used candy wrapper.

Leo's skin is going to curdle when I tell him the story.

As we headed for the door, I realized it wasn't too late to make up for my insensitive decision. Leo was going to be angry when I told him about how I had spent the morning drawing in public, and out of all the gazillion graves in the cemetery, I had zeroed in on his buddy's wife's memorial.

But, my window of opportunity was closing. When we reached the door and said our goodbyes, Stefano paused and took one last look at my collection of guardian angel paintings.

I nearly choked on my guilt. I would never forgive myself if I didn't give him the sketch he desperately wanted. "Wait," I said to Stefano. "Before you go, I want you to have this." I offered him the drawing.

Stefano waved his hand and refused my offer. "I respect your decision not to part with your art. I cannot ask you to compromise your morals."

Relieved he had given me an out, I slid the drawing back into my purse. "Well, if there is anything I can do for you, please don't hesitate to ask."

Stefano raked his hands through his thick, dark hair as he considered my offer. "You know, Evelyn. I think there is something you can do for me."

"Anything," I said.

"Nicoletta's passion in life was helping people. She started a foundation that served hospitalized children while they received life-saving medical care."

Stefano shifted his attention to the angel section of the

gallery. "Her charity fundraiser is coming up next Saturday. This is the first event since her passing. I don't want her memory to be forgotten."

"What can I do to help? Donate a painting for the silent auction?"

"No. I want you to paint Nicoletta's portrait."

CRASHED—LEO

I loved Evelyn. I trusted her and was confident she had a reasonable explanation of why she had gone to a cemetery to sketch today. But the idea of her drawing Nicoletta and sharing details of her gift with Stefano Vanzetti had my blood boiling.

Was this her idea of staying out of trouble?

My gut told me to get ahead of this situation before it went any further. I never wanted to be the kind of man who forbade his girlfriend from doing something, but this whole "I need my freedom" spiel this morning seemed calculated.

Did Evelyn get her gift back and fail to tell me?

What if Nicoletta visited her in a dream and pointed her toward the cemetery? As my detective's brain tallied the evidence that suggested Evelyn had lied to me, I considered the facts.

First, Evelyn had *not* drawn Nicoletta as a corpse or any gory scenes from the accident. The sketch showed Nicoletta as an angel—not a ghost.

Nicoletta died in an accident. No foul play, no need for

revenge. It was possible that Evelyn's drawing of Nicoletta was meant to affirm that her soul was at peace.

While that seemed plausible, the evidence contradicted that theory.

Evelyn sees ghosts, not spirits. I had no idea there was a difference until I met a medium. A ghost is a restless soul with unfinished business. Something in this life that was holding them back from the next—that's why they came to her for help.

Spirits, on the other hand, were at peace. They were the glowing, happy souls who crossed over and lived the good life in the Great Beyond. But Evelyn had only seen spirits once—when she was about to die at the hands of a serial killer.

Secondly, Stefano Vanzetti was an old friend from the neighborhood. The timing of Evelyn's freedom proclamation landed on the six-month anniversary of Nicoletta's death. Had Evelyn's sixth sense alerted her to go to the cemetery today?

Did she sense Stefano's connection to me?

Lastly—and this was the most disturbing reason—today was the first day since the abduction that Evelyn had gone out in public alone. This was a significant milestone in our relationship, and I would've never let her go if it had been up to me.

Her gift was dangerous. She could communicate with the dead—a resource money could not buy. And on the first day, in the first hour, the first time she went out in the city without me, my old buddy showed up out of the blue and made a connection with her.

My brain kept circling back to the same question—*why?*

Only two scenarios made sense:

Evelyn had been drawn to the cemetery by a paranormal force.

Or Stefano had been waiting in the wings until he found his moment to contact her.

I didn't have enough information yet to make a judgment call, but there was something suspicious about this *chance* meeting at the cemetery today. I didn't want Evelyn near Stefano until I knew who or *what* had caused this setup.

"The event is next Saturday? That doesn't give you much time, Evelyn." I needed to give her an easy out. Everything was happening too fast, and we needed to hit the brakes.

Stefano shook his head when he realized he had gotten ahead of himself. "Of course, it is impossible for you to create one of your masterpieces on such short notice. Forgive me for—"

"I can do it," Evelyn said. "But I have to start right away. I need pictures, details about Nicoletta's life, things she loved, places that made her happy—"

"The lake house," Stefano replied. "She loved everything about it. The birds, the water, the serenity of nature. It's not far. Only an hour away in Wisconsin."

"Perfect," Evelyn said. "I can swing by and do some preliminary sketches. Then we can talk about what I should incorporate into the painting."

I stood there, stunned, watching Evelyn and Stefano cook up a plan that seemed impossible. I'd seen Evelyn work, and she only painted that fast when she sketched her automatic drawings—art that came to her from the dead.

"I have an idea," Stefano said. "You and Leo will be my guests at the lake house this weekend. I'm heading there after work. We can spend some time together, Leo and I can catch up on old times, and you can experience firsthand how Nicoletta lived her life."

"Perfect! Leo just told me this morning that he would take a couple of days off."

It was like watching a train derail in slow motion. One minute we were chugging down the tracks, saying our good-byes, then a split second later, the conversation veered toward a dead woman. *Boom!* The entire weekend crashed into a Big. Fucking. Disaster.

HEADLIGHTS—LEO

Evelyn cranked up a country music playlist as we cruised out of the city and crossed the border into Lake Brickell, Wisconsin. While her car was in the shop, she rented a convertible Mustang for our road trip.

With the windows down, the warm summer breeze blew through her gorgeous long hair as she sang along to her favorite songs. Even though I didn't love the idea of spending the weekend at Stefano's place, I still had reservations about the whole thing, I was happy to see my girl having fun and doing what she loved—painting the dead.

Life had been crazy busy for us over the last several months. Evelyn's career had skyrocketed, and her paranormal-themed gallery was the hottest ticket in town. She constantly had art shows, tours, and tons of publicity surrounding her cool and edgy paintings.

I knew she was upset about losing her ability to communicate with ghosts, but even though I never wanted to see her sad, I was relieved her gift had not returned. Playing junior detective for the dead almost got her killed. I never wanted her to go through that trauma again.

"What do you want to listen to next, babe?" Evelyn reached over and slid her fingers under my shirt collar and lightly scratched my neck with her long, black-painted fingernails.

Her touch excited me, and I stole glances at my sexy girl-friend. Her perky breasts bounced when we went over a bump in the road. I was ready to strip that pale blue summer dress off her toned and sexy body.

Evelyn lowered her shades and tossed me a flirtatious grin when she busted me checking her out. "See something you like, Detective Ricci?"

Damn. Evelyn was the hottest woman on the planet and knew how to turn me on. When she called me *Detective,* I wanted to steer off the road, slam the car in park, and devour her.

She turned down the music, brought her hand to my leg, and squeezed my upper thigh. She gave me a sultry smile as she slid her dress up her leg, giving me a taste of what I had to look forward to when I got her alone.

"Show me your panties," I said.

"Sorry. I'm not wearing any."

God, help me.

Evelyn cracked up at her sexy little joke then her expression turned serious. "Before we get there, can you tell me about Nicoletta?"

"Like what?"

"How did she die? I've meant to look it up online but haven't had a chance."

"She was killed in a car accident not far from the lake house."

Evelyn nodded as if something about her cause of death seemed to answer a question.

"Did Nicoletta make contact with you at the cemetery?" I didn't want to ruin our peaceful drive, but asking the necessary questions now was better than waiting until we got to the house. I hated surprises and wanted to know what, if anything, was heading our way.

"I'm not sure," Evelyn said. "I got a clairaudient message at the cemetery. But in a memorial garden packed with dead people, I had no way of knowing where it came from."

"What was it?"

"*Lago.*"

"That translates to lake in Italian."

"That's what steered me out of the cemetery's older section. There was a small pond over by the modern area—the same section where Nicoletta was laid to rest."

"So, you don't know *who* lured you to that section?"

"Correct."

Once we turned off the highway, we left the city behind. The road to the lake house was lined with trees, and instead of the omnipresent hustle of street noise, Lake Brickell offered a symphony of cawing crows paired with the wind rustling through the leaves.

We were quiet as the road wound around the bend and headed toward a one-lane covered bridge. As we approached, Evelyn's eyes widened. She sat up straight in her seat as if something ahead had spooked her. "Can we take another route?"

The old wooden bridge was as rickety as an old toolshed. It looked creepy, and I had faith that if Evelyn got a bad vibe from it, she was probably right.

"There is only one way to the lake house, and it's through that bridge. We'll have to turn back if we don't cross here."

Evelyn frowned, unhappy with her choices. "Okay. I'm going to close my eyes. Tell me when we're through."

Evelyn curled onto her side and covered her face with her flowy summer dress. I rolled forward slowly, as she requested, then waited at the entrance to check for incoming cars. Once I was sure it was clear, I rolled through, but when I crossed over the water, Evelyn's breathing got heavier, and she covered her hands over her ears.

Once we reached the other side, Evelyn placed her hand over her heart and took a few deep breaths to calm herself. She shot her gaze to mine and said, "*Fari.*"

I'd been around Evelyn long enough to understand what was happening. She had just received another clairaudient message—a word that comes from the spirit world.

"Do you know what it means?" she asked.

The driveway to the lake house was just ahead. According to the news article, Nicoletta Vanzetti was killed in a single-vehicle crash less than a mile from her vacation home.

Judging by the accident's proximity and the fact that *lago* and *fari* were both Italian, I feared the sender of the messages could have come from my friend's late wife.

I met Evelyn's weary gaze. "Headlights."

HAUNTED—EVELYN

Stefano Vanzetti was a liar.

I knew it when we rolled up to his not-so-humble abode. This was not simply a lake house. It was an early 1900s-era sprawling mansion with multiple properties tucked behind a security gate that spanned the entire complex.

Leo checked the GPS and then stared at the address placard on one of the massive stone pillars that marked the entrance.

"This is Stefano's place?" I pointed to the two-story main property with pointy turrets and gables, multiple chimneys, and an ornate fountain that curved around the water's edge.

As we stared at the house, a heavy security gate opened, inviting us into the compound.

"Apparently so." Leo rolled through the open gate and parked in front of a set of garage doors. He grabbed our bags from the trunk, and as we padded to the front door, I studied the architecture of the historic mansion.

The home had several wings of varying levels. The section on the right was all glass and appeared to be a garden room. The sun shone through, giving a jaw-dropping view of the lake and the botanical garden with colorful flowers in full bloom.

There were so many windows on the second level I estimated the mansion had at least a dozen bedrooms. As I considered the size of the estate, I wondered if it had been originally designed as a private residence or if it had been built as a hotel.

"Want to place a bet?" I shot Leo an ornery grin.

"What kind of bet?"

"I'll bet you a million bucks this place is more haunted than the nine levels of hell."

"That's not funny."

"Nothing screams, *"I'm haunted!"* louder than a secluded mansion tucked away on about twenty acres of lakefront property without a neighbor in sight."

This century-old house with its flowing white curtains, creaky weathervane, and windows resembling spooky eyes was a restless spirit thirst trap. My goal was to get my gift back—no better place to start than a haunted lake house.

Leo's expression turned serious. "If you don't want to stay here, we can leave after dinner."

"Are you joking? This place is a medium's playground." I knocked into his shoulder as I cracked up, but Leo didn't appreciate my humor. "Seriously, though. I don't feel like myself anymore. I want my gift to come back. This place might help me get back to normal—well, my version of normal, anyway."

When we reached the entrance, I rang the doorbell. A bong chimed, alerting our host that we had arrived.

Leo gave me one last out as we waited for Stefano to answer the door. "If anything happens here that makes you uncomfortable, say the word, and we're out."

An ominous shadow as thick as a rhinoceros appeared on

the other side of the frosted glass. A lock clicked. The door slowly opened. Dino opened the door. "Welcome to the Vanzetti Estate." He gave us each a once-over, paying particular attention to Leo.

Since he oversaw security, I figured he was checking to see if Detective Ricci was packing heat—which he was not. Once we were cleared, Dino swept his arm forward and invited us inside. He spoke to Leo in Italian and then motioned to the bar where we were apparently meant to wait for the boss.

"Wow, the décor is stunning." White leather furniture. A gourmet kitchen with an island that wrapped around to a fully stocked bar. Windows from floor to ceiling showed off a gorgeous view of the lake as far as the eye could see.

I marveled at the white marble floors, the massive crystal chandelier, and the open staircase that led to an open-style balcony with a black iron railing. Most of the furniture had been updated to a more modern style, but the fixtures appeared original, giving the home a cool retro vibe.

Dino grabbed our bags and carried them off—I assumed to some guest suite on the far side of the house. Seeing a guy bigger than Leo was rare, but Dino had at least thirty extra pounds of pure muscle on him.

Stefano must really be concerned about his safety.

A moment later, the boss man greeted us with a broad smile and open arms. Stefano had ditched his suit and opted for a more casual and relaxed lake life ensemble of a breezy linen shirt, white slacks, and leather loafers.

His shirt was unbuttoned a couple notches, and I snuck a peek at a cross pendant resting atop a thick blanket of dark chest hair. Stefano was a handsome man, and I wondered how long he would wait before he was ready to find love again. A sexy, billionaire bachelor like him would have a line of intelligent and beautiful women waiting to meet him.

"Ciao, bella." Stefano leaned in and kissed my cheeks. His warm lips lingered on my skin a moment longer than I had become accustomed to with Leo's Italian family. When Stefano pulled back and met my gaze, his aura was glowing.

"Welcome, friends. Thank you for coming." He greeted Leo in kind, and the two conversed in Italian.

Leo hadn't initially been thrilled I had planned this whole trip without talking to him about it first but seeing him enjoying a conversation with his old friend gave me hope that he would have fun on our impromptu trip.

I never had the chance to ask Leo why he and Stefano had fallen out of touch. They seemed to have grown up like brothers, and I wondered why Leo had never mentioned him. I had been to his mother's house plenty of times, and Silvia never spoke of Stefano, either.

Her living room was plastered with photos of the Ricci family and their friends from the neighborhood over the years, but I couldn't place Stefano in any of them. I knew photos existed because Stefano showed them to me on his phone.

Did something happen that tore their friendship apart?

THESE WALLS HAVE EYES—LEO

Our evening kicked off with a round of drinks outside on the veranda and the promise of a tour of the largest lakefront estate in the county.

Stefano's phone buzzed a few times since we had arrived. He'd been ignoring it but finally gave in and checked his messages. "Forgive me, I must take a call," he said. "I will ask Mira to give you a tour while I attend to business."

A moment later, Stefano's sophisticated driver joined us on the veranda and stepped in to show us around. He introduced her as the resident expert on the history of the estate and assured us we were in good company.

Evelyn and I held hands while Mira led us down a stone-lined path. There were multiple guest cottages, a carriage house, and a retro-fitted garage that housed Stefano's exotic sports cars.

"An infamous real estate tycoon built the Hillcrest Estate during the Prohibition Era. There are six properties on the grounds. While it was officially designed as a hunting lodge, it was notoriously referred to by the locals as the Bootlegger Estate."

"No way," Evelyn said. "This place was a lake house speakeasy?"

Mira twisted her red-painted lips and nodded. "Chicago's high-class clientele enjoyed live music, dancing, and the whiskey flowed like water. The house where I stay allegedly served as a brothel." She pointed to a two-story home next door to the main house.

"When Nicoletta was alive, she and Stefano hosted lavish parties every weekend. The guest houses were full, and the fun never ended. But now—"

Overcome with sadness, Mira paused. "I'm grateful the two of you are joining Stefano this weekend. This is the first time I've seen him happy since Nicoletta passed. I hope this is a sign that he is ready to start living again."

Mira touched her heart. "The four of us were like a little family. Losing our dear Nicoletta has been difficult for all of us."

"The four of you?" I asked.

"Stefano employs a full-time security detail. Dino was Nicoletta's primary bodyguard. I know he comes off as cold, but he is a sensitive soul. He was distraught after the accident and cried every night for weeks."

Interesting. My detective's brain zeroed in on a key detail —Nicoletta was alone when she was killed in the wreck. Strange for a woman with around the clock security. "Why wasn't Dino with Nicoletta on the night of the accident?"

Evelyn squeezed my hand, letting me know my question was insensitive.

"Good question, Detective Ricci. Unfortunately, we will never know," Mira said. "Nicoletta and I were like sisters. We shared everything, but I do not know why she left the hotel alone after her charity event." Mira was quick to drop the subject and continued the tour.

"I've saved the best for last—The Grand Ballroom." She

led us inside a detached room connected to the main house by a covered breezeway.

When we reached the ballroom, Evelyn rubbed her arms as if shaking off a chill. This side of the estate was hotter than Hades. No air conditioning was running on this wing, and if Evelyn had felt a cold blast, it hadn't come from an air vent.

Evelyn's bright blue eyes sparkled as she scanned the room and admired the massive hanging candelabra and about a hundred candles ready to illuminate the room when night fell.

"Can you imagine the energy in this room when all these candles are burning?" She squeezed my hand.

I didn't want to be a killjoy, but the idea of Evelyn in the midst of all that "elemental energy" was a paranormal Molotov Cocktail I hoped she never got the chance to light. I moved to the wall and studied a collection of black and white photographs that dated back to the Roaring Twenties.

There were pictures of flapper girls and dapper gentle-men, dancing and imbibing in this room alongside family portraits of the original owners who built the estate a century ago. One photo, in particular, caught my attention. It was a sepia-toned oval portrait of a little girl with pigtails and big, sad eyes.

"That was Miss Bridgette Hillcrest, the owner's baby daughter. Poor child died during the influenza pandemic at the age of five. Her parents were so distraught they carved out a small parcel of land to serve as a family burial plot. Mrs. and Mrs. Hillcrest wanted their family to remain together forever. The entire Hillcrest family is buried on these grounds."

"Do you think the estate is haunted?" Evelyn asked excitedly.

"Nicoletta believed these walls have eyes." Mira pushed

her dark-rimmed glasses up her nose and grinned mischievously. "I do not believe in ghosts, but I will confidently tell you that strange things happen here at night."

She leaned in closer as if telling a secret. "One time, Nicoletta told me she heard a child laughing in one of the bedrooms upstairs. She checked all the rooms, but there wasn't a soul around. But, a single light was on in the bedroom that had once served as the nursery."

"Did Nicoletta believe it was little Bridgette's ghost?"

"There are no ghosts here." Mira corrected herself as if feeling guilty for being disloyal to her employers by spreading a rumor. "Nicoletta had a wild imagination."

Great. The entire Hillcrest family probably haunts this place.

LIKE THE DEVIL—LEO

*S*tefano dismissed his household staff for the evening so we could have our privacy. Dinner was warm in the oven. All we had to do was carry a tray of appetizers outside and open a bottle of wine to enjoy before the Italian feast.

Evelyn was delighted when our host asked her to light the candles on the veranda and choose a playlist for the dinner party. I watched her through the window as she spread out a tablecloth, arranged fresh-cut flowers in a small vase, and placed a cluster of candles around the table to serve as our centerpiece.

"Where did you meet?" Stefano nodded to Evelyn as he poured a bottle of vino into a decanter.

"At a coffee shop. I busted her drawing my portrait. It gave me an excuse to strike up a conversation."

Stefano grinned. "Same way I met her."

I had yet to grill Evelyn about every detail leading up to her meeting Stefano. Still, it irked me that she had set up shop in a cemetery, essentially inviting strangers to watch her draw and initiate a conversation.

"Yeah. Drawing is her thing."

Evelyn shaded her eyes with her hand and watched a blue heron cruise over the water toward a small undeveloped island a good distance from the house. The evening summer breeze blew the fabric of the gauzy white dress she had changed into for dinner.

When the bird had flown out of sight, she turned her attention back to the table and lit the candles. Her sixth sense must've alerted her that she had an admirer. She looked up and met my gaze as I watched her through the window.

Then my beautiful, easygoing girlfriend blew me a kiss.

"You are a lucky man, Leo." Stefano carried the wine outside just as Evelyn turned on the music.

True to her style, she selected an upbeat playlist to set the tone and rocked her shoulders in time to the music. When Stefano approached her, he set down the wine and waved his hand over the table, probably complimenting her fine work of setting the table.

I grabbed the tray of apps and went outside to join the party.

Evelyn pulled me to the veranda's edge to watch the sunset over the lake. "Can you believe this is our view for the entire weekend?" Evelyn's complexion glowed as she watched the sky turn a soft shade of pink.

I wasn't angry with her for wanting her freedom, but I was concerned that she was oblivious to the fact that she was a gorgeous and talented woman that attracted a lot of attention. I imagined when Stefano Vanzetti spotted Evelyn drawing in the cemetery, he was more interested in meeting *her* than he was in the sketch of his late wife.

Stefano focused all his attention on my girlfriend as we shared marinated vegetables, cheeses, dry sausages, and fruit from the charcuterie board.

"I must ask you a question, Evelyn," Stefano said. "Something you said at the gallery has stuck with me, and I can't get it out of my head."

"Really? What?" Evelyn sipped her wine as she eagerly waited for his answer.

Stefano shook his finger at her playfully. "You said before you died, you had your heart set on a career in finance. What were you planning to do?"

I stabbed an olive with a toothpick and popped it into my mouth. I had known Evelyn for months and never asked about her life as the overachiever *Lauren Murphy*—her name before she changed it. She never talked about her life before the accident. I figured it was because she wanted to leave the past behind her.

"Get a job with one of the Big Four and work my way up the corporate ladder. Or dive into a career on Wall Street. Or become the CFO for a venture capitalist and score a couple million before I turned twenty-one."

Evelyn laughed at her ambitious goals, but she was being humble. Her current investment portfolio was in the seven figure range.

"You may not know this, but I am the CEO of a financial services company, Vanzetti Investments." Stefano drummed his fingers on the table. "What is the square root of 576?"

"Seriously?" she scoffed. "Is this a test because you think I'm exaggerating my skills?" She sipped her wine and stared at the lit candle on the table, something she did while trying to calm her mind.

After a moment of uncomfortable silence, Stefano spoke. "My apologies, Evelyn. I meant no disrespect. I simply—"

"Twenty-four," she answered. "There isn't a math problem I can't slay. Have you ever heard the term *mathlete*?"

Stefano's eyes were wild with excitement as Evelyn elaborated on her love of high school math competitions and how she holds some record for the highest score at some brainiac state conference.

Good to know a little bit about you, Lauren.

Over a dinner of all my favorite Italian dishes, Stefano and I reminisced about our childhood. We told lively stories about getting into trouble with my best friend, Christopher Santoni.

"You won't believe me, Evelyn, but I was as innocent as a little lamb when I met Leo and Christopher. For a couple of guys who grew up and became cops, they got into more trouble than all the other boys in the neighborhood."

"What about you? Are you saying you didn't do anything wrong?" Evelyn asked.

"No." Stefano patted his mouth with a napkin. "I worshiped Leo and Christopher. I went along with every bad idea they came up with, but—I was smarter than them and never got caught."

"Ouch. He burned you, Leo." Evelyn patted my leg and laughed at Stefano's recollection of the past.

Stefano was right. Santoni and I were the only ones who got into trouble, but it wasn't because Stefano was smarter than us. It was because when we were confronted, we owned our mistakes and accepted the consequences that followed.

Stefano, however, lied like the devil to keep himself out of trouble.

BUBBLES—EVELYN

That evening, Leo and I cuddled in bed and listened to the chorus of nature outside our window. I yawned and rested my head on his chest. The soothing sound of his heartbeat helped me relax.

I was exhausted and ready to sleep, but I had a nagging question I had been meaning to ask Leo about. "Did you know Nicoletta?"

"Stefano and I had lost touch over the years. My family wasn't invited to their wedding."

Leo's answer surprised me. He and Stefano had once been close friends. I understood they had taken different paths in life, but I sensed a touch of bitterness in Leo's voice, leading me to believe there may have been a rift that caused them to distance their relationship.

"Why did Mira allude to a mystery about Nicoletta's accident? There's more to the story than just a car wreck. What was she talking about?"

Before I went to sleep under Stefano's roof, I needed to know a few basic questions about his late wife. The clairaudient messages I had received were vague, and I wasn't sure they had come from Nicoletta, but I couldn't rule it out either.

"Nicoletta died a few hours after her charity fundraiser. She and Stefano were staying at a hotel in Chicago on the night of the party. Sometime during the night, Nicoletta left the hotel, drove to Wisconsin—presumably on her way to this house—and skidded off the snow-covered road."

"That's awful," I said. "Why did she leave the hotel alone to come here?"

"That is the mystery."

"Did she die instantly?"

"This part is even stranger than the mystery of why she left the hotel," Leo said. "After she crashed into a tree, she survived the initial impact. She must've been delirious from a head injury because she exited her vehicle and wandered into the woods, where she slid down an embankment and hit her head on a rock."

I flinched from the horrific image of Nicoletta's cause of death. "That seems *strange*."

"There was a winter storm that night. Six inches of snow accumulated around her car after the accident."

I shook my head in disbelief. "Did she die close by?"

"Less than a mile from here."

Near the covered bridge. I felt a sense of dread when we passed through. Places have a way of holding onto the memories of past events and preserving the terror.

When tragedies occur, the emotions of the living are imprinted on the landscape where the event happened. Battlegrounds, hospitals, prisons, and sites of natural and manmade disasters with large death tolls. Crash scenes.

"Do you think my clairaudient messages are coming from Nicoletta?"

"I don't know." Leo kissed me on the forehead and rubbed

warm circles on my back. "What do you want me to do if you have a nightmare?"

A reasonable question given the fact that we were spending the night in a presumably haunted house. "People have nightmares. I'm sure Stefano will understand if I wake up screaming, especially given my history—and the back-story of the Bootlegger Mansion."

I cracked a smile and sat up to face him. "There's a family graveyard on the grounds, Leo. If a restless spirit doesn't contact me in this place, I'm out of the ghost business for good."

Leo's stern expression alerted me that he was not as excited as I was about dreaming of the dead. I kissed him softly on the lips. "Good night. Love you."

"Are you too tired to…" He slid his hands down my back-side and squeezed my ass. "Want to give the Hillcrest ghosts something to think about?"

"Leo, we can't do it here. Everyone will hear us. Sorry, babe. I'll make it up to you when we get home."

I rolled on my side and thought about the mystery of Nicoletta's accident as I drifted off to sleep.

DRIP...DRIP...DRIP...

The sounds of dripping water roused me from a deep sleep. I sat up in bed and glanced around the room. The sheer white curtains billowed from the gentle breeze blowing outside. I was certain we had closed the window before bed.

Had Leo opened it in the night?

As I pondered the thought, a woman appeared from the shadows. She lifted her arm and pointed over my shoulder. Water dripped from her fingers as she moved past me in a trance-like state.

Through the darkness, I couldn't make out her features. She was tall and wore a dress that clung to her body. Her hair was long and stringy from being soaking wet.

"Who are you?"

The woman whipped her head around and rushed toward me when she realized I could see her. She tried to speak, but her mouth was full of water, and she was choking on her words.

Water spewed from her mouth as she shook her head violently, trying to expel the massive volume she had swallowed. The woman lumbered toward me with her finger still aimed out the window as she desperately tried to communicate.

"I'm sorry, I can't understand what you're saying."

The woman drifted past me and beckoned me to follow her. When I stepped out of bed, my toes squished in the mud when I planted my bare feet on the floor. I was no longer in the bedroom. I was outside the mansion by the water's edge.

This is a dream.

Lake water lapped at my ankles as the moon illuminated the night sky. A horrible stench of death lifted from the lake. I covered my nose and mouth to block the smell. The woman who had entered my dream pointed into the darkness as if she wanted me to follow her into the water.

Her violent choking fit had calmed, and it seemed instead of telling me what she wanted me to know, the woman wanted me to follow her out to the putrid-smelling water so she could show me.

Slowly, I backed away. There was no way I would follow a restless spirit into the abyss. When the woman suspected I was taking a hard pass on her invitation, she reached out and tried to grab me.

Horrified, I ran back toward the house. When I had nearly reached the veranda, a pair of ice-cold, bony hands grasped my ankles and dragged me all the way back and into the water. As my body went under, I screamed for help, but my plea was reduced to a violent rush of bubbles.

I struggled to free myself as my body sank deeper and deeper. Something heavy was attached to my ankles, dragging me down like an anchor. I flailed my arms and tried to break free, but I was powerless against the weight.

"Wake up, Evelyn!" I told myself. *"Wake up!"*

A strong set of hands grasped my upper arms and pulled me upright.

I panted for air as I shoved Leo away and jumped out of bed. I dropped to my knees, placed my hand over my heart, and forced myself to breathe as I recovered from my nightmare.

"Are you okay, Evelyn?" Leo smoothed my sweaty hair off my forehead.

"I'm okay." I stood to reorient myself and stared out the window into the darkness of the lake as I replayed the details of my nightmare. The scene was so graphic, I felt as if I had witnessed a murder firsthand from the victim's point of view.

The lingering sensation of icy cold hands grasping my ankles. My body being dragged into a watery grave. The helpless feeling of sinking while choking on water, knowing death was imminent. The dream felt so real. I couldn't shake the unsettling feeling of drowning.

There was no mystery about what this ghost wanted—revenge. I never had a nightmare through the eyes of the victim like this before. I buried my head in my hands and tried to push away the horror from my mind.

"Want to talk about it?" Leo asked.

"I need to draw."

Leo grabbed my sketchbook and pencil pouch while I lit a large three-wick candle sitting on the coffee table in the seating area by the window. I concentrated on the wax pooling around the wicks and inhaled a blend of aromatic essential oils used to scent the candle.

As the flames danced, I focused on their energy and closed my eyes to bring myself into a deep state of relaxation. I placed the tip of my pencil on a blank sheet of paper and held my hand in ready position as I counted down and invited the spirits to guide me and help make sense of my dream.

One hundred, ninety-nine, ninety-eight...

My hand moved across the page.

THE POINTING WOMAN—LEO

 atching Evelyn's gift unfold was the most miraculous thing I had ever witnessed. Six months ago, I didn't believe ghosts existed—let alone that the smoking hot artist I'd met at the coffee shop could communicate with them.

While her body relaxed and her mind was on another plane, her hand moved across the page, bringing images to life that would drop a non-believer to his knees. As a homicide detective, I had a front-row seat to some of the most gruesome crimes ever committed. But I was a professional. My job was to process the nasty details and seek justice for the victims and their families.

Evelyn wasn't like me. She never volunteered to speak with the dead or draw these horrific pictures to bring peace to restless spirits. Even so, she handled her gift with class and a level of bravery I had never witnessed outside of my fellow law-enforcement officers.

While I admired Evelyn's commitment to the dead, I hated to see her experiencing graphic nightmares and seeing her draw her horrid sketches. But Evelyn believed her gift was her calling in life and would never walk away from a restless soul in need.

Once her hand stopped moving, she let the pencil roll out of her hand, and then she collapsed from exhaustion. Drawing for the dead zapped her energy, and she needed to rest after completing her work.

I blew out the candle, covered her with a throw blanket, and slid her sketchbook away so I could study her work. I flipped through the pages and tore out the three automatic drawings Evelyn had completed.

As I watched her draw, her hand partially obstructed my view. I had gotten a glimpse of the images but only part of the picture. The first sketch was of a long, skinny bird gliding over the water—like the one that had caught Evelyn's attention earlier.

The bird had its head cocked and looked straight at me as it did a fly-by over the lake.

I slid that one aside and studied the next one drawn from the vantage point of a person looking up from the belly of a ditch or possibly a shallow grave. Dirt was piled around her, and a set of hands raised in a defensive position had been drawn in the foreground.

Above the hole stood three shadowy male figures, peering down at the apparent victim below. I studied each figure, searching for clues about their identity, but Evelyn had not sketched any facial details.

Her drawings were never delivered on the nose. Never once had a ghost come to her, announced their identity, then outed their killer. That was not how Evelyn's gift worked. At best, she got a couple of puzzle pieces, and the rest of the information was up to us to figure out.

When I flipped to the last drawing, I looked at the subject and winced. It was a female form in a long dress, drenched to the bone as if she had just crawled out of the lake. Her soaking-wet hair covered her face, making it impossible to make out her features.

Is this the ghost that visited Evelyn in her dream?

What was most striking about the drawing was the woman's pose. Evelyn had drawn her from the side. Her head was bent forward, her back hunched, and her arm was outstretched, pointing at something or someone not visible in the drawing.

I flipped over the bird sketch and placed the other two drawings side by side to study the details. *Are the women in the two sketches the same person?*

The Pointing Woman had long hair, but the woman in the shallow grave was drawn more like a dark shadow. Neither of their features was visible, making it difficult to identify them as two separate people or the same.

There was no way to make that determination using only the sketches, but Evelyn's dream would likely provide more details about the trio of killers and the woman or women in the drawings.

Evelyn's lapse in dreams had lasted several months, but it was clear her gift had returned in full force. I understood why Evelyn felt lost without her ability to communicate with the dead. Still, as I watched her nightmare unfold and witnessed the terror in her eyes after what she had seen, I was reminded of the old saying:

Be careful what you wish for.

LADY IN THE LAKE—EVELYN

In the morning, Leo was already up and out of bed by the time I woke up. We could talk about the drawings and disturbing details of my dream later, but today was a painting day, and I wouldn't let ghosts bring me down.

Outside the window, I spotted Leo on the dock, prepping Stefano's speed boat for a day on the water. His muscles rippled as he loaded a heavy cooler on deck. His back glistened with sweat, and I reasoned he had gotten up early for a boot camp-style workout before dawn.

I slid into my bikini, covered up with a tank top and a pair of frayed cutoff jeans, and went outside to meet Leo.

"Good morning, babe!" I waved from the veranda.

He met me halfway on the stone-lined path and greeted me with a kiss. "Congratulations."

"For what?"

"You got your gift back."

"Right," I said. "I guess you hid the drawings?"

Leo nodded. "Want to talk about it? I can stay if you don't want to be alone."

"No. We can do that later. I'm relieved my dream wasn't

about Nicoletta. The mystery woman died or was murdered in the lake. *Lago* was a spot-on clairaudient message."

Leo leaned down and kissed me again. When I spotted Stefano headed our way, I realized it was my boyfriend's subtle way of alerting me to stop talking about ghosts.

"*Buongiorno,*" Stefano said as he cruised past us on his way to the dock. He was ready for a day on the boat and dressed in swim trunks and deck shoes.

He was shirtless, and I got a glimpse of his tight abs and thick blanket of chest hair. His body was lean and muscular, and he moved with the confident swagger of a swaying king cobra.

His vibe pulsed a conflicting blend of personality traits. Stefano was kind and generous, funny and outgoing, but something hidden under the surface of his façade didn't blend with his outward appearance.

I wasn't an aura reader, but if I had to guess what it was, I believed Stefano was only showing the side of himself he wanted us to see. Everyone does that to an extent, but I sensed there were parts of him he didn't want Leo and me to meet.

Maybe the off vibe I was getting had something to do with his past. I didn't want to grill Leo about what had come between them that caused their friendship to drift apart. Leo seemed to be proceeding with caution and wasn't a hundred percent all-in for his rekindled friendship.

The problem could've revolved around me. I could communicate with dead people. Knowing Stefano's wife had recently died may have made both the guys uneasy around me because of my gift. Leo knew a ghost was communicating with me, and Stefano might have been worried I would dream of Nicoletta while staying at the house.

"Are you sure you won't come with us, Evelyn? The weather is perfect for boating."

The last time I went out into the lake, I died. I won't make that fatal mistake again.

"You guys have fun. Painting outside on a gorgeous day is my idea of heaven."

"She's afraid of the water," Leo explained.

"Not true. I'm only afraid of lakes. I'll be enjoying the pool later this afternoon."

"As you wish, Miss Sinclair."

"Before you leave, I would love to ask you a few questions and get some photos of Nicoletta. I start my painting process with watercolor studies to create a color palette and make some samples of your preferred poses and expressions for the final piece."

"Of course, Evelyn. I have everything you requested. We can have our meeting over breakfast."

As we enjoyed fresh fruits, pastries, and fluffy omelets prepared by the chef, I interviewed Stefano about his fondest memories of Nicoletta. His eyes shined with adoration as he shared heartwarming stories about their charmed lives and how she loved volunteering at the children's hospital.

He provided an album he had recently put together with his favorite photos and cherished memories. By the time we finished our bountiful breakfast, I believed Stefano was right —Nicoletta and I would've become fast friends.

I smiled when the boat motored up and sped away, radio blasting, grateful the guys would have a fabulous day on the water skipping over the waves and reminiscing about their glory days.

I flipped through the album and selected a candid photo of Nicoletta. She was here, on this veranda, with the wind blowing back her long dark hair. The sun was shining down on her, giving her skin a healthy glow. Her eyes were bright, and her smile gentle and loving.

This was Nicoletta in her natural element.

As I set out my art supplies, I had the eerie sensation of being watched.

I turned to look behind and yelped when I found Dino hovering behind me. "Oh, good morning, Dino. I didn't see you there."

He was dressed casually and assumed the more relaxed lake house style. "Nicoletta loved the birds." He handed me a small journal. "She had names for all of them and believed they were her *angeli*—angels." He forced a smile as he scanned my open bag that held my art supplies.

What do you think I'm hiding in there, a sawed-off shotgun?

I opened the book and flipped through the pages. Dino was right. Nicoletta had made a bird-watching journal and filled the pages with photos, drawings, and observations about her beloved water birds. She described their habits and gave each one a cute nickname.

"Thank you for sharing this, Dino. I can work some of these details into the painting."

He lifted his chin and nodded as if honoring Nicoletta's memory was as important to him as it was to Stefano. "Boss gave me the afternoon off. I was going into town, but I can stay with you if you don't want to be alone." Dino widened his stance and assumed the bodyguard position.

There was a zero percent chance I could work with Dino hovering over me. "Don't change your plans for me. I prefer to paint alone. You would be doing me a favor by giving me time to myself."

Dino did a visual sweep of the perimeter. "Mira is staying next door. If you need anything, she will assist you."

I was relieved when Dino left and was ready to get to work. With the sun shining down, I sketched the outline of her face. As I filled in her features, my mind drifted back to the covered bridge where Nicoletta had died.

Why had Nicoletta left the hotel alone? Why hadn't she woken Stefano and asked him to go with her?"

I stared at her photograph as my mind raced with questions about the accident, her seemingly perfect life, and why she had desperately tried to reach the lake during a winter storm.

I dipped my brush into a pool of pale blue paint and drew a horizon line that separated the lake from the sky. I closed my eyes and tuned in to the sounds of nature to inspire my art.

When Nicoletta was here, she'd heard the same chorus of birds. The same sounds of the water slapping against the dock. The distant high-pitched hum of boat engines…

After painting for what felt like hours, I opened my eyes and gasped at what I had drawn—a watery portrait of Nicoletta floating naked under the water. She held a package in her hands and wore a chain on her ankle attached to a briefcase. Her long hair fanned out around her bloated face and vacant eyes.

This was not the portrait I wanted to paint.

This seemed more like a scene from my dream last night.

On closer inspection, I'd used a pencil and drawn detailed tattoos up and down both arms. In the photos I'd seen of Nicoletta, there was no visible ink on her skin.

Then I found another tattoo. This one was on her hip. It was a heart-shaped charm with the letter 'L' engraved across the center and was attached to a small chain. Was this Nicoletta's tattoo? I had no way of knowing unless there was a picture of her in the nude in one of the photo albums.

Wait a minute. I flipped through the album again and found a picture of Nicoletta wearing a charm bracelet—the same bracelet that appeared in my painting as a tattoo. However, it was an actual piece of jewelry.

Interesting. I wondered if Nicoletta really had that tattoo

on her hip. She didn't have tattoos on her arms, so the ink was symbolic and not meant to be taken literally.

I'll talk to Leo about this later and get his perspective.

I glanced around to ensure no one had seen my disturbing painting of Nicoletta. The boat was still gone, so Leo and Stefano had yet to return. The only other people on the property were Mira and possibly Dino, if he had returned from town.

I checked my watch. Several hours had passed. I looked over my shoulder at the lake house. As soon as I turned my head, I spotted a shadowy figure standing in front of the window on the second level.

Someone is inside the house.

I did a double take, but when I looked again, the shadow was gone. Had I imagined a figure standing there, or had someone been watching me? Mira? No. She stayed in the house next door. Why would she be roaming upstairs in the main house?

I tore the large sheet of watercolor paper off the easel and folded it a million times, making it as small as possible. Then I stuffed it into the bag that held my art supplies to hide the morbid watercolor painting.

Leo had stashed away my drawings from last night, and when we had a moment to ourselves, I could lay them out and compare them.

For now, I needed to focus my energy back on Nicoletta and away from the mysterious, tattooed Lady in the Lake.

BLOODLINE—LEO

It had been years since Stefano and I had been out on the lake together. We'd spent plenty of weekends out on the water with our friends from the neighborhood in our teen years, but never as adults.

Time had ticked on, and we no longer ran in the same circles. Stefano left the neighborhood and moved into a penthouse condo downtown, and I planted my roots close to home.

While he had become a rising star in the business world, I was a beat cop working my way up the ranks to detective. Stefano was a resourceful, hard-working kid, and I never doubted he would grow up to be a successful guy. His parents died when he was young, and he moved to America with his Uncle Luca who raised him.

He had a rough childhood, and I was happy he had grown up and lived a better life, but when I found out he'd become a millionaire and then a *billionaire*—I admit, I never imagined he would be *that* successful.

Once Stefano had found his fortune, he stopped coming over for Sunday dinners, no more flowers for Mom on special occasions, and never dropped by to have a beer and a slice of pizza with his old buddies.

I wasn't mad at the guy for wanting to move on from his past, but it hurt my mom's feelings when he stopped returning her calls and acted like he was too good to be a part of our family anymore.

As Stefano's cigarette boat skipped over the waves, he cranked up the music we used to listen to growing up and joked about all the girls that had turned him down in high school. I thought about what Mira had said about Stefano not having people over since Nicoletta had died.

Seeing him happy and enjoying our day on the water made it impossible for me to hold a grudge against my old friend. Once we sped around the lake for hours, Stefano slowed it down, and we cruised while we had a couple of beers and some sandwiches.

"How did you meet Nicoletta?"

A grin spread across his face. "She arranged a meeting with me to discuss a donation to her charity. When this raven-haired goddess stepped into my office in a curve-hugging suit, I knew one day she would be my wife the moment our eyes met. I didn't know her name or a single detail about her. All I knew was that I had to make her mine," Stefano said.

"As Nicoletta shared her charity's mission statement and showed me pictures of the little angels she volunteered with at the children's hospital, all I could focus on was our future together. Not only was she the most attractive woman I had ever seen, but her passion for helping others made her so desirable. All I could think of was how to convince her to marry me and bear my children one day."

"I'm sure she felt the same way, buddy." I lifted my beer in salute.

While he spoke of his whirlwind romance with Nicoletta,

my detective brain wondered what had happened the night of her charity event that had led her to leave her husband in the middle of the night.

Years of experience as a law-enforcement officer led me to believe something caused Nicoletta to flee the hotel room without waking her husband. That didn't mean Stefano was responsible or even had knowledge that something was wrong, but whatever it was, Nicoletta had chosen to leave without telling him what was bothering her.

As we popped open a couple more beers, we caught up on what was happening in our lives. He asked about Mom and the rest of the family. Then it occurred to me. He hadn't mentioned a word about his Uncle Luca.

"Whatever happened between you and Luca?" I asked.

Stefano took a long swig of his beer. "We had a falling out a few years back. He was going through hard times, so I let him move in with me until he got back on his feet. I was careless with my bank account information, and Luca bled me dry to cover his gambling debts."

"Oh, shit. What did you do?" I asked.

"I take no pride in this, Leo, but I settled the score with my fists."

Damn. That was a side of Stefano I had never known. "Was that the last time you saw him?"

He laughed bitterly. "Luca and I are the only surviving members of the Vanzetti bloodline. I did what needed to be done, but I could never turn my back on my only living relative."

CHILDHOOD MEMORY—EVELYN

By the time the guys got back, I had recouped my lost time and completed a series of watercolor studies of Nicoletta in different poses, angles, and with different expressions.

My arms ached, and I was dehydrated from a long day of working in the sun. I had stayed on the veranda and didn't want to venture inside to grab more water or anything from the fridge because I was worried about the shadowy figure I'd seen in the window.

Stefano's security was tight. No one with more than a single brain cell would enter the property uninvited. Still, my sixth sense warned me something was off about the house—or possibly the people in it.

Maybe I was paranoid, but I was relieved when the guys returned from their boat trip. Leo greeted me with a hot and sweaty hug while Stefano gushed over my paintings.

"Have you been working this whole time?" Stefano asked.

"Yeah. Once I get into the groove, it's hard to stop."

He glanced at his Rolex. "We've been gone for hours. Did you take time to eat? Take a dip in the pool?" His gaze drifted down my bikini-clad body. I had on a t-shirt and shorts, but I felt as if he had undressed me with his eyes.

"I lost track of time. No big deal."

Stefano scoffed. "You are a guest in my home, working yourself to the bone. Leo, please take your girlfriend to the pool while I find something for her to eat. We have let her suffer long enough."

I cracked up at his melodramatic humor as Leo and I headed toward the luxurious, vanishing-edge pool. When I started to unfasten my jean shorts to slide them off, Leo touched my hand and stopped me.

"That's my job."

I blushed and glanced back at the house to ensure Stefano was out of sight.

Leo turned me around and pulled me toward him so my back was against his bare chest. He held one hand on my hip and unfastened the closure with the other. As he slid down my shorts, he trailed kisses down my neck.

I inhaled a sharp breath as his touch brought a wave of warm ripples of pleasure to my core. In response, I wiggled my backside against him as he pulled down my shorts over my string bikini bottom.

"Careful, Evelyn," Leo growled. "I've been thinking about your smoking hot body since you came outside in *this*." He snapped the string of my bathing suit against my skin. "I can't wait to get you alone, beautiful."

"Leo!" I pinched him teasingly in the side. "We can't do it while we are here as Stefano's guests. You're too loud."

I bit my lip and peeked up at him to gauge his reaction. I was the more vocal one, but Leo never met a headboard he couldn't bang against a wall with enough force to knock an entire building over.

Leo nibbled on my ear as his hand slid to my thigh. My body tingled with excitement as he squeezed my ass and whispered what he would do to me once we returned to our room.

"Stop it." I swatted at him playfully as I broke free from his roaming hands, stepped into the pool, and eased into the warm water. Leo's magical touch excited me on every level imaginable, but I didn't want our public display of affection to make Stefano uncomfortable.

I glanced back at the house to see if Stefano had made it back yet. I couldn't see into the kitchen from the pool, but I could see the light in one of the bedrooms upstairs.

The same bedroom where I thought I'd seen someone watching me.

Keeping with the pool party vibe, we enjoyed a more casual dinner than the previous night.

The chef had prepared some mouth-watering steaks, locally caught fresh fish and veggies, a Caprese salad with sliced mozzarella, beefsteak tomatoes with olive oil, aged balsamic vinegar, and fresh basil leaves.

Before we sat down to eat, Stefano invited me to his wine room to choose a couple of bottles for dinner. His selection of French and Italian wines was impressive, but seeing a healthy stash of California cabs in his collection was a fun surprise.

Stefano noticed me reading the labels from his domestic section and commented that he and Nicoletta had gone on a wine tour in Sonoma. "One of the vineyards had a stable. My wife loved animals, and I wish you could've seen her joy when the owner brought her a bucket of vegetables to feed the horses."

"No way. I love wine, but that would've been the highlight of the trip for me."

"I bought a hundred cases of their finest wines to show my appreciation." Stefano smiled at the memory as he lifted a couple of bottles from the rack.

When we returned to the kitchen, Stefano opened the wine and asked, "Did you have any more questions about Nicoletta?"

I was curious about the mysterious tattoos I had penciled into the painting today, but I needed to be subtle about how I broached the subject. "Well, now that you mention it, I thought of a few things. They're personal questions, so you don't have to answer if you don't want to."

"Ask me anything."

"Did Nicoletta have any tattoos?"

So much for being subtle, Evelyn.

"She had a little flower tattoo right about there." Stefano smiled and aimed his finger at my hip. "It was tiny, and she had it done before we met. What made you wonder about that?"

"Oh, it's something I always ask. Some clients want me to incorporate special little details into the painting."

Hmm...Nicoletta did have a tattoo on her hip, but it wasn't the charm bracelet I had drawn.

"What else would you like to know?"

"Are there any material items you want me to add? Something like a family heirloom, a favorite article of clothing, or any special *jewelry?*"

Stefano leaned against the counter and swirled a sample of wine in his glass as he contemplated my question. "Her wedding ring, of course. Let me think if there is anything else. Can I get back to you with an answer?"

"No problem." We joined Leo outside and had drinks as the guys swapped stories about growing up in the old neighborhood. They apparently had a wonderful afternoon as both guys seemed more relaxed around each other than before.

Leo told a story about how Stefano started his first business when he was nine and earned more cash than most adults in their working-class neighborhood. "Stefano was skinnier than a broom handle when we were kids and had all the moms on the block hypnotized with those big brown eyes."

Stefano shook his head at Leo's over-the-top description of him.

"He went door to door asking if anyone needed help mowing the lawn because he was saving up for his first car. Remember, he was only nine years old. In no time, he was pushing a mower up and down every lawn in the neighborhood."

Leo lifted his hand to the horizon as he recalled his childhood memory. "This went on for years until he finally turned sixteen and was ready to buy the Camaro he'd been dreaming of for years."

"So, you had enough money to buy it?" I asked.

Leo motioned to Stefano to finish the story.

"I was lucky to have saved up a small fortune from my little business. Instead of spending the money on a car, I learned how to invest and grow my savings. When I turned eighteen, my vision of what I wanted had changed. Instead of buying a car, I bought a *house*."

Leo laughed with his old friend, and it seemed like whatever had happened in the past no longer affected their friendship. I loved seeing the guys truly enjoying themselves, and I was thankful we had agreed to spend time together this weekend.

UNSAVORY—EVELYN

After an indulgent and amazing dinner, Stefano went inside to grab a bottle of dessert wine. I'd already had plenty to drink, and my body was loose and relaxed as I lounged on an outdoor loveseat.

I cuddled up to Leo and wrapped my arm around him. No service weapon strapped at his waist. No badge. No cell phone. No signs that our weekend getaway would get derailed by his high-intensity job.

I slid my finger along the waistband of his pants and gave his leather belt a little tug, letting him know what I was in the mood for later.

"You better be ready to put out when we get back to our room," Leo warned me playfully. "No one likes a tease, Evelyn."

"Don't worry, babe. I'll take care of you." I straightened up when Stefano returned with a bottle of limoncello. The sun had gone down, and a cool breeze kicked up as the three of us followed the dimly lit path to another seating area on the massive estate close to the water.

The evening air was crisp, and I was chilly in my strapless sundress. I rubbed my arms to chase away the goosebumps.

"Here you go, Evelyn. This will keep you warm." Stefano, the gracious host that he was, brought me a gorgeous floral pashmina to keep me warm.

When I wrapped it around my shoulders, the lingering scent of a woman's perfume reminded me that the wrap had belonged to Nicoletta.

The ambient glow of candles drew me to the water's edge. Stefano's staff had set up a dreamy conversation area that incorporated all my favorite things.

A crackling fire pit surrounded by a foursome of Adirondack chairs and dozens of candles artfully placed in lanterns and hurricane glasses. Rows of string lights twinkled overhead, and clear bowls filled with water held a collection of floating candles shaped like lotus flowers.

It's like one of my Pinterest boards had come to life.

Instrumental music played through the outdoor speakers, creating a relaxing soundtrack that paired nicely with the natural sounds of the nocturnal lake life. I hated to sour the mood with an ungrateful thought, but this setting seemed too romantic for the three of us.

Had Stefano gone to all this trouble for me?

Arrogant, I chided myself. Even so... This ambient outdoor scene was my idea of perfection.

Stefano poured a round of drinks and initiated a toast. "To friendship."

Leo and I repeated the toast, clinked glasses, and sipped. Stefano grinned as I licked my lips and savored the sweet, lemony dessert. Pleased, it seemed, that I enjoyed the fruits of his hospitable labor.

"Hey, you guys down there!" a man hollered from the veranda.

We all turned to see who it was. Dino and Mira were

there, but I didn't recognize the other guy. Leo did, though, and looked angry enough to spit venom.

Stefano responded in Italian and motioned for the guy to join us.

"Who is that?" I whispered to Leo.

"Luca Vanzetti, Stefano's uncle."

The tall thin man with a slight hunch to his back padded down the walkway with a rocks glass in hand. "When I heard Chicago's finest was our guest for the weekend, I had to come by and see with my own eyes."

Luca set down his drink and came at Leo with open arms. He spoke in Italian as he moved in for an awkward hug, then focused his attention on me.

"Ah, Evelyn Sinclair, the famous artist of Halsted Street." Luca reached for my hand and clasped it with both of his. His palms were sweaty, and his chummy vibrato seemed forced. "Listen, I don't know diddly about art, but your work is freaking cool, you know?"

"You've seen my paintings?"

"Of course. Everyone in Chicago knows who you are."

I supposed that was true, considering I had made headlines last fall when I helped end the reign of the Windy City Stalker. Then it occurred to me that when I'd met Stefano, he acted like he had no idea who I was.

"You and Leo, huh?" Luca's gaze bounced between us. "Let me tell you something, sweetheart. You couldn't have found a better man in the city than this guy. Unless, of course, you would've met my nephew first."

He erupted in a boisterous round of laughter at his unsavory comment, then slapped Leo on the back as if to say it was all in good fun.

Seriously? I glanced at Stefano. The man was still mourning the loss of his wife. But he seemed to let the comment slide. They were family, so he was probably accustomed to his uncle's awkwardness.

"So, Evelyn." Luca was so close I could smell the whiskey on his breath. "I have to know something. Are you for real with the paranormal gift thing? Do you really see ghosts, or is that some gimmick for your art shows?"

Leo was holding my hand, and I could feel him tense up. He was putting up a good front but seemed uncomfortable around Luca. Leo was as protective as a Belgian Malinois and would shred Luca if he inched too close to my personal safety zone.

"It's true," Leo said. "Ghosts visit her in her dreams. She doesn't see them outside of that. No, she can't talk to them, communicate with them, or ask them any questions."

Apparently, Leo had memorized the Q&A section of my website. I was grateful he had answered on my behalf and would tease him later about his curt response. Although, I was sure he had a valid reason for not liking Luca.

"Whoa, that's amazing. I've never met anyone with a gift like yours. I have to say, though, with all due respect, I don't believe a word of your story, Miss Sinclair." Luca turned to Stefano. "What about you, kid? Do you believe in ghosts?"

I wasn't violent, but I felt the urge to shove Luca into the lake. Where was his filter? He'd been rude to exactly everyone in the room in two minutes flat.

Stefano swept his hair out of his face and stared into the darkness. "I believe all things are possible. If Evelyn says ghosts visit her in her dreams, I have no reason to doubt her credibility."

Leo stayed out of the conversation, probably hoping that it would end.

"Fine. I can accept that I might be a little closed-minded. Prove me wrong," Luca said to me. "Convince me you're telling the truth. Tell me one of your best ghost stories, and maybe I'll change my mind."

"Sorry, Luca. I'm exhausted. I need to get some sleep." I let out a yawn to drive my point home.

Leo and I stood, thanked Stefano for hosting, and wished Luca a pleasant evening. While I was truthful about being exhausted, I would rather do a cannonball off the dock into the murky lake than share one of my personal stories with Luca.

"Hey, Leo. Kiss your mother for me, all right?"

When he spoke, a chill ran through my blood. I pulled Nicoletta's pashmina tight as Leo placed his hand on my back and ushered me away.

I didn't know what it was about Luca Vanzetti, but my instincts warned me to stay the hell away from him.

BANGED—EVELYN

*L*eo locked the bedroom door behind us and checked the windows to ensure they were secure. Running a security sweep was expected, but he seemed uneasy. Was it Luca? The vibe definitely changed when he joined the party.

"Why don't you like Luca?" I asked as I sat on the edge of the bed and unbuckled my strappy wedge sandals.

"Stefano spent the night at our house a lot when we were kids. Mom fed him, made sure he had clean clothes, and looked after him like he was one of her own."

"That sounds like Silvia."

Leo paused as he was seemingly choosing his words carefully. "There were a couple of times when I noticed the skinny little guy had bruises on his face and defensive lacerations on his arms that I've since learned are tell-tale signs of self-defense, maybe against a strap or a stick. All I knew as a kid was they weren't something Stefano did to himself."

I covered my mouth, horrified at the images of poor Stefano suffering abuse as a child.

"Luca had a temper when he drank. We took care of our

own in our neighborhood, but we also kept to our business—Italians don't rat on each other."

My heart ached for Stefano, but I was grateful the Ricci Family cared for him. But if Luca had physically hurt Stefano, why did he still have a relationship with him now that he was an adult?

While I pondered the idea, Leo undressed in front of me. He locked his gaze on mine as he stripped off his shirt, exposing his sun-kissed skin and rippling muscles. He dropped his pants, then got down on his knees and parted my legs as I sat on the end of the bed.

"Leo, we can't." I was tipsy from all the alcohol I had consumed over the evening and giggled as Leo inched my dress up my thighs. I placed my hands on top of his and tried to slow him down, but he had been ready to go since he stripped my shorts off at the pool.

"Fine. If you don't want to sleep with me, I'll have some fun with *Lauren* tonight."

I busted out laughing. "I hate to ruin your fantasy, Leo, but the former *me* wasn't very cool—Unless you're into horse-loving girls with frizzy hair, an obsession with home makeover shows, and an insatiable desire to collect academic trophies?"

Leo gave me a sultry grin. "Did Lauren volunteer to tutor her fellow students?"

"Yes."

"Did she bake cupcakes for the class?"

"Yes."

"Did she wash shelter dogs on the weekend to help them get adopted?"

"Yes."

"I'm going to devour every inch of you, *Lauren Murphy.*" He flung my panties on the floor and was kissing me between the legs before I could mock-protest any further.

I dove my fingers into his hair and moaned softly as his warm tongue explored my body. His strong hands grasped my thighs as he pleased me orally. I found Leo's strength and control over me sexually gratifying, and I loved how he dominated me in the bedroom.

He slid his finger inside as he lashed his tongue over my sweet spot, bringing me on the verge of orgasm.

I swiveled my hips and pulled his hair as I panted with pleasure. When at last I peaked, I groaned my satisfaction as Leo savored my sweetness. I collapsed back on the bed to recover, but Leo wouldn't give me a break.

He rolled me on my side, unzipped my dress, and tossed it on a chair beside the bed. Then he unhooked my front closure bra and massaged my breasts, bringing each one inside his mouth while I stroked his length to bring him to rock-hard status.

He pressed his body on mine and then was inside me in a hot second.

"Oh, Leo." I gasped when he thrust deep inside my core. My body was slick and ready for a wild ride underneath the weight of his muscular body. Leo was a big guy in every sense of the word, and nothing was more satisfying than when he put all his energy into our lovemaking.

He thrust slowly at first, easing himself in and out as I wrapped my legs around him, moaned with satisfaction, and scratched my fingernails lightly down his back. Once we got into a steady rhythm, our bodies became slick with sweat, and Leo's need intensified.

He sat on his knees and lifted my hips onto his thighs to shift us into a different position. When my body was at this angle, he entered a special erogenous zone that brought us pleasure on a new level.

The antique bed squeaked as our passion heated up.

"Leo," I whispered. "Everyone will hear us."

"Good," he panted. "Then Stefano can have a party to celebrate that we had a good fuck under his roof tonight."

Even though my boyfriend had me in the throes of passion, I laughed at Leo's spot-on observation.

As if to prove his point, he thrust harder, and the old wooden headboard banged against the wall in a syncopated rhythm that undoubtedly could be heard throughout the twelve-bedroom mansion. I reached orgasm again as Leo quickened his pace on his way to join me.

Leo grasped my thighs and groaned a throaty exhale when he released inside me. He held me firmly and closed his eyes as sweat trickled down his body, and his chest heaved as he came down from his sexual high.

We cuddled under the sheets and listened to bullfrogs croaking and bats screeching as the moonlight spilled into our room. As I cuddled into my lover's arms, I was grateful to the universe for bringing us together.

I hoped we could cap off our evening with a peaceful night's sleep, but that seemed impossible in Stefano's haunted mansion.

CAPTIVE—EVELYN

Someone knocked on our bedroom door.

I glanced at the clock: 4:06 a.m.

Leo was sound asleep. I got out of bed, moved to the door, and opened it a crack.

No one was there.

I stepped into the hallway and searched the living room. "Hello?"

The house was quiet and dark at this hour, but moonlight shone enough to illuminate the room. I didn't see anyone, but I heard a woman sobbing. The house was massive, and I couldn't tell where the sound was coming from. "Hello?" I called again.

I moved through the living room, but I didn't see anyone. Standing at the foot of the staircase, I realized the sound was coming from upstairs. I climbed the stairs and noticed a light on in one of the bedrooms.

The door was open, and I was sure the crying woman was there. I held my arms out so I wouldn't bump into anything as I moved down the hallway.

When I reached the door, I tapped and then let myself

into the room. A woman with her back to me was seated in a rocking chair.

She had long dark hair and was wrapped in the warm pashmina I had worn earlier in the evening. As far as I knew, Mira was the only woman on the property aside from me, but the woman in the rocking chair was not her.

"Are you okay?" I whispered.

When the woman didn't answer, I figured I had spoken too softly, and she hadn't heard me. I stepped closer and placed a hand on her shoulder. "Do you need help?" I asked a little louder.

The woman stopped crying and froze as if startled by my intrusion.

As my hand rested on her shoulder, the woman snatched my wrist and shoved me so hard that I stumbled backward and fell to the ground. As I lay there, stunned, the woman straddled my body and pinned my wrists to the cold hard floor.

Now that I could see her face, I recognized her immediately—Nicoletta Vanzetti.

I tried to scream, but my words wouldn't come out. I struggled against her, but she held me captive in her cold dead hands. I was terrified and feared I was going to have a panic attack.

Nicoletta hovered over me as she opened and closed her mouth like a mummy returning to life after a couple thousand years. Her ghost had a deep, ruddy gash on her forehead, and her eyes and mouth were open wide with a panicked expression that read like she had taken her last breath while screaming in horror.

"What do you want?" I managed to eke out the words.

Nicoletta began talking, but I didn't understand her because she was speaking in Italian. Her words came out slow at first, and then she got on a roll and spoke faster as she told me a long story I didn't understand.

I shook my head, trying to communicate that her words were lost on me. As if she had understood my message, her spirit dissipated into a fine, blue mist.

Then she was gone.

SUSPICIOUS—LEO

$\mathcal{I}$ woke up just after four o'clock and was alarmed when Evelyn wasn't beside me. I checked the bathroom. She wasn't there, but our bedroom door was wide open.

I jumped into a pair of shorts, grabbed my phone to use as a flashlight, and stepped into the hallway to track her down. The alarm panel in the hallway glowed red, meaning it had not been deactivated during the night.

Evelyn is still inside the house.

The living room and kitchen were clear. Stefano's bedroom door was closed. I headed upstairs to check the other dozen or so bedrooms up there. Mira said she stayed at the house next to this one, and I assumed Dino and Luca slept somewhere in the mansion, but I didn't know which bedrooms they occupied.

When I reached the hallway, I froze.

Evelyn was no more than six feet in front of me, standing as still as a statue in her nightgown.

"Evelyn?" I called her name.

When she didn't answer, I moved closer.

Her eyes were open, and she pointed straight ahead into one of the rooms. She was breathing heavily like she did when she was experiencing a nightmare. I repeated her name, but she didn't react. Then it dawned on me—*Evelyn is sleepwalking.*

This was uncharted territory for us, and I needed to think before I startled her awake. Evelyn was experiencing something on a paranormal level. Whatever was going on, it was apparent it revolved around whatever was in that room.

My instincts as a detective urged me to find out. I stepped inside the room and shined the light from my phone from left to right as I surveyed the area. The bedroom appeared to be used as an office. There was a desk with a locked drawer that had been pried open.

The contents had been dumped on the floor and rifled through.

I aimed the light at a stack of boxes around the room. They were all open, and the contents ranged from photo albums and keepsakes to what appeared to be work-related files and stacks of receipts bound with rubber bands.

I shifted the light to the corner of the room. There was a rocking chair next to a small table, a lamp, and a pair of reading glasses. Aside from the busted desk drawer, nothing else suspicious stood out.

I turned off the light and went back to Evelyn.

I approached her carefully as if she were a bomb I had ten seconds to diffuse.

Is she going to scream when I wake her? Will she be angry I didn't let her finish whatever the hell it was she was experiencing?

I took a deep breath and braced myself as I smoothed her hair out of her face and gently tapped her cheeks. "Evelyn, sweetheart. Wake up."

She blinked rapidly as she snapped out of her trance. Then she inhaled a sharp breath, clutched my shoulders, and choked out a single word: *"Braccialetto."*

Translation: *"Bracelet."*

Another Italian clairaudient message.

eo and I got back to our room without waking anyone up.

My hands shook as I replayed my dream, including a horrifying encounter with Nicoletta's ghost. Leo showed me my drawings from last night and spread them out on the bed.

The first one was of a native bird soaring over the lake. The next was a group of shadows standing above a shallow grave or a ditch where a female form raised her hands in a defensive position.

The last one was of the woman from my dream—The Lady in the Lake. I had drawn her from the side, aiming her finger at something off the page. Her face was shielded by her hair, making her features unrecognizable.

Leo tapped his finger over her image. "That was you tonight."

I shook my head, not understanding.

"I found you in the hallway, pointing into that fucking haunted room upstairs just like *this*." He tapped his finger over the drawing.

Acid came up my throat as an image played in my mind. I had no memory of standing in the hallway like that, but I remembered going upstairs and getting flung to the ground by an angry ghost.

"Something else happened today." I rushed to get my bag that held my art supplies. "While I was painting, I produced this." I pulled the large watercolor paper out of the bag, unfolded it, and smoothed out the wrinkles.

Leo studied the image of the woman who appeared to be Nicoletta under the water along with the weird tattoos I had penciled into the painting. His expression remained calm as he took in the details, but he seemed shocked when he noticed the charm bracelet tattoo on her hip.

He picked up the painting and hastily folded it back up, gathered the other drawings, and shoved them all into his suitcase.

"What's wrong?" I figured he noticed something I hadn't, but Leo didn't answer me. He opened all the drawers and tossed our clothes on the bed.

"Get dressed."

Without arguing, I obeyed as Leo pulled on a shirt, shoved all our belongings back into our suitcases, and carried them to the door. He did a quick visual sweep of the room and then focused his attention on me.

"We're getting the fuck out of here—*now*. Don't breathe a word of this to Stefano."

GROUND RULES—LEO

I peeled out of Stefano's haunted mansion like a demon making a break from the gates of hell.

Evelyn slunk down in the passenger seat and held her stomach as she recuperated from the unsettling chain of events.

The radio was off. Neither one of us spoke a word. I kept my eyes on the road and clenched my jaw to settle my emotions.

I was angry at Evelyn for getting us into this mess. I was ticked off at Stefano for manipulating Evelyn into painting his dead wife. I was horrified that Nicoletta Vanzetti was haunting the lake house...

"Leo?" Evelyn asked. "Are you mad at me or the situation in general?"

I was too fired up to have this conversation right now, but my blood was boiling, and if I didn't let my frustrations out, I was going to blow.

"When did you decide to go to the cemetery, Evelyn? *Before* you gave me that spiel about wanting your freedom or *after*?"

She collected her thoughts before she spoke. "If I would've told you I was going to the cemetery, you would've ordered me not to go."

"*Before.* So, you lied to me?"

"I have the right to make my own decisions, Leo. My intention wasn't to *lie*. I just wanted to spare you the task of worrying about me all day."

"Did you go there to connect with ghosts?"

"Yes."

"Are you happy about that decision now that you connected with my buddy's dead wife?"

Instead of coming at me and defending her actions, Evelyn shut down and put up her shields whenever she felt threatened. Instead of lashing out, as I had done, she stared out the window, shifted her attention to a flock of geese flying in V formation, and mentally clocked out of the argument.

Now that I had unjustly unleashed my frustrations on her, I felt horrible for making her feel guilty for wanting to be herself again. I had no right to restrict her freedom. Still, I wished she would understand, for her own safety, she needed to draw a boundary line to protect herself from dangerous situations—*like going ghost hunting in a fucking cemetery.*

Before I said another word, I took a moment to bottle up my frustration, calm myself down, and come up with a solution to the tsunami of problems headed our way.

"I'm sorry I didn't tell you I was going to the cemetery," she said.

"You were right. I would've told you not to go." I apologized for lashing out and blaming her for things she had no control over.

Then as we sat in silence, I came up with a solution for moving forward. Now that the ghost was out of the graveyard, we had to confront the problem. "We need to set up some ground rules about how we are going to handle this with Stefano."

"Agreed," Evelyn said.

"Number one: I don't want you to return to that cemetery to connect with Nicoletta."

Evelyn nodded in agreement.

"Number two: You're not going back to that haunted mansion."

"Okay."

"Number three: You're not going to paint Nicoletta's portrait. I'll talk to Stefano on your behalf and get you out of it. The last thing you need is to get wrapped up in another homicide investigation."

"Whoa, Leo. Time out." Evelyn sat up and turned to face me. "You can't order me not to paint—it's my job. Secondly, Nicoletta came to me for help, and I won't turn my back on her. Lastly, what homicide investigation? The only thing I'm certain of is that Nicoletta is a ghost—but that doesn't mean she was *murdered*."

I stole glances at her as I steered down the winding road. I was glad Evelyn was still speaking to me and willing to compromise. But when I threatened to come between her and her ghost, she came back at me with the fierceness of a ticked-off tigress.

"You recited the Q&A section of my website verbatim to Luca last night. Have you forgotten the three reasons why a restless spirit remains earthbound?"

"Fear, love, or revenge," I said.

"Correct. Nicoletta died in a tragic accident. I think it's safe to scratch *revenge* off the list. She started a foundation to help hospitalized children find joy while receiving life-saving treatment. I'm scratching out *fear of judgment* as a reason, too."

"You believe Nicoletta stayed behind because of *love*?"

"Love is our most powerful emotion. She died unexpectedly and never got to say goodbye to the man she loved. What if her unfinished business is *Stefano*?"

I understood where Evelyn was going with her train of thought. While we didn't know why Nicoletta was haunting the lake house, the fact remained that Evelyn was going to help her find peace whether I wanted her to or not.

She wanted her freedom, and it wasn't my place to stop her. But I had to be myself, too, so while Evelyn searched for answers, my job was to protect her.

CONNECTED—EVELYN

$\mathcal{L}$eo's mom wanted us to drop by Sunday evening. We hadn't been to her place in a few weeks, and she insisted we come over for a bite to eat and catch up.

More likely, the Italian neighborhood gossip mill had caught wind that we had spent the weekend at Stefano Vanzetti's lake house. Silvia was disgruntled that she had learned the news secondhand from someone down at the deli, the beauty shop, or the corner market and wanted information straight from the source.

"You two got a little sun this weekend? Where did you go?" Silvia peeled the plastic wrap off a plate of sandwiches and set them on the counter.

Leo gave me a nod to indicate I should tell the story. Given how I had met Stefano, he wanted me to control what part of the story I wanted to divulge.

"I ran into an old friend of Leo's the other day. Long story short, I'm painting a portrait of his wife. He invited us to his lake house this weekend so I could do some preliminary sketches."

"An old friend?" Silvia asked. "What's his name?"

"Stefano Vanzetti."

"Oh." Silvia was a warm and loving soul, an eternal optimist, and a generous person who never spoke ill about anybody. Still, she seemed put off by the idea of us spending time with him.

After hearing the stories about Silvia taking in Stefano as a child, feeding him, teaching him to speak English, and giving him safe refuge from an allegedly abusive uncle, I expected a much different reaction.

She checked herself and plastered on a smile to soften her bitter reaction. "How is he?"

"Great. He misses Nicoletta, of course, but we had a wonderful—"

"Why'd you make that face, Mom?" Leo wasn't going to let her reaction slide without an explanation.

"I didn't make a face, *patatino*. I was just surprised to hear his name." Silvia touched her heart necklace that held all her grandchildren's birthstones and fidgeted nervously. She pushed the plate of sandwiches closer to Leo and offered to get us some drinks.

Leo let her flounder as she exhibited the telltale signs that she was not being honest. As shameless as it was, I was dying to find out what she was hiding.

"Mom." Leo cocked his head and stared at her, prodding her into answering his question.

While a part of me hated to see Silvia squirm, I was relieved I wasn't the only one who couldn't talk her way out of giving Leo the answers he wanted. When he was locked and loaded in detective mode, Leo didn't give anyone—not even his own mother—a pass from his interrogation.

"Nothing is *wrong*. I was just surprised you, of all people, wanted to rekindle your friendship with him."

I side-eyed Leo to gauge his reaction.

"What makes you say that? Do you know something I don't?"

"I'm sure it's just a rumor I heard at the beauty shop. Forget I said anything."

"What rumor?"

"People around the neighborhood are saying Stefano is *connected*."

Leo's gaze sharpened. "Connected? Like to the Chicago Mafia?"

Silvia tipped her hand. "Well, he has done very well for himself. For a guy who never went to college, Stefano sure moved up in the business world faster than anyone I know. A billionaire with his name on a skyscraper before the age of thirty. That's quite a come-up for a kid from the neighborhood."

Holy crap. Silvia was not the type who spilled the dirt on anyone—let alone someone she once considered family. She must've believed some part of it was true.

"Mom, that's ridiculous. Mobsters are ruthless bloodsuckers who will do whatever it takes to get what they want. You know Stefano. He's a smart guy who chased his dreams all the way to the top. Don't listen to the haters down at the beauty shop."

While Leo and Silvia sparred over the neighborhood gossip, I had the eerie sensation that something unsettling had been set into motion. I couldn't explain how or why I felt this way or what led me to this conclusion.

I sensed a vibe as subtle as a bird landing on a wire or a single drop of water dripping from the faucet. Things your brain was aware of but not something you consciously thought about. A leaf falling to the ground. The hum of electrical currents. A childhood memory tucked inside a brain cell.

The sensation that someone is watching you, but no one is around.

MIXED SIGNALS—EVELYN

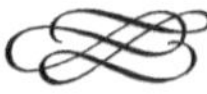

The morning birds cooed outside our window, waking me before dawn.

I rolled over and touched Leo's side of the bed. The sheets were cool, which meant he had been up for a while. The smell of fresh coffee wafted in from the kitchen and lured me out of bed.

Leo got up early to make breakfast.

I slid on a robe and went to the kitchen to embrace my thoughtful boyfriend. Instead of finding a hot guy flipping omelets, there was a note on the counter next to a bakery bag from the market across the street.

A sweet gesture, but it meant Leo had left to get a head start on a busy week, and I wouldn't get to see him until dinnertime.

The note read:

> *Good morning, beautiful.*
> *Call me if you need anything.*
> *Love, Leo*

I smiled as I set down the note and looked into the bag. *Yum.* A bear claw. Leo was in a rush and didn't have to run out and get me breakfast before work. I appreciated the gesture but wondered if he had left early to avoid seeing me.

Leo had asked me to cut ties with Stefano and back out of our agreement to paint Nicoletta's portrait. He was spooked after my encounter with Nicoletta's ghost and alarmed over my drawings and string of Italian clairaudient messages: Lake, headlights, and bracelet.

While I understood his apprehension, I refused to back off the project. When he wasn't in bed this morning, I worried he had left early because he was still mad at me for going through with the painting.

Jeez, Evelyn. Can't your boyfriend do something nice without you suspecting he had a motive?

I chastised myself for being ungrateful as I poured a hot cup of coffee from the carafe and stirred in cream and sugar. I had slept peacefully through the night, which was rare for me.

Ghosts didn't care if I was tired or busy or had no interest in getting involved with their unfinished business. Once they had my attention, they usually hung on until I helped them resolve their issues.

With Nicoletta, I was ninety-nine percent certain she wanted me to deliver a message to Stefano, but my drawings sent mixed signals. My working theory was that I was getting my psychic wires crossed with another ghost vying for my attention.

A mystery woman with tattoos who had possibly drowned in the lake.

I didn't want to play favorites, but I needed to find out what Nicoletta wanted from me first, then I would revisit the watery ghost with the tattoos. Speaking of the dead, I had to get a jump on my day to squeeze in some time to work on Nicoletta's painting.

I had plenty of pictures and reference photos of the lake house, but I needed Stefano's input on my preliminary sketches to see what pose and expression he wanted for her portrait.

I retrieved my phone to send a message to Stefano, but I was surprised he had beaten me to it.

STEFANO VANZETTI: Greetings, Evelyn. I trust you had a good trip back to the city. Please let me know when you will arrive today for our meeting, and I will clear my calendar. *Ciao.*

When your name was on the skyscraper, that made you the most important person in the room. Who would argue with him if he wanted to boot everybody out of the board-room to meet with an artist?

RATTLED—LEO

I never lied to Evelyn. Honesty and loyalty were the bricks and mortar of our relationship—along with our passionate sex life and undying attraction and love for one another.

However, something was gnawing at me about what had gone down over the weekend. I wasn't ready to talk to Evelyn about it, so I contacted my partner to get some clarity on a disturbing paranormal matter.

When I got to Parker's apartment two hours before our watch began, he was ready to roll. He was stoked to have the opportunity to dive into the ghostly waters and swim with the undead, literally, in this case.

My partner poured a couple of cups of coffee as I spread Evelyn's art across the kitchen island. Parker was fascinated by her ability to communicate with the dead through her art and was a valuable resource for paranormal phenomena.

"Full disclosure, I have Evelyn's permission to share these with you. I'm not going behind her back or anything."

Parker eyed me suspiciously. "Thank you for confirming that we have Evelyn's consent." My partner was a criminal profiler and a genius beyond his years. We worked together on the Violent Crimes Task Force, a joint effort between the F.B.I. and Chicago P.D.

Even though Parker still got carded when we went out for beers, he had the instincts and talent of a seasoned agent. He was a good friend, and I trusted him with our paranormal secrets.

"How many drawings?"

"Three plus a watercolor painting."

"Did she draw them all while at the lake house?"

"Yes. Three the first night, then a painting the next day." I placed the first sketch of the bird on the table.

"A blue heron," he said. "Seems simple enough."

"Yeah. On our first night, Evelyn saw one flying over the lake. For some reason, it caught her attention."

"Noted," Parker said as he jotted down the information.

We slid that one aside, and I set out the drawing of the three men hovering over the shallow grave.

Parker crossed his arms as he examined the drawing. "That's horrifying," he said under his breath. "A cruel way to end someone's life. Looks personal, doesn't it?"

I pointed to the trio of shadows. "Agreed. Three men taking the life of one—"

"Four," Parker corrected. "Look, here." He pointed out a dark gray shape, stretching across the dirt, that appeared to be another shadow.

I nodded in agreement. "You might be right about that."

"Did Evelyn have an opinion about it?"

"No." I pulled out the pointing woman sketch and explained Evelyn's dream and how she had embodied the pose while sleepwalking.

"Interesting." Parker took notes and studied the work. "She could be pointing at the previous scene. Perhaps she witnessed the crime?"

"Good point." I tugged at my shirt collar as I prepared to show him Evelyn's watercolor painting. "I need to give you some context before I show you the next one. This is the one I have a problem with."

"You have a *problem* with something Evelyn has drawn?" Parker seemed surprised to see me uneasy. We had been in the trenches of heinous murder investigations together. After all we'd seen and been through, I never flinched.

I was a trained detective. Nothing rattled me. But this was different—the following sketch was personal. I unfolded the larger watercolor drawing of a naked Nicoletta Vanzetti covered in tattoos. The ones inked on her arms were not true to life. She had zero tattoos on her limbs or back. But the one of a tiny charm bracelet with a heart engraved with the letter L was in the right place, but not an accurate design.

"Wow." Parker's eyes widened at the graphic image. Nicoletta was a gorgeous woman in life, but in death, Evelyn's interpretation of her was haunting. Her vexing glare. Ghostly post-mortem decay around her eyes and mouth. The black and blue watercolors in the painting bled together and gave the eerie work of art an extra layer of morbidity.

"The tattoos on her arms don't belong to Nicoletta. The only tattoo on her body was in that spot, but it was a little flower, not a bracelet." I pointed to the tattoo on her hip.

Parker crossed his arms and studied the painting. He was well-educated and had a tireless thirst for knowledge. He was a speed reader who devoured facts. Without blinking, he could recite the name of every serial killer in recorded history along with intriguing details he'd compiled along the way.

While he processed the information about the tattoos, I was sure he was recalling his extensive research into the paranormal as he developed a theory.

"Did you confirm the information about Nicoletta's

tattoos through crime scene photos? The autopsy report? Witness statements?" Parker asked.

"No." I scratched the back of my neck and let out a sigh. "I know from personal experience."

"What kind of personal experience? You've seen her without her clothes on?" As soon as he finished the sentence, the realization hit him. "You slept with Nicoletta Vanzetti?"

Now it was his turn to be rattled.

I held out my hands and shook my head. "She was Nicoletta *Russo* at the time, but yes. I slept with the woman who married my buddy and is currently contacting Evelyn from beyond the grave."

"Holy. Fucking. Shit." My straight-laced partner raked his hands through his freshly gelled hair and stepped away to catch his breath. "Does Evelyn know?"

I shot him a guilty look.

"Does Stefano know?"

I shrugged. "I knew her before they met. Our relationship didn't last long, and when I found out Nicoletta and Stefano were engaged, I kept my distance. They were happy. I didn't want to mess anything up between them."

Parker downed his coffee and refocused his attention on the drawing. "Million-dollar question. Do you believe Nicoletta Vanzetti is the woman in the pencil sketches?"

"She died in a car crash. These drawings don't seem to correspond with her accident."

"Do you recognize the false tattoos on Nicoletta's arms? Have you seen them before on anyone, alive or dead?"

"No."

Parker nodded as his gaze shifted between the black and white drawings and the watercolor of Nicoletta. "What if the tattoos on Nicoletta's arms belong to the woman in the lake? Is it possible two ghosts are trying to contact Evelyn simultaneously?"

Parker reached into his desk drawer, pulled out a magnifying glass, and set it on top of the drawing of the woman in the shallow grave. The two of us squinted as we assessed the finely sketched details.

Her arms were raised in a defensive position, and upon closer inspection, there appeared to be marks on her arm.

"There." I pointed to what appeared to be a Celtic cross. "Do you see that?"

Parker bent over the sketch. "I'll be damned. It's faint, but I see it, too. The woman in the grave has the same tattoos as the ones on Nicoletta's arms. This painting appears to be a joint effort."

"What do you think it means?" I asked.

"The cases are connected?"

"How?"

"Maybe the women knew each other."

"Or they were killed by the same person—or people." I pointed to the Trio of Killers and the Shadow Man.

We were silent a moment as we processed the new information.

"How well do you know Stefano?" Parker asked. "I mean no disrespect to your friend, but he seems to be the common denominator between the women. Unless you ...had relations with the Lady in the Lake."

I couldn't be pissed at Parker for being a top-notch investigator. In our line of work, we had to follow the evidence, even if it was unpleasant for the parties involved.

"I don't recognize the tattoos and have never slept with a woman with that much ink. I'm not connected to her in any way I can think of."

"Then we need to take a closer look at your friend."

"Agreed."

Now that Parker and I had made our first significant discovery, the next step was identifying the tattoos. Since

Evelyn had drawn The Lady in the Lake, it was reasonable to assume she was a ghost. And if Evelyn's drawings accurately depicted a murder, Parker and I could research homicide and missing persons cases to find a match.

As I packed up the drawings, Parker asked a tricky question. "Are you going to tell Evelyn you had a relationship with Nicoletta?"

CHARMING—EVELYN

Stefano's office was on the billionth floor of a high-rise on Michigan Avenue. When the elevator reached the moon, the doors opened, and I was greeted by a smartly dressed receptionist with platinum blonde hair pulled back in a tight bun.

I glanced down at my casual weekday wardrobe of a skirt, wedge sandals, and a breezy cotton shirt with a couple of long layered strands of my favorite crystal necklaces. I felt underdressed and wanted to kick myself out for not choosing something more professional for my meeting today.

"Good morning, Miss Sinclair." The young woman glided out from behind her desk and welcomed me with a firm handshake. "Mr. Vanzetti is expecting you." To the right of her desk, a slick security guard in a dark suit gave me a visual frisking while the receptionist led me down the hallway toward Stefano's office.

As we walked away, the guy lifted his cell and spoke in Italian, presumably updating his team that a guest had entered the building.

Stefano sure has a lot of security.

As we breezed past a posh, modernly designed waiting area with black leather furniture and plush pillows that added pops of color, my attention turned to the breathtaking view of the city. Stefano's penthouse office suite was designed with floor-to-ceiling windows to capture the best views of the lake on one side and the skyline on the other.

"That's quite a come-up for a kid from the neighborhood." Silvia's comment about Stefano's rise to power came to mind. She was right about that, but it didn't mean Stefano had done anything wrong to reach the top.

The receptionist pressed an intercom button to announce our arrival then a set of double doors opened into an immaculate office. Dino, Stefano's bodyguard, swept his arm forward and permitted us to enter the boss's den. He gave me a once-over, as the other guard had done. Dino eyed me suspiciously, and I wondered if he would search my portfolio for a cache of weapons.

With his tough as Teflon exterior, I found it hard to imagine him crying for weeks after Nicoletta's death as Mira had described. I was certain those close to him were accustomed to his softer side, but as he regarded me as a potential threat, I saw no trace of the compassionate soul Mira had described.

Around the corner by the window, Stefano was seated behind a modern glass desk with reading glasses on, intently staring at something on his monitor. Whatever he was studying had his full attention, and it wasn't until the receptionist spoke his name that he realized we were there.

As soon as he saw me, he slid off his glasses, cruised around his desk, and greeted me affectionately. *"Buongiorno,* Miss Sinclair. Thank you for squeezing me into your busy workday."

"My pleasure. I'm excited to show you some preliminary sketches so that I can get started on Nicoletta's portrait."

Stefano dismissed his receptionist, who left with the promise to return with refreshments. He also dismissed Dino, but instead of exiting the boss's office, he kicked over to at-ease mode and settled into a chair on the opposite side of the room.

Is the security team expecting an assassination attempt this morning?

Stefano was just a businessman. Was it common for billionaires to have this level of constant security? I supposed he could be considered a high-value target, susceptible to kidnapping for the sake of ransom demands. If that were the case, I understood why he was overly cautious.

Being kidnapped sucks.

I set my portfolio on Stefano's desk and opened it to show him my landscape studies and some scenes of the natural habitat. I painted several watercolors that showed different views of the lake and the birds Nicoletta loved.

Stefano slid his glasses on again and examined my sketches.

After we discussed the background, I spread out the samples I had drawn of Nicoletta. Stefano's eyes glistened as he studied the series of pencil drawings. He held up each one as we discussed the poses and expressions of each sketch.

"They are all lovely, Evelyn. I don't know how to choose."

"I'm going to sound artsy for a moment, but I want you to understand my process and how I come up with the final design."

Stefano gave me all his attention. "I devote the entire day to the creative process. I hole up in my studio and don't resurface until my work is done. I begin with a deep meditation where I concentrate on my subject to fuel my artistic muse."

I explained how I surrounded myself with photos and immersed myself in my subject's world before my brush touched the canvas. "Your feedback is important, but ultimately, I don't know what will inspire me that day."

Stefano nodded as if he understood my method. "Ah, speaking of that. I have something you requested." Stefano reached into his jacket and pulled something out. It was the charm bracelet I had seen Nicoletta wearing in the photos—the one I had painted on her hip.

"I would like you to add this special piece of jewelry to Nicoletta's portrait. It is simple, but it held deep sentimental value to her."

As I studied the cheap trinket, I wondered why a woman dripping in diamonds and precious gemstones would continue wearing something that clashed with her upper-class style. "This is great. I'll snap a picture. If it was important to Nicoletta, I don't want to lose it."

Stefano clicked his tongue as he lifted my hand and clasped the bracelet on my wrist. The sensation of the metal was cold at first, then warmed instantly from the heat of my skin. As I examined the jewelry, a woosh of euphoria spread through my body.

My mind drifted back to the lake house and the gorgeous view from the veranda. Birds flying overhead. The warm breeze blowing through my hair. Stefano and I drinking wine and laughing at nothing in particular...

"You're shivering. Are you all right, Evelyn?" Stefano picked up my hand and pressed it to his heart. "Your hands are ice cold."

My pulse quickened as a confusing and uncomfortable sexual tension pulsed between us. I pictured his tight abs and broad chest underneath his suit and imagined myself running my fingers through his thick black hair as he made love to me right here in his office.

With our fingers laced together and still pressed against my chest, I moved closer to feel the heat of his body. As Stefano and I stared into each other's eyes, my lips parted in anticipation of his kiss. I lifted my free hand and slid my fingernail along the collar of his shirt.

What is happening?

I loved Leo with all my heart, but there was an erotically charged chemistry between me and Stefano that was hot and sensual and undeniable. His energy pulled me to him like the force of a magnet I was too weak to resist.

Stefano whispered something charming in Italian then leaned down to kiss me—

Someone knocked on his office door, interrupting our *almost* kiss. Stefano's assistant had returned with refreshments, and the distraction brought me back to center.

I pulled my hand back and blinked away the steamy sexual fantasy playing out in my mind. "Thank you for the bracelet. I'll take good care of it. I need to get back to my studio."

"Not yet," Stefano said. "First, I will take you to lunch."

I was about to explain why I couldn't join him, but the urge to spend more time with him was greater than my resolve.

PUBLIC ENEMY—EVELYN

*S*tefano and I enjoyed a glass of champagne as Mira drove us to lunch near the old neighborhood where Leo and Stefano grew up.

Stefano was in a good mood and was giving me Italian lessons as he showered me with affection in the back seat of his limo. We rolled up to a quaint local place with a neon sign in the window that read: "Sal's Family Restaurant."

Stefano's security team had arrived ahead of the boss and was stationed at the entrance. Why the need for security at this quaint little joint? The suits opened the door, and Stefano led me inside. I inhaled the aroma of fresh baked bread and garlicky pasta sauce as we breezed into the room.

The restaurant's nostalgic décor had a cozy charm with black and white vintage photos of wineries, bountiful dinner tables, and Italian family portraits. The chairs, wallpaper, and carpet were designed in flashy red and green patterns that shouted: *This is a traditional Italian ristorante!*

A middle-aged man in a white jacket greeted Stefano with open arms and a friendly kiss on the cheek. Stefano introduced him as the owner, Sal Baldacci.

Sal shook his head and wagged his finger emphatically. "No, no. This beautiful restaurant belongs to your family now, Mr. Vanzetti. Your Uncle Luca runs this place. I am just the humble cook." His expression remained cordial, but his eyes held a glint of bitterness.

What is it about Luca that rubs people the wrong way?

A slim hostess with cascading brunette ringlets, red lipstick, and a short black dress offered to take my jacket.

"Thank you," I said.

"Allow me." Stefano was much taller than me, and as he stood behind me, he had a nice shot down the front of my casual, buttoned-down shirt. He took his time peeling off the sleeves, enjoying the view. He tossed me a shameless grin when I busted him checking me out.

I glanced away, pretending I hadn't noticed, but the butterflies fluttering in my stomach reminded me I was skidding into dangerous territory.

Sal led us into the bar area while Dino trailed behind us. The regulars greeted Stefano like a king with waves and well-wishes in English and Italian. He acknowledged every man by name and introduced me as the lovely Evelyn Sinclair.

Luca came out of his office and greeted us with open arms. "The two of you. I knew something was happening between you when I saw you acting cozy at the lake house."

Oh, my God. "No, no, no. You've got it all wrong. Stefano is my client—"

"Hey, everyone!" Luca lifted a rocks glass and waved it at the crowd. "Look who's back on the market. My nephew has found himself a looker, eh?"

An older man with a thick mustache lifted his glass. "*Salute* to you and your beautiful new girl, Stefano."

The men raised their glasses and gawked at me like I was a slab of prime beef served up for the crowd to devour. It was barely noon on Monday afternoon, and the bar was packed with mostly men, drinking and noshing on long skinny breadsticks.

This was low, even for Luca. He knew Leo and I were a couple. I had to right this wrong. I waved my hand dismissively and was about to defend myself when—

"You are mistaken, Luca," Stefano said. "Miss Sinclair and I have a business relationship—nothing more."

The bar went silent. All the attention in the room fell on Luca. Stefano had called him out and embarrassed him in front of his clientele, and the crowd went still as they awaited his uncle's reaction.

Luca responded with a boisterous laugh and addressed the crowd in Italian. I had no idea what he said, but I was certain I didn't want the translation. I was grateful Stefano had righted Luca's wrong, but I couldn't understand why Stefano let his uncle trample over him.

Sheesh. Luca was the most toxic human being I had ever met. Every word out of his mouth was with a passive-aggressive tongue-lashing aimed at his only living blood relative— Stefano. Was Luca jealous of his nephew? The bigger question was why Stefano allowed it to continue.

When our celebrity bar tour ended, Sal led us into the dining room and pulled out a chair for me at a cozy and romantic table in the corner of the restaurant. It was a straight shot from the door to the table, yet Sal had paraded us through the bar first.

At the risk of letting my imagination run wild, Stefano wanted to be seen or possibly wanted *us* to be seen together. Maybe it was his way of showing his buddies he was ready to move on from Nicoletta.

He certainly wasn't going to move on with me—*I am in love with Leo.*

A waiter approached our table, lit a candle, and asked us what we would like to drink.

"Macallan twenty-five, neat." Then he turned to me. "Same for you?"

"Perfect."

The waiter nodded and hustled to the bar to grab our drinks.

Dino stationed himself between the bar and our table while another burly guard in a black suit positioned himself by the front door. Stefano's crew had assembled at the entrance and exit points. No one was getting in or *out* without permission from the guards. This was a casual Italian restaurant off the beaten path.

Why did Stefano require this level of protection?

He must've had at least six or seven guards securing the perimeter while we dined. This was not normal—not even for a billionaire.

The waiter delivered two rocks glasses that held a healthy volume of liquid gold. Stefano lifted his glass and offered a toast. "To you, my dear Evelyn. You have come into my life unexpectedly, and although we have only known each other briefly, you have become one of my most cherished friends. You are my angel. *Salute.*"

We clinked glasses then I looked away to hide my embarrassment. As I glanced around the room, all eyes were on us as if Stefano's toast had sent some secret message to the roomful of Italians. I zeroed in on Luca.

He was eyeing me like I was his Public Enemy Number One—same as Dino had regarded me when I entered the boss's office. Luca wasn't pleased to see me in his restaurant, but I couldn't understand what I had done to have earned the ire of Stefano's inner circle.

After a long day on the job, I drove home and parked across the street from our apartment. Our living room window was visible from the road. The blinds were closed, but the lights were on, which signaled Evelyn was home.

I kept the car running and cranked up some music to clear my head. Crimes were never-ending in the big city, which meant my team was always busy hunting down killers and vicious criminals. And the Violent Crimes Task Force saw the most disturbing crime scenes. Head clearing was essential.

Plus, I didn't want to face Evelyn right now because I hadn't decided which way to go on the Nicoletta situation. I drummed my fingers on the steering wheel in time with a classic Led Zeppelin song.

Do I tell Evelyn the truth about my past relationship with Nicoletta, or do I keep my mouth shut and hope she never finds out?

I hated that I had reservations about being honest with Evelyn. In the past, keeping secrets had nearly cost Evelyn her life. But was sleeping with someone years before we met a secret? Or did it fall into the category of things that happened long ago that we never had the opportunity to talk about?

Evelyn had never asked about my past relationships. Never once. But she had shared with me that she had only been with one guy before me—her high school sweetheart. She never slept with the rich pricks she dated and never had a serious boyfriend after her accident.

As for me, the list was much longer. I'd never wanted to be tied down in my personal life. It wasn't until I'd met Evelyn that my feelings about love and relationships had flipped.

My cell buzzed with an incoming text:

EVELYN: Almost home? Missed you today.

God, I fucked up.

She deserved to know, and I should have told her before we went to the lake house.

Before she started working on Nicoletta's portrait. Before she looked at Nicoletta's pictures. Before Nicoletta's ghost contacted her. Before Evelyn had drawn the tattoo of the charm bracelet on Nicoletta's hip that *I* had given her years ago.

I stared at Evelyn's message but didn't respond.

The right thing to do was to go inside, kiss my girlfriend, and tell her the truth. If I let this go on any longer, or God, didn't tell her and she found out on her own, it'd be a hundred times worse.

Then an even more disturbing thought crossed my mind. What if Evelyn learned the truth from Nicoletta instead of me? What if Evelyn sketched me and Nicoletta together?

For fuck's sake.

It wasn't a crime that I slept with another woman years before I met Evelyn. The subject would've never come up if

Evelyn hadn't met Stefano. The only thing I was guilty of was withholding the truth between Friday morning and Monday evening.

Not the worst sin in the world, and it was forgivable—If I copped to it now.

Evelyn would be angry I hadn't told her sooner, but she would forgive me. I had to do it. I had to face her and confess before this situation spiraled out of control.

When I entered our apartment, Evelyn was freshly showered and wrapped in a throw blanket on the couch, watching TV. Her hair was wet, and her face was clean and makeup free.

Her eyes lit up when I walked through the door. "Hey, babe. I missed you." She tossed off the blanket, met me at the door, and wrapped her arms around me. I kissed the top of her head and pulled her into my chest.

The scent of her citrus body wash and minty shampoo smelled like home.

"How was your day?"

"The usual." I went into the kitchen and poured a glass of water.

"Do you want me to warm up some dinner?"

"I already ate."

Evelyn nodded, sensing my sour mood. "You were up early this morning. Did you meet with Parker?"

"Yes."

"And you showed him my drawings?"

"Yes."

"Did you find out anything about the tattoos or—"

"I can't discuss the details of an open case with you."

"An open case? Does that mean you discovered the identity of the Lady in the Lake? Who is she?"

Evelyn's gift was amazing and defied every logical sensibility I had. While I didn't understand how or why she received information from the dead, I knew her gift was accurate and dangerous.

We had both found that out the hard way. Theoretically, Evelyn had a right to know what our research had turned up. But as a detective working a missing persons case that may be evolving into a murder investigation, I could not divulge any evidence about the crime or details about the victim we had dubbed the Lady in the Lake.

"I'm sorry, Evelyn. I can't answer your questions until, or if, information regarding the case is released to the public."

"I understand." Evelyn covered her mouth to mask a triumphant smile. "Thank you for taking my gift seriously, Leo. I am so relieved I don't have to keep secrets from you anymore."

Speaking of secrets, I had a confession to make.

ATTACHED—EVELYN

Something was going on with Leo.

He had been acting strangely since he returned home. His job was dangerous, demanding, and depressing at times, but I sensed there was something he was keeping from me—beyond what he had found out about the Lady in the Lake.

Leo continued to work well into the night. He was focused on whatever he was researching on his laptop and had barely spoken to me since he had returned from work—other than to tell me not to ask him any questions.

Maybe I could lure him to the bedroom. I was feeling guilty over my sudden attraction to Stefano this afternoon. I had no idea what had come over me, but I would be careful next time and decline any invitations outside his office. I would finish the painting this week, Leo and I would go to the fundraiser on Saturday night, then my obligation to him would be fulfilled, and our business relationship would come to an end.

For now, all I wanted was to spend the night in the arms of the man I loved with all my heart. No one would ever come between us, and I wanted to show Leo how much I cherished our relationship.

"Ready for bed?" I strolled out of our bedroom in a silky nightie and struck a sexy pose by the door to entice him.

"Sorry, I need to catch up on some work tonight," he answered without looking up from his laptop.

"Oh, okay." I *un-struck* my sexy pose. "I'm going to read a little bit before bed."

"Don't wait up for me." Whatever he was working on had his complete attention.

I snuggled under the sheets, stuffed some pillows behind me, and settled into the perfect reading position. My friend Tess lent me a shifter romance novel starring a small-town sheriff who shifted into the alpha of a wolf pack by the full moon's light. His love interest was a new girl who left her big city job to take over her dearly departed grandmother's failing bakery.

Tess had already spoiled the plot by revealing the grandmother was haunting the bakery—but only Sheriff Wolf could see her ghost. Granny had vowed never to rest in peace until her uptight, bossy C.E.O. granddaughter returned home and found her true love and fated mate.

Between devouring the book and battling to stay awake past my bedtime, I kept checking the clock. It was after one o'clock now. Leo was still working. I knew I couldn't ask him about his investigation, but I hoped it was the Lady in the Lake case.

Or maybe he'd found out something about Nicoletta.

All I knew was that she was a ghost, but since she died in an accident, I reasoned her motivation to remain earthbound was because of her love for Stefano.

A kind and giving soul like her wouldn't fear judgment. She wasn't out for revenge. All that was left was love. I hoped Nicoletta's message became clear when I worked on her painting. I wanted her spirit to find peace, which would only happen once she resolved her unfinished business.

Let me help you, Nicoletta. Tell me what you want Stefano to know.

I ran my finger over the heart-shaped pendant on her charm bracelet. Sometimes ghosts were attached to objects, so it might help Nicoletta and me connect if I left it on.

I let out a yawn. I was losing my battle to stay awake. I set my book on the nightstand, clicked off the light, and turned on my side. The heart charm on Nicoletta's bracelet jangled against the cheap silver chain.

Why was this bracelet special to you, Nicoletta?

WICKED—LEO

A cold hand touched the side of my cheek.

I opened my eyes and found Evelyn leaning over me. I was sleeping on the couch in the living room because I hadn't wanted to risk waking her while she was sleeping peacefully.

"Hey, sweetheart. I'm sorry I didn't—"

Evelyn planted her lips on mine and kissed me deeply. Her long hair fell over my face, shrouding me in a curtain of golden-brown locks. She was naked, and her bare breasts rubbed against my chest as she ran her fingers through my hair and slid her tongue inside my mouth.

Damn. My body reacted to her sexy ambush, and I was ready for whatever my girlfriend had in mind. I got off the couch, slid off my clothes, and pulled her body close to mine. She grazed her teeth on my neck—harder than I expected from Evelyn. Then she scratched her nails down my back and grinded against me, arousing me with pleasure and pain.

"Want to play a little rough tonight?" I growled in her ear.

She responded with a hard slap to my ass.

I didn't know what had gotten into her, but I was excited to play her game.

I wrapped my arms around her petite frame and rubbed my erection against her flat abs. "You make me crazy, Evelyn." I squeezed her ass and fantasized about the various positions I would put her in. She was feisty and aroused and hungry for my attention.

My primal need to spread her legs, push inside her, and harness her sexual energy had me throbbing with anticipation.

Evelyn guided me down to a sitting position on the couch. Then she grabbed a bottle of oil and squirted it over her chest. She locked her sexually charged gaze on mine and massaged her breasts as she spread the oil over her body and between her legs.

All my blood went south when Evelyn touched herself and prepared her body for a wild night under the sheets. When she was ready for me, she dropped to her knees before me.

She put her hands on my knees and parted my legs as she cozied up close. In this position, I expected she would give me oral pleasure, but Evelyn was full of surprises tonight. She laid her chest across my lap and sandwiched my length between her breasts.

I groaned from the pleasure of her oil-slicked bosom rubbing against my erection. Evelyn had never done this before, and I didn't know where she got the idea, but it was the hottest act of pleasure she had ever performed.

"Oh, fuck. What are you doing to me?"

She cupped her breasts and rocked her body as she pleased me. When I had reached rock-hard status, she brought me into her mouth and swirled her tongue around my head as she stroked me.

My girlfriend had me twisted, and if she kept it up, I

wouldn't reach the bedroom. I wanted her to stop so I could last, but her mouth was warm and wet, and I was ready to explode.

My primal instinct to control her was greater than letting her blow my mind orally. I craved her femininity. The sensation of being inside her and hearing her moan with pleasure as our bodies synced into a sensual rhythm.

"You are the sexiest woman in the world, Evelyn." I found a moment of self-control, grasped her elbows, and brought her back to her feet.

I steered her to the bedroom, laid her back on the bed, and pressed my body on top of hers. Evelyn let out a pleasurable groan as my strength excited her. She craved my alpha male control in the bedroom, and I planned to follow her lead and please her in every imaginable way.

Evelyn had been uncharacteristically quiet and more aggressive than usual. Not that I was complaining. If my girl was in the mood for a rough, domineering ride, I would happily play out that fantasy.

I slid my finger between her legs and massaged her to get her wet and ready for an energetic ride. Evelyn placed her hand on mine, encouraging me to go faster as she panted excitedly. I couldn't see in the dark, but she had on a bracelet that jingled as she encouraged my touch.

I lifted her knees and slid my tongue between her legs as she headed toward orgasm. Her body tasted heavenly, and I got an erotic rush of pleasure as she reacted to my touch. She dug her fingers into my hair as I pleasured her and let out a breathy exhale loud enough to wake the neighbors.

She fell back on the bed as her breathing slowed as she came down from her sexual high while my need to be inside her intensified.

"Want to play rough tonight?"

Evelyn's eyes burned with desire as she nodded her

consent. She got on her hands and knees and smacked her backside—*hard*. She gave me a sultry smile and wiggled her ass, inviting me to have a turn.

She wants me to spank her?

I would never hurt her, but Evelyn's energy felt different tonight, and I wanted to live up to her sexual expectations. "Buckle up for a rough ride, sweetheart. Tell me to stop if it gets to be too much." I grasped her ankles and pulled her across the silky sheets toward the end of the bed.

Her skin was cold, but her body was slick with sweat.

When I flipped her on her stomach, she looked over her shoulder and gave me a naughty grin, letting me know she liked where our lovemaking was headed. I would introduce Evelyn to a tolerable amount of pain for the first time in our relationship. "Get on your knees."

She followed my command as I saddled behind her, wrapped one arm around her waist, and held her firmly against me. I brushed her hair over her shoulder and kissed her neck as I rubbed my erection across her femininity and massaged her breasts.

Evelyn leaned her head back on my chest and groaned from my touch as I whispered dirty thoughts in her ear. Evelyn didn't speak a word, other than her sexy sounds, while we dove deeper into our foreplay.

"Get ready for the *Beast*, Evelyn."

When we were both excited and ready to go, I stacked a couple of pillows in front of her and gently pressed my hand on her back. "Bow for me." With her hips raised, I spread her legs and positioned myself behind her. I scooted her forward until she could reach the headboard.

"When we are heading to climax, hold on." I was going to give it to her hard and fast, and when we were in the throes of passion, she would need something to hold on to keep her on the bed.

"You want me to spank you?"

Evelyn nodded her consent.

When I slid inside her V in that vulnerable position, I groaned as I sank inside her warm and wet body. I moved slowly at first to ease Evelyn into our lovemaking. I wouldn't last long in this position, so I sped up as my excitement headed toward climax.

Evelyn began to pant, and I knew she was about to come undone, too. I gave her a good smack on the ass, then another, and another as I thrust harder. Our skin slapped, and Evelyn's breasts shook as our lovemaking intensified. "Hold on to the headboard."

She grasped the metal frame while I wrapped my arms around her waist to hold her steady. When we reached our climax, I grasped her hips, held firm as we peaked, and then collapsed on the bed.

Our hearts raced as we came down from an erotic high. After our role-playing game ended, I reverted to loving boyfriend mode. I snuggled up with Evelyn under the covers and cradled her head in the crook of my elbow.

"That was amazing, sweetheart. How do you feel?"

"*Il nostro amore non morira mai*," Evelyn said. It was an Italian phrase that translated to: Our love will never die.

"Where did you learn to say *that*."

Evelyn closed her eyes as a wicked smile crept up on her lips.

SECRET—LEO

*M*y alarm went off too damn early in the morning.

Parker and I were meeting again to review the Lady in the Lake case. While working late last night, I switched gears and studied Nicoletta's accident report.

I didn't like what I found—a sloppy investigation.

A Lake Brickell snow truck driver was the one who discovered the scene of the accident. When he found Nicoletta's crashed car in the embankment, he rushed to the vehicle to see if anyone needed help.

When no one was in the car, he noticed footprints leading away from the vehicle and down an embankment toward a creek bed. He followed the trail and found Nicoletta's body. He called in the accident then waited for help to arrive.

According to the report, the call to the station came in at 4:46 a.m. The problem was it had taken first responders *three* hours to arrive at the scene. During that time, significant snowfall had accumulated, covering up tracks, footprints, and any trace evidence that would've normally been collected at the scene of a fatal accident.

No tire tracks. No skid marks. The snow had covered up everything that held significant evidentiary value. The report described the accident as a single-car crash caused by inclement weather.

That was an assumption, not a fact. Without photos of the scene, there was no evidence to dispute the report. The only witness was the snow truck driver. Initially, he had said multiple sets of footprints led him to Nicoletta's body.

Later, he corrected his statement during an interview and said he only remembered seeing a single set of tracks.

While following the evidence, I couldn't get Evelyn's drawings and the details of her nightmare about Nicoletta out of my head. Nicoletta was a ghost. Not only was she trying to contact Evelyn, my gut told me she was trying to get a message to me.

Why else would Evelyn have drawn the charm bracelet I had given Nicoletta years ago? The answer was clear—her ghost was trying to get my attention.

I was eager to share the news with Parker and get his input. I rolled over to turn off my alarm and noticed Evelyn wasn't in bed. It was five in the morning. The bedroom door was open. All the lights in our apartment were still off.

"Evelyn?" I called out as I hopped out of bed and slid on shorts.

No answer.

Memories of our wild lovemaking made me smile as I ventured into the living room, where I expected to find Evelyn meditating, drawing, or getting in some early morning yoga.

The apartment was empty.

I clicked on the light. Her cell phone was not at the charging station, and her purse and car keys were also gone.

Where the hell did she go?

I went to the kitchen and found a handwritten note beside the coffee maker.

Good morning! Getting an early start.
Painting today. I will be home late.
Love, Evelyn

Something was off about her. She was a creature of habit, and sneaking out of the house early without waking me was way off the mark. Was she mad and left early to avoid seeing me? If so, I could only think of two reasons she was upset.

Evelyn knew I had found out information about the Lady in the Lake. Was she ticked off that I wouldn't share information about the case?

Doubtful. Evelyn seemed happy I was investigating and hadn't appeared miffed that I had found something out and refused to share details.

The other reason was more personal. Had I been too rough in bed? What if I'd gone too far with the spanking?

I hoped to God that wasn't the reason. Her energy was off the charts last night. Our sex life had always been bold and playful, and we loved trying new things. We experimented with toys and lotions and made love in different positions on the couch, in the shower, standing, sitting, lying down…

Being adventurous was part of the fun. I had never gone too far or done anything she wasn't one hundred percent up for in the past. If Evelyn didn't like something, she would've told me. From my perspective, we both enjoyed last night's rough-and-tumble romp in the bedroom.

Since both reasons seemed implausible, I trusted Evelyn was telling the truth. She had never lied to me before, and I had no reason to suspect she would start now. I retrieved my phone and checked my messages—none from Evelyn. I tapped on her name to send a text, but her notifications were silent.

I didn't want to be that guy who checked up on his girlfriend, but in the interest of her safety, I needed to make sure Evelyn was where she said she would be.

I checked the security app to see if she had cleared her alarm at work. The record showed she had entered the gallery less than an hour ago.

While everything seemed fine, my gut told me Evelyn was keeping a secret from me.

SEXT OF SHAME—EVELYN

WHAT HAVE I DONE?

I have never felt more humiliated in my life. I didn't know why, when, or how *this* happened, but I was sick to my stomach trying to devise a solution to right my horrifying wrong.

Sometime in the middle of the night, I had taken a full-frontal nude in front of the mirror and sent a naked selfie to Stefano Vanzetti. On top of that, I also sent him a message to accompany the photo:

"Il nostro amore non morira mai."

I had hit the Translate option to know what I'd texted: "Our love will never die."

This morning, I left in a panic and came here to my studio to wallow in self-pity while figuring out a solution. I had no memory of taking the photo or sending it to Stefano. I didn't speak Italian and had never heard that phrase before. The last thing I remembered yesterday evening was reading before bedtime, turning off the lamp, and settling in for the night alone.

Whatever had happened between then and 4:30 a.m., when I woke in a cold sweat, was a mystery. I had no memory of getting out of bed, taking naked selfies, or sexting Leo's buddy in the middle of the night.

I plopped down in my office chair and winced. My body was sore *down there*, and my muscles ached as if I had squeezed in a Pilates workout during the night. When I'd gotten dressed this morning, I noticed a few faint blue finger bruises on either side of my hips and a red mark on my backside.

There was no doubt I was home alone with Leo last night, which meant either he had put those bruises there or I had done it to myself. Had we made love last night?

Did we get a little rough with each other?

I loved Leo's big strong body, and I felt no shame admitting that I found his strength and alpha dominance sexually gratifying. It seemed obvious we had made love, but the question that frightened me was, why didn't I remember?

The more pressing question was, why had I snapped a sexy selfie and sent it to Stefano? What in the name of all things holy was I thinking? When I admitted to Leo what I had done, would he forgive me? Hiding out in my studio with my phone turned off wouldn't solve my problems—I had to go straight to the source to fix this.

Time to face Stefano.

My stomach felt queasy as the elevator ascended. A disgusting rush of shame oozed through my veins as I mentally prepared to face Stefano.

When the elevator door opened, Stefano's receptionist seemed surprised to see me. "Evelyn, good morning. Is Mr. Vanzetti expecting you? I don't have you on the schedule for today."

I wiped my sweaty palms on my pants and avoided eye contact with the security guy standing guard by the entrance to the main lobby. "I don't have an appointment, but I have an urgent matter to discuss with Stefano. If you could squeeze me in for ten minutes, I will be on my way."

She glanced at her monitor and then gave me a sympathetic smile. "I'm sorry. Mr. Vanzetti is completely booked today, but I'll be able to get you in next Tuesday afternoon. What shall I say is the nature of your visit?"

"It's a personal matter. And it can't wait until Tuesday."

The bodyguard in the tight black suit eyed me suspiciously, probably assuming a personal problem meant something romantic. In my haste to escape this morning, I had left the apartment without paying attention to my appearance.

I arrived at the boss's office wearing a yoga outfit and tennis shoes. I wasn't wearing a stitch of makeup, and my hair was pulled back into a messy bun.

My appearance had one-night-stand drama scribbled all over it. I had no idea if Stefano was dating anyone, but six months had passed since his wife died, and I would bet I wasn't the first woman who had stepped off the elevator hoping to squeeze in some time with the most eligible bachelor in the city.

"I don't mean personal like, you know, *that*. It's just a matter that is not related to business." I grimaced at the sound of the words coming out of my mouth. "Can you please just buzz him and tell him I'm here?"

"I'm sorry, he's in a board meeting and cannot be disturbed." His assistant's smile faded as she stood her ground. "We'll see you Tuesday at 3:45. Have a wonderful day, Ms. Sinclair."

I returned to the elevator to give myself one last chance at a Hail Mary. I whipped out my phone and sent a text to Stefano.

EVELYN: I'm at your office. We need to talk.

While the porter held the elevator door for me, I pretended to trip over my shoelaces and went down on one knee to tie them. I took my time tying and re-tying the laces, hoping to give Stefano a moment to read my message.

While I got an impatient glare from the elevator operator, I tried to replay the events from last night. *Why can't I remember anything?* No alcohol was involved. No sleeping pills. Last night was the same as any other—

"Miss Sinclair."

I sighed with relief when Stefano called my name. I stood to face him, but the moment we locked eyes, a rush of guilt from my *sext of shame* flooded my soul. The problem was Stefano was an incredibly handsome man. I would be lying if I said I hadn't noticed. Hell, everyone noticed. I had gotten accustomed to women drooling over Leo and wasn't blind to the fact Stefano received the same reaction.

The attraction had begun yesterday when we met in his office and then went to lunch. His eyes were more playful and loving than I had noticed before. The way he grinned when I said something funny. The affectionate way he touched the small of my back when we left the restaurant together.

But even though I thought Stefano was handsome, that didn't mean I was *attracted* to him. At least, that was the story I was sticking to until I found out why I had texted him at four in the morning.

"Please, let's go to my office to speak in private."

Stefano escorted me past a boardroom with glass walls and a commune of executives seated in posh office chairs around a long conference table. All eyes were on us as we breezed past the gawking business pros.

Had Stefano ditched a board meeting because of me?

Once we entered his office, Stefano dismissed Dino to his break area on the opposite side of the room. I was so nervous about how to handle this unprecedented situation. My hands were shaking, and I couldn't stop thinking about how I would explain to Leo about what I had done.

Stefano offered me a chair and then sat across from me at his desk. His expression was a mix of curiosity and excitement as he waited for me to explain the nature of my urgent, early morning meeting.

"I don't suppose there's any chance you failed to check your messages this morning?"

"No, Miss Sinclair. I'm all caught up." He leaned back in his chair and grinned, seemingly enjoying watching me squirm with embarrassment.

"Right. First, I didn't mean to send that message to you. I didn't mean to send it to anyone. I blacked out last night. I have no memory of taking the picture or sending it to you. I'm still trying to figure out what happened. I love Leo with all my heart, and I would never—"

I couldn't finish my sentence. Tears welled in my eyes as an overwhelming fear of losing Leo shook me. Disappointing Leo to the point that he would leave me was my worst nightmare, and after what I'd done, I wouldn't blame him if he broke up with me.

Stefano placed a gentle hand on my shoulder to soothe me. My first instinct was to shove his hand away and chew him out for being so affectionate with me. We had a business relationship. Nothing more. But I was so emotionally wrecked, I couldn't think clearly.

"This is a serious problem, Evelyn. Did something happen that caused you to black out?"

I shook my head. "I don't think so. I didn't drink or take any recreational drugs or medicine. I was reading in bed, fell asleep, and woke up in a cold sweat early this morning. It wasn't until I checked my phone that I realized what had happened."

"What did Leo say about this?"

I slink down in the chair and winced. "I haven't told him yet. I left early to avoid him. I was so freaked out and scared and needed time to process what had happened. I left the house before he woke up."

He exhaled and shook his head. "Leo has quite an ego. This will not be easy for him. When are you going to tell him?"

I swallowed a lump in my throat the size of a toad. "When he gets home. I don't want to distract him while he's at work."

"Did you send this photo to anyone else?"

"No. Only you."

His expression turned serious as he pulled out his phone and set it on the desk between us.

My nude photo taunted me from the screen. My breasts glistened with oil as I sat on the edge of our bed with my legs crossed in front of my floor mirror. While the pose was tasteful, my *come fuck me* expression was the most damning part of the photo.

My survival instincts urged me to grab the phone, slam it against the wall, and smash it into a million pieces, but Stefano lifted it off the desk before I had a chance.

"You did the right thing by coming to me about this." He leaned back in his chair and held up the phone. "I understand your relationship with Leo is on the line, and as my friend, I will never let any harm come to you."

While he spoke, my skin prickled as an unsettling feeling came over me. As Stefano sat behind his expensive desk in a rich black leather chair, I conjured up an image of making a deal with the devil. Stefano wasn't doing me a friendly favor —his gracious offer to help would come at a price.

"Your problem is solved, Evelyn." He tapped the screen

and deleted the photo along with the unsettling message that had accompanied it. "Your secret is safe with me. Leo never needs to know."

TROUBLE—LEO

When I arrived at Parker's before work, he took one look at me and knew something was up. He was a criminal profiler and an expert at reading people. An invaluable tool on the job, but in this case, I wish I could steer my personal life away from his scrutiny.

"What happened to you?" Parker touched his neck in the same spot where Evelyn had left a *love mark* as deep and vast as Lake Michigan. I had short hair, and it was summertime, so I couldn't easily hide my giant hickey with a scarf or a jacket.

I let myself inside his apartment and shook my head. "Nothing. Do you have a first aid kit?"

"Sure." Parker returned a moment later and set a small case of medical supplies on the table. He remained silent as I selected the largest bandage in his stash and attached it over the incriminating mark.

"Did you get into a fight?" Parker glanced at my hands to check for bruising. You couldn't get away with anything when all your buddies were law enforcement officers and FBI agents. There was no bullshitting my partner.

"No. It's a *love mark*. Evelyn gave it to me last night." I told him the truth so we could focus on our case.

Parker's cheeks flushed with embarrassment. He waved his hand as if he could erase the conversation.

Now that the awkwardness was behind us, Parker pulled out his laptop and gave me a smug grin. "Ready to meet the Lady in the Lake?"

"You found her?"

"Shay Adams. A twenty-four-year-old recovering drug addict reported missing by her sister last December." He explained Shay's unstable employment history. How she moved frequently and only came to Chicago when she ran out of money, and her sister took her in.

"Shay was never identified as a missing person?"

"No. Detectives found no evidence a crime had been committed, and with her history, it was likely she had run off and didn't want to be found. Shay had gone to work one day and never come home," Parker said.

"She left her sister's house with her purse and computer bag and hadn't made contact since. Single. No kids. Nothing tied her to the city except her older sister, Amanda, who admitted the two weren't getting along at the time of her disappearance."

"Then how did you find her?" I asked.

"Social media. I did a keyword search using words to describe her tattoos. That's when I found Amanda Lockhart's profile." He turned his laptop around so I could see the post.

"Help! My little sister is missing!" The post was pinned to Amanda's page, along with a smiling picture of Shay. She had pink hair, dark-rimmed glasses, and a sleeveless blouse that exposed her heavily tattooed arms.

The same tattoos that appeared in Evelyn's drawing.

The post had all the pertinent information about when she went missing, where she was last scene, how to contact

Amanda with any information, along with an angry jab at Chicago P.D. for not taking her sister's disappearance seriously.

"Nice work, Agent."

Parker held a copy of Evelyn's drawing up to the light. "The gravity of what Evelyn can do defies logic. Her gift is phenomenal."

Evelyn was the only person in six months who had made contact with Shay Adams. Parker and I had only begun our investigation, but we both believed Evelyn had uncovered crucial, albeit unconventional, evidence regarding her disappearance.

"Terrifying is a more accurate description," I lamented. "I dug into Nicoletta Vanzetti's accident report last night. It's suspicious. We need to take a closer look, but we have to make certain nothing we investigate ties back to Evelyn."

"Right. I understand, partner. We will keep Evelyn out of our investigation."

"Without a body or evidence of a crime, how do you suggest we proceed?"

Parker twisted his lips as he considered our options. "We contact Shay's sister. Tell her we are following up on Shay's disappearance. She will be willing to talk to us, and we can gather more information that might lead us to her killer."

I agreed that was the safest way to proceed. I had devoted my life to helping victims of violent crimes, but this case was hitting too close to home. My job, above all else, was to protect Evelyn.

I had two ghosts. Two possible murders. And a hundred different ways to get Evelyn into trouble.

FORBIDDEN ATTRACTION—EVELYN

When I returned to my studio, I collapsed in my chair and hung my head in shame. I had hit rock bottom emotionally and didn't know how to undo the relationship damage I had caused.

Why can't I remember what happened last night?

I checked my phone.

No messages from Leo.

It was Tuesday. The fundraiser to honor Nicoletta's memory was in four days. All I wanted was to complete my obligation, paint the portrait, and never see Stefano Vanzetti again. Even though I was responsible for my own actions, I was angry at him for shamelessly seducing me.

He had technically not done anything *wrong*, but his actions were calculated. He had flirted with me, invited me out to lunch, and treated me like his prized possession in front of his buddies at the restaurant.

Stefano had overstepped his boundary as my client, and while I owned half the blame for letting him get away with it, I had no doubt he was seducing me.

And I stepped willingly into his trap.

My stomach churned with anxiety as I contemplated whether I would tell Leo about the selfie. In my defense, I had no memory of taking it or anything that happened after I closed my eyes and went to bed.

Instead of spending the day lamenting my choices and blaming others for my mistakes, I sucked up my shame, gathered my reference photos of Nicoletta, and stormed over to my painting corner to finish the portrait.

I clicked on my opera music, silenced my phone, and switched off the guilt and confusion that had become my life since meeting Mr. Vanzetti. I squeezed paints onto my palette, set out my brushes, and taped Stefano's favorite photos of Nicoletta to the wall to inspire the final design.

As I blended my colors and thinned the paint, I hummed along to *La Traviata* as I visualized Nicoletta living her best life at the lake house.

The wind blowing her long hair as she watched her beloved lake birds...her husband wrapping his arms around her in a loving embrace...sipping wine and enjoying a beautiful sunset...

I marked the canvas with random swipes of neutral colors to serve as an abstract background. Then I rolled a thin brush in paint and outlined Nicoletta's face and long, luscious locks as I studied the happy photos of the late Mrs. Vanzetti plastered across my wall.

I touched the charm bracelet on my wrist that had held sentimental value to Nicoletta and imagined her life when she was among the living. The Italian opera music was grating on my nerves, so I switched to a Fleetwood Mac playlist that suited my style and energized my soul.

While I sang along with Stevie Nicks and swayed my shoulders in time with the music, I let go of my obligation to paint the perfect portrait of the perfect woman who had been cheated out of her perfect life.

I wasn't a blue sky, yellow sun kind of artist and refused

to compromise my artistic vision to conform to a billionaire's desires. Stefano had told me that Nicoletta would've loved my paintings. If that were true, I would pay tribute to her memory by giving her something imaginative that suited her style.

It's just us now, Nicoletta. Show me the way. Let's do this together.

When my favorite song played, I cranked up the music, poured myself a whiskey, and downed it in one shot. I was tired of feeling guilty about my gift and for actions I had no control over.

My insecurities will not pollute my artistic soul.

I held my brush in one hand and my palette in the other. With "Dreams" playing as my theme song, I unleashed my inhibitions and let the spirits guide me.

After what felt like hours, I finished the portrait. I set down my brush, stretched my arms, and downed a glass of water. While working, I was in a productive groove and needed to step away for a fresh perspective.

I moved to the back of the room to study Nicoletta's portrait from a distance. I loved the loose and carefree pose of her sitting on the edge of the boat dock with her feet dangling in the water. She looked down at her beautiful reflection with a soft smile and an aura of peace.

But there was something *off* about Nicoletta's likeness.

Her long hair was styled like she usually wore it, but the color was golden brown like mine. I took a few steps closer and focused on her face. I had painted her characteristic thick black eyelashes, but her eyes were blue—not dark brown.

The dress I had painted didn't belong to her, either. It was the white summer dress I had worn to dinner on our first night at the lake house.

I rushed back to the painting to examine the fine details.

My nose.

Her lips.

Our charm bracelet.

My heart pounded as I backed away from the unsettling portrait. Subconsciously, I had painted Nicoletta and myself as one person.

Half her, half me.

Feeling violated, I crossed my arms—the charm bracelet jangled from the sudden movement. I stared at it in horror when I considered that this object attached to my wrist held a deep sentimental value to the original owner.

Was it possible Nicoletta's ghost was attached to this bracelet? Could this be the reason for my forbidden attraction to Stefano?

MYSTERY BOYFRIEND—LEO

After a long day of solving murders, Parker and I got back to work on Shay's case. Starting with a meeting with the missing woman's sister.

When we arrived at Amanda's house in the suburbs, she was grateful we had taken an interest in her sister's disappearance six months ago—just before Nicoletta's fatal accident.

"I swear to you, something happened to Shay. She would never stay away this long."

Parker and I joined Amanda at her kitchen table and took notes as she recalled the last time she had seen her sister and where she had been the day of her disappearance.

"Was Shay involved with anyone romantically?" Parker asked.

"I think so, but she got mad at me when I asked her about it. She had come home in the middle of the night a few times. I asked her where she'd been and what she was doing, but she never answered. I just wanted to talk, but she thought I was accusing her of using drugs again."

Amanda wiped her nose on a tissue. "Shay was angry

because she thought I didn't trust her. That's why we weren't on speaking terms when she disappeared. When she hadn't come home for a few days, I figured she was staying with someone to cool off, but she never came back."

"Can you think of anyone who would want to harm her? Jealous exes? People she owed money to? Drug dealers?"

Amanda's lip quivered at the mention of drugs. "The other cops think Shay was some junkie who ran off when she needed a fix, but I'm telling you, she was clean. She paid her share of the rent on time. She got up every single day, made coffee and breakfast for the both of us, then went to work."

"It sounds like Shay was on the right track with her recovery. You are a great sister for supporting her." Parker was the kindest person I had ever met. For a guy with a soft heart like his, he had chosen a career that revolved around tragedy.

I had feelings too, but I never let them show on the job. I took an all-business approach to solving cases. "Where did she work?"

"Shay was a freelance bookkeeper. She had a couple of accounts that kept her busy."

"Can you give us the names of her clients?"

Amanda shrugged. "I don't know who they are. She worked on a laptop she had with her on the day she disappeared. It's gone, along with her purse."

Parker stared at the ceiling as he considered his next question. "Could you show us her bedroom? Maybe she has some work files or a pay stub that might help us figure out who she worked for."

She gave him a hopeful smile. "Of course. She stayed in the guest bedroom. You guys are a lot smarter than the other two suits they sent over."

Once the homeowner permitted us to search her home, Parker and I found several boxes of work folders and papers stashed in Shay's closet. There was too much information to sort through in an evening, so Amanda allowed us to take it with us.

When we got back to the car, Parker and I were hopeful something in those papers might lead us to a motive for Shay's departure or evidence of foul play. When Amanda mentioned Shay was a freelance bookkeeper and that her laptop was missing, we considered her disappearance might be connected to money—a common motive for murder.

Our next steps were to search the paperwork, track down the purse and laptop, and discover the identity of the mystery boyfriend.

ESCAPE—EVELYN

I had my phone turned off all day and hadn't spoken to Leo since last night—at least, that was the last time I remembered talking to him. I sent him a text to let him know I had turned my phone back on:

EVELYN: Hey, babe. Miss you. I'm finished painting for today. On my way to yoga with Tess. Can't wait to see you later. Love you!

Leo didn't respond immediately, and I wished I could skip out on Tess, rush home, and give him a big hug. The guilt of sending the nude selfie to Stefano was eating me alive. I needed to explain what had happened and free myself from this anxiety before the guilt consumed me.

I rechecked my phone.

No response.

Please text me back, Leo.

It was Tuesday night. The day of the week my friend and fellow artist Tess and I had a standing order for a girls' night out. Normally, we went out for drinks, but we planned a yoga class this evening followed by a healthy dinner.

The fitness studio was only a couple blocks away from

the gallery, so we decided to meet here and then walk there together. While I waited for her to arrive, I stretched by the window and watched the foot traffic go by.

Joggers zigzagging around the slow folk, business pros jawing on their phones, families pushing strollers, tourists hugging their purses for fear of being mugged…

I lifted my hands over my head, interlaced my fingers, and leaned to the right to stretch the aching muscles in my back. Holding the pose, I noticed a man across the street staring at me through the glass.

He was dressed in dark jeans and a black t-shirt with a cigarette dangling from his lips. Mid-thirties. Baseball cap. White sneakers. When he noticed I had spotted him, he shifted his focus to his phone. I stepped back from the window to escape his line of sight.

Stop being paranoid, Evelyn.

I was in an art gallery. My self-portrait was on display in the window. Maybe the man had seen my portrait then made the connection that it was me. Or he was staring at one of my ghostly—

Someone banged on the gallery door, startling me half to death.

I hugged the wall and checked around the corner to see who was there.

Tess waved when she spotted me. She was wearing a cheetah print yoga ensemble and had her rolled-up mat tucked under her arm. "Sorry, I didn't bring my key!"

I sighed with relief, knowing it was just my friend trying to get my attention. As we left the gallery, I glanced around to see if the man who had been watching me earlier was still lingering on the street.

No sign of him.

Breathe.

DISTURBED—LEO

 tried to call Evelyn, but she must've been in her yoga class. I texted her and told her I was going out to grab a beer with the guys—and that I loved her very much.

If anyone in the world could set me straight about how to handle the Nicoletta situation, it was my best friend and fellow law enforcement officer, Christopher Santoni. I asked him to meet me at a bar we'd never been to before so I could talk to him privately.

When I arrived at a spot outside our neighborhood, my buddy had a bucket of Pabst Blue Ribbons at the corner table and a basket of peanuts to snack on. As I approached the table, his eagle eyes landed on the bandage I had on my neck.

Our job was dangerous, and any number of things could've happened that resulted in an injury, but when Santoni read my expression, he seemed to understand what had happened. I'd known him my entire life, and this wasn't the first time I had to cover up a love mark before going on duty.

Santoni crossed his thick arms and shook his head as I

approached the table. I was in for a good-natured razzing, and the only way to get it over with was to go headfirst into the shitstorm. "How's it going, Detective Ricci? Looks like you had a nice weekend at the lake house."

Santoni popped the top of a PBR and slid it across the table. Our moms talked daily, and I had no doubt that Mrs. Santoni had already informed her son about my reunion with our old friend Stefano.

I raised my glass in salute and took a swig of beer. "It was eventful." I leaned on the bar and checked out the scene. It was early, so the bar wasn't too crowded. Just a line of regulars seated at the bar, watching sports recaps, and the after-work crowd enjoying half-price wings, loaded potato skins, and happy-hour drink specials.

"What's on your mind, buddy?" Santoni must've read my mood and realized something was troubling me. I had never been in a serious relationship before Evelyn, and I trusted him to steer me toward a resolution that didn't end with Evelyn hating my guts.

The only people I trusted with information about Evelyn's gift were Santoni and Parker. I didn't want to bring my partner into my relationship with Evelyn, and what I was about to say to Santoni included intimate details of my love life.

"Last night. Evelyn was *different*." I peeled back the bandage and revealed the dark red and blue bruise on my neck to give him context.

"Was that an act of violence or passion?" Santoni loved being a cop and serving his community. He knew Evelyn was not the violent type but questioned me the same way he would a stranger.

"Passion. We were both into it. I got a little rough with Evelyn, too."

"Is she hurt?"

"No. I don't think so. She left early this morning before I woke up. She told me it was a painting day and didn't want to be disturbed. I got a text from her an hour ago. She said she loved me."

Santoni took a swig of beer and processed the information. "Well, if you were both into it, then—"

"There's more to the story. It has to do with Evelyn's *gift*."

I backed up the story to Evelyn's chance meeting with Stefano at the cemetery, how we ended up going on a weekend getaway at the lake, and that Evelyn had agreed to paint a portrait of Nicoletta for her memorial charity event this coming weekend.

And that the ghost of Nicoletta Vanzetti had contacted Evelyn through her dreams.

Santoni slowly blinked as if my information had short-circuited his brain waves. "Does Evelyn know about your past relationship with Nicoletta?"

"No. That's what I want to talk to you about. I don't know which way to go on this one. I've waited too long. If I confess now, she's going to be angry I didn't tell her right away."

"True. But if she finds out from someone else, she'll feel betrayed."

As we went back and forth with different scenarios, the consensus was that Evelyn would be ticked either way. I would be livid if Evelyn failed to tell me the truth if our roles were reversed. Especially when there was the possibility that she might find out from the source—Nicoletta.

We finished our first beers and were on to the next round when Santoni seemed perplexed about one detail I had yet to expound upon. "I'm missing something here." He snagged a peanut from the basket, cracked it open, and popped the nuts into his mouth. "How does this ghost story factor into your passionate romp last night? What caused Evelyn to want to get rough with you?"

Now we reached the part of the story I never wanted to consider. Back in the day, when Nicoletta and I were dating, we both found it sexually gratifying to play rough in the bedroom.

Spanking, safe words, blindfolds, bondage…Nicoletta and I loved discovering new and exciting ways to satisfy each other by combining pleasure and pain.

Evelyn was different. We loved playing around with toys and lotions and trying different positions, but I had never spanked or been rough with her until last night.

I had already spilled my guts to Santoni, and there was no turning back now. I downed the rest of my beer, set the empty bottle on the table, and came out with it. "I believe the ghost of Nicoletta Vanzetti possessed Evelyn last night."

STAY AWAY—EVELYN

When Tess and I reached the yoga studio, I couldn't go through with the class. My body was twisted in knots, and my kundalini was coiled up and hissing at the base of my spine. It would be impossible to unwind or even breathe until I decided how to handle my naked selfie situation.

My head was spinning with indecision, and I was about to crash from the emotional pressure.

"Is something wrong, Evelyn? You look ill." Tess touched my arm to steady me before I face-planted on the sidewalk.

"Do you mind if we skip the class? I need a drink."

"You had me at *skip*." Tess hooked her arm with mine and steered me toward the closest bar. The city was ripe with watering holes, and I didn't care where we went as long as they poured with a heavy hand.

We found a quaint corner bar with an outdoor table. Tess and I had on our yoga clothes, but the place was casual and dog friendly, so I didn't feel underdressed.

I ordered a double vodka on the rocks with a splash of

soda and a twist of lime. Tess opted for a cosmopolitan and an order of mozzarella sticks.

"My diet will start two days from *never*." Tess cracked up at her own joke and adjusted her hat to avoid the sun. "How's Leo? Did you guys have fun at the lake?"

Her question caught me off guard. I must've looked like I was about to cry.

"Hey, sweetie. What's going on? Are you guys okay?"

I wanted to tell Tess everything, but I had never shared the true nature of my gift to anyone outside of Leo, Santoni, and Parker. Like everyone else in the city, Tess only knew that ghosts visited me in my dreams. I never shared information about my automatic drawings or my new ability to sketch premonitions.

I trusted my dear friend, but my gift was too dangerous to share with anyone outside of my inner circle. "We're fine. I just—something strange happened last night."

"What?"

As I prepared to confide in Tess about my blackout and naked selfie situation, a man standing on the corner of the street caught my attention. Jeans and a black t-shirt. Baseball cap. White sneakers. It was the same guy who had watched me at the gallery.

I jumped, startled to see him. Tess turned to see what had caught my attention and asked what was wrong.

I looked again, but the man was no longer there. "Oh, nothing." I waved my hand to excuse my strange behavior. "Someone darted across the street, and I was worried they were going to get mowed over by a car."

Tess nodded, but I didn't think she had bought my excuse.

"I'm going to run to the bathroom. Back in a sec." I weaved around the tables, hopped over a golden retriever, and entered the restaurant. If the man following me was still hanging around, I wanted to see if he was hiding out on the other side of the building.

I cruised the indoor dining section and checked out the windows to see if I could find him lingering outside, waiting for me to leave.

He must be gone.

Since I was already inside, I went to the bathroom before returning to the table. Inside the stall, I noticed someone had come in behind me. I looked under the door and was relieved to see a woman's feet instead of a pair of white sneakers.

I opened the door and found a woman waiting by the sink. She smiled awkwardly while I washed my hands as if getting up her nerve to say something. "Uh, sorry if this is weird, but your friend asked me to give this to you." She offered me a pack of cigarettes.

"My friend? You mean the woman outside in the cheetah-print yoga ensemble?"

She shook her head. "No, not her. It was a man. He said you asked him for a smoke."

"Sorry, not me. Must be meant for someone else." I smiled politely and started to leave.

"No. I'm sure it's meant for you. He pointed to you specifically." She placed the pack into my hand. "I don't care what you do with it, but the man paid me twenty bucks to deliver it." The woman laughed and left the bathroom before I thought to ask for a description of the guy.

As I held it in my hand, it felt empty. I tore open the pack and found a handwritten note tucked inside. I unfolded the paper and read the message.

Stay away from Stefano Vanzetti.

My mouth went dry.

I wasn't being paranoid. He was following me. Why would a man I had never met warn me to stay away from Stefano?

No more guessing. I called Leo. He picked up on the first ring.

"Hey, sweetheart. How are—"

"I need you to pick me up." My words came out shaky. I didn't want to scare him, but the discretely placed note and the guy following me had me freaked out.

"Where are you?"

"A place called Ruby's a couple blocks away from the gallery."

"Are you safe?"

"Yeah. I think so. I'm here with Tess."

"What happened?"

A door opened, and a couple of women entered the bathroom. I couldn't go into details while I was in public. "I can't talk now. I'll explain when you get here."

When Evelyn got into the car, her hands were trembling. She looked exhausted and stressed and all I wanted to do was find out what happened so I could make her problems disappear. I dropped her friend Tess off at her place, and as soon as she waved goodbye, tears streamed down Evelyn's cheek.

"What happened?"

Evelyn pulled out her sketchbook and began to draw. "A man followed me tonight. I saw him watching me through the gallery window and again when I went to the bar with Tess. I tried to get a picture of him but lost him."

I kept my eyes on the road and stole glances at Evelyn's composite sketch of a tall man wearing plain clothes, a baseball cap, shades, and high-top white sneakers.

"Had you seen him before tonight?"

"No. But something else happened right after he showed up at the bar." She reached into her purse and pulled out a cigarette pack. "A woman gave this to me in the bathroom. There was a note inside."

"What did it say?"

"Stay away from Stefano Vanzetti."

Back at our place, Evelyn tossed her yoga mat on the floor, wrapped her arms around me, and hugged me as if we hadn't seen each other for a year.

I rocked her gently as she buried her head on my chest and told me she loved me. There was more going on than what she had told me, and it seemed like something was weighing on her conscience.

Does this have something to do with Stefano? Everything else seems to.

"I blacked out last night," she said. "The last thing I remember was reading my book, turning off the light, and going to bed. I have no memory of what happened between that time and when I woke up early this morning."

She pulled back from my embrace and met my eyes. "Did we make love?"

As I stared into her eyes, my heart sank. Guilt flooded my soul knowing Evelyn didn't remember being intimate and possibly had no control over her own body last night. A sickening sense of dread washed over me as I realized my theory that Nicoletta's ghost had possessed her was valid.

The question that was eating me alive was how did it happen?

"Yes. We made love last night." No matter the consequences, I had to tell Evelyn about my past relationship with Nicoletta and share my opinion about the possibility that she had somehow taken control of her body without her knowledge.

"Evelyn, there's something I need to tell you—"

"Can it wait?" She crossed her arms and shook off a chill. She was wearing a long-sleeved wrap, but her body was trembling as if she was freezing. "I feel sick. I need to lie down."

THE PACKAGE—EVELYN

*L*eo tucked me into bed and stayed beside me as I came down from a dizzy spell.

"I'm exhausted from painting all day. I'll be fine. I just need a catnap then we'll talk later."

Leo smoothed my hair out of my face and stared into my eyes. "Are we okay?"

A fresh round of guilt came over me. "I love you more than anything in the world, Leo. Nothing will ever come between us."

He kissed me softly, turned off the light, and left the room. I took a deep breath and turned on my side to settle in for much-needed rest.

"Your secret is safe with me, Evelyn. Leo will never find out." Stefano's words replayed in my mind like a soundtrack from hell. I never wanted to keep a secret from Leo, and that devil was using my sin to drive a wedge between us.

What kind of person would coerce a woman to lie to her boyfriend? A man with questionable morals. It was a calculated move on Stefano's part—a means for a spoiled billionaire to get what he wanted—*me.*

I closed my eyes and vanquished the glossy-haired demon from my mind as I drifted off to sleep.

SCREEECH...

A sharp scraping sound like nails on a chalkboard woke me from my sleep. I sat up in bed and checked around the room for the source of the noise. A woman was curled up outside my window like a cat, scratching her long fingernails down my bedroom window.

Her face was covered by a sheer black veil, making it difficult to make out her features. When I got out of bed and approached her, she pressed a package wrapped in brown paper against the window.

Water dripped from the package, and ink bled over the pages. It appeared the contents were disintegrating from being submerged in water.

I stepped closer to inspect the package and noticed handwriting on the paper, but the ink was smeared, and the words were illegible.

The woman banged her fist on the glass, desperate for me to take the package.

The moment I lifted the window, she held it out and shoved it toward me. I was about to take it from her but stopped when I could make out her features.

She wasn't a woman—she was a *corpse*.

Rigor mortis had settled into her skin, leaving her face blotchy and distorted. Her eyes had melted away, leaving two dark, cavernous holes devoid of life. The fingers that clutched the package were bones wrapped in a greenish-black shroud of decayed skin.

She shoved the package into my hands. I tried to hold onto it, but it became watery mush and dripped through my fingertips like a heaping scoop of lumpy oatmeal.

"I'm sorry. I can't help you." I backed away from her, but the corpse grabbed my wrist and dragged me through the window.

I closed my eyes and screamed as my stomach turned from the sickening falling sensation. When I opened my eyes, I was alone in the dark on a secluded road. A wintery mix of ice and snow fell, chilling me to the bone.

As I walked toward a covered bridge, headlights cut through the darkness. Three male figures got out of the car. Their shadows stretched across the road, blanketing my body in darkness. A crushing sense of fear settled over me, as the realization set in that the men were there to harm me.

Wake up, Evelyn. This is a dream. Wake up!

I tried to run, but my feet were chained to a heavy briefcase, making it impossible to escape. While I stood there, helpless, the shadows swooped down on me like angels of death and feasted on my flesh.

I screamed in terror—then strong hands grasped my arms and pulled me to my feet, helping me to escape my nightmare.

"I've got you, Evelyn. You're safe with me."

ABSTRACT IMAGES—LEO

$\mathcal{A}$fter Evelyn's nightmare, she spent the next couple of hours drawing for the dead. When her hand stopped moving, she was so exhausted that she collapsed on the floor in a heap.

I carried her into the bedroom and tucked her back into bed, hoping this time, she could rest peacefully through the night. "I love you, sweetheart. We're going to get through this." I slid under the sheets beside her and rubbed her back to soothe her.

I understood Evelyn's resolve to use her gift to help others, but her selflessness was draining the life out of her. When her gift had gone dormant, I was relieved. The thought of Evelyn never communicating with the dead again had given me hope that she would be safe, and we could live a normal life.

My love for Evelyn was unconditional, but communicating with the dead was a dangerous practice. If I had my way, Evelyn's gift would disappear for good, and ghosts would never interfere in our lives again.

In the morning, I beat the alarm and texted Parker:

LEO: Rough night. More drawings. Meet at my place?

PARKER: I hope Evelyn is all right. See you soon.

Before my partner arrived, I cleared the candles off our dining table and spread out Evelyn's latest series of nine drawings. This batch seemed different than the others she had drawn in the sense that they were all abstract images.

When Parker got to my place, Evelyn emerged from the bedroom. Thankfully, she had rested after her nightmare and had gotten her energy back. "Hey, guys."

"Hi, Evelyn. How are you?" Parker asked.

"Fine. Aside from the horrible nightmare. What did I draw?"

I kissed her good morning and then led her into our dining room to examine her work. As she studied the drawings, she rearranged them and turned them in different directions to get a new perspective.

"Hmm…" She walked around the table and squinted as if studying a pattern. Then she stood on one of the dining chairs to get a bird's eye view. "They're not in the right order. Can you grab some masking tape, Leo?"

She hopped down from the chair and shifted the placement of her work while I grabbed the tape from the utility drawer. Parker stood back and watched, enthralled by her creative process.

Once she had everything in order, she turned them all over and attached the nine pages. Then she taped it to the wall, and we stood back to assess her work.

"You guys see what I see?" Evelyn asked.

Holy hell. The abstracts were puzzle pieces. When placed in the correct order, the combined images created a creepy image of Nicoletta Vanzetti holding a water-soaked package.

"That's how she came to me last night. She was desperate

to give me the package, but when I tried to take it, the papers disintegrated into mush."

"What do you think it means?" Parker asked.

She took a deep breath. "I believe whatever is inside the package got her killed. If we find it, we'll uncover the truth of why she left the hotel room in the middle of the night."

SPOOKED—EVELYN

My only objective today was to deliver Nicoletta's portrait to Stefano's office. Normally I would have my gallery manager Gibson oversee the delivery, but I wanted to set things straight with Stefano and give Nicoletta's charm bracelet back to him.

The sooner I could fulfill my obligation, the better.

My life had been a blur from the moment I met Stefano at the cemetery. Leo and I needed to get our lives back on track. I hadn't had a chance to talk to him about my naked selfie fiasco, but I would tell him everything as soon as the time was right.

I knew something was bothering him, too, but I had faith that once we had a moment to ourselves, we would reconnect and make everything right between us.

I would drop off the painting to Stefano, and then I wouldn't have to see him again until the charity event on Saturday night—then my business with him was over.

When the delivery driver arrived at the gallery to transport the painting, I asked him if I could catch a ride. Mike was our regular guy and was happy to give me a lift since he was returning to the Arts District for another job anyway.

When we arrived, Stefano's assistant escorted us to a private room where we could display the painting. We set up an easel, unwrapped the protective cover, and placed Nicoletta's portrait near the window.

It was a tradition to place a silky white cloth over the art before the official unveiling. Yes, it was dramatic, but delivery days were special occasions between me and my clients. Our joint effort to create a work of art was a moment to celebrate, and I often got teary-eyed after the big reveal.

"Mr. Vanzetti will join you momentarily, Miss Sinclair," Stefano's assistant said.

Then she offered the delivery driver a coffee as she escorted him back to the lobby. I promised him I wouldn't be long, but he assured me he had an hour before his next job and wasn't in a big rush.

As I waited for Stefano, my stomach fluttered with nervous excitement. Even though I was annoyed with him over his flirtatious behavior, I was proud of the portrait I had painted. I had made the necessary fixes to her facial features and hair color and ensured that no part of myself was still visible in the art.

Now that the job was complete, I hoped Stefano loved the beautiful tribute to Nicoletta's memory as much as I did.

While it pained me to know that Nicoletta was not at peace, I would do everything I could to help her—without getting myself into trouble.

There was a knock on the door, then Stefano led himself into the room. He grinned when he saw the painting staged for the big reveal. "You didn't go to all this trouble for me, eh?" His eyes lit up as my efforts seemed to warm his heart.

"Ready?" I stood next to the painting and grasped the cloth.

"Ready," he said.

"One, two, three!"

As Stefano marveled at the endearing portrait of Nicoletta, I rested my hand over my chest to calm my racing heartbeat. Now that the painting was complete, a rush of conflicting emotions whooshed to the surface.

I was happy I had finished the job, and my life was about to return to normal, but I also felt a sense of dread knowing I had not yet helped Nicoletta find closure.

"My dear Evelyn, I couldn't imagine a more perfect tribute to her memory than this. You captured the essence of Nicoletta's spirit. For this, I am forever in your debt." Stefano tore his gaze away from the portrait as he noticed my panicked expression.

"What's wrong? Did you think I wouldn't like it?"

I laughed to cover up for my weird reaction. "No, no. I love it, too. Reveals always make me a little nervous."

Stefano opened his arms and invited me in for a hug, but I offered a business-like handshake instead.

Stefano grinned as he shook my hand. "Your work should hang in the world's most famous museums, Evelyn Sinclair. Nicoletta would be honored."

He seemed sincere. Maybe I'd misread his intentions. The guy's wife died tragically just six months ago. He was lonely, and it was egotistical of me to think he was trying to steal me away from Leo.

Give him a break, Evelyn.

"You're too kind." I reached into my pocket, retrieved the charm bracelet, and returned it to Stefano. "I hate to cut our reveal short, but I must return to the gallery. I'll see you Saturday night at the fundraiser."

As I turned to leave, I noticed Dino in the doorway, staring at the painting. His gaze was fixed on the lower portion of the canvas, and he seemed spooked by what he was looking at.

I pretended to get something out of my purse and glanced at the painting. I followed his gaze and quickly scanned the area, but nothing strange stood out.

Stop being paranoid, Evelyn.

I wished Dino a good day as I breezed past him, but he was on my heels in a hot second. "Boss told me to make sure you get home safely," he said over my shoulder.

"Thank you, but I have a ride. My driver is in the lobby waiting for me."

"No," he said sharply. "The guy left. He said you were taking too long."

I glanced at my watch. Mike had said he wasn't in a rush. He had only waited for fifteen minutes.

"I'll drive you home." Dino escorted me to the elevator and pushed the button.

As the elevator went down, I felt like I was stuck in a tank with a great white shark. The bad vibes reverberated off the walls as Dino fidgeted nervously. My sixth sense alerted me that I was in danger.

I glanced at the elevator buttons. Dino had pressed the lower-level button—not the lobby stop where I usually got on and off. Why was he taking me to the basement of the building? I didn't know, and I sure as hell wasn't going to find out.

I touched the lobby button. "You pressed the wrong one."

The veins were popping out on the side of his head. "My car is in the garage on the lower level."

A reasonable explanation. I believed him, but I wasn't going to get into his car. When the elevator door opened, I was relieved to see a swarm of businesspeople buzzing around the lobby.

I tried to exit, but Dino put his arm out to block me. "Wait. We'll get off at the next stop."

Knowing he wouldn't try to stop me, I pushed past him and joined the crowd. "Thanks for the offer, but Leo will pick me up."

I felt the heat of Dino's stare as I left the building alone.

SWEET & SEXY—LEO

I spread a tablecloth over the dining table, set out a vase of fresh flowers, and lit Evelyn's favorite candles. Dinner was in the oven. The wine was in the decanter. Dessert was in the fridge. And my apology was on the tip of my tongue.

Today was a big day for me—I learned something about myself. Before I went to bed last night, all I wanted to do was protect the woman I loved. From ghosts, from murder investigations, and most importantly—I wanted to protect Evelyn from *herself.*

Why was Evelyn upset when her gift went on hiatus? How could she possibly want those horrifying ghosts that woke her in the middle of the night, tapping on our bedroom window, showing her their dead bodies? How could that be something a sane person would want anything to do with?

I got the answer to the question while working on a case today.

Using Evelyn's drawings as our guide, Parker and I gathered enough evidence to open a missing persons case for Shay Adams. This was a monumental accomplishment. The information that led us to investigate Shay's disappearance had originated from a *dream*.

Her drawings of the tattoos allowed us to identify the victim, then we found the sister, then we got the box of Shay's work records and personal notes that led us down a path to financial fraud from one of the victim's freelance clients.

Now that there was an open investigation, our team could find out who Shay had worked for at the time of her disappearance. We were also trying to discover the identity of the mystery boyfriend Shay didn't want her sister to know about.

What I learned about myself through this process was that I was a jerk for wishing Evelyn's gift never came back. Like my fellow law enforcement officers, Evelyn was a hero. She selflessly put her life and well-being on the line to help homicide victims find peace in a way no one else could.

Instead of trying to change the woman I loved, I should've supported her and thanked her for her service—the same way she treated me.

Keys rattled outside our apartment door. Evelyn was home. I picked up the vase of fresh flowers and met her at the door. "Welcome home, sweetheart."

Evelyn scanned the room and seemed confused by the romantic setting. "What's going on?"

"We're celebrating tonight."

"What are we celebrating?"

I gave her a peck on the lips. "You."

"Why? What did I do?" She slung her purse onto the couch and eyed me suspiciously.

"I'll show you." I wrapped my arm around her and led her to the kitchen bar.

Instantly, she zeroed in on a file folder I had placed next

to the wine. She seemed worried about what I had to show her, so I wanted to put her mind at ease.

"Because of *you*, we were able to identify a missing person and open an investigation into her disappearance."

"Really? Is that…*the Lady in the Lake?*"

"Ready to meet her?" It may seem morbid to people outside our profession, but seeking justice for victims was our calling, and Evelyn's information led us to a crime no one believed had ever happened. I opened the folder and revealed a Missing Person flyer for our victim, Shay Adams.

Evelyn's eyes welled with tears as she focused on Shay's smiling face. The picture her sister provided showed her full sleeve of tattoos on both arms, including the Celtic cross Evelyn had drawn, which led Parker to Amanda's social media post about her missing sister.

"She had pink hair." Evelyn smiled through her tears. "I'm sorry I couldn't help you before you died, Shay," she whispered as she traced her cross tattoo with the tip of her finger. "We'll help you find peace. Show me how to help you."

Seeing Evelyn's compassion toward a woman she had never known wrecked me. I never wanted her to change. I loved her sensitive soul, and from that moment on, I vowed never to treat Evelyn or her gift as a burden again.

"Did you find out if Shay and Nicoletta knew each other?"

"The investigation has just begun, and of course, I can't discuss any details about the case with you. But I can promise that my team will dig into every aspect of Shay's life. If there is a connection between her and Nicoletta, we'll find it."

Evelyn wrapped her arms around me. "Thank you for believing in me. I'm so thankful the universe brought us together. I love you so much."

I kissed the top of her head as we embraced. Her tears

soaked through my t-shirt and flooded over my heart. Now was not the time to tell her about my prior relationship with Nicoletta, but I would tell her everything as soon as the moment was right.

"I love you, sweetheart. I can't imagine my life without you." I lifted her chin and kissed her softly on the lips. Being close to Evelyn and having this moment to share how much she meant to me was something long overdue in our hectic lives.

Evelyn snaked her hands up my back and massaged the ripple of muscles under my shirt. She slid her tongue inside my mouth and kissed me deeply as I embraced her. "Make love to me, Leo." I was happy to know Evelyn and I were thinking the same thing. I picked her up, carried her into our bedroom, and set her down on the bed.

As she lay there, looking up at me with those gorgeous blue eyes, I was grateful to have this remarkably brave and selfless woman in my life. I turned on some music and dimmed the lights to create a romantic mood for our special night.

Then I gave Evelyn my undying attention and undressed her slowly so I could appreciate every inch of her incredible body. I slid under the covers with her and made love to her slowly as I savored the warmth of her body, the faint scent of citrus on her skin, and the sweet and sexy moans of satisfaction that escaped her lips as I pleased her.

I was the luckiest man in the world and wanted to spend a lifetime showing Evelyn how much I loved her.

BOLD MOVE—EVELYN

Leo held my hand as we strolled into the ballroom and joined the black-tie charity event. A jazz quartet played as our fellow guests sipped champagne, perused the bid-and-buy auction items, and noshed on elevated appetizers.

"Have I told you how amazing you look tonight, Evelyn?" Leo's gaze drifted down my body, as he admired how the layers of my midnight blue formal gown swayed as we moved through the crowd.

Detective Ricci looked jaw-droppingly gorgeous in a tux. The tailored suit accentuated his broad chest and tight abs, and I wasn't blind to all the attention he was attracting from the ladies in the crowd. "That's quite a compliment, coming from the hottest guy in the room."

I squeezed his thick arm and tossed him a sultry smile. Leo had been showering me with affection since we put all the Stefano drama behind us, and I was excited to get through this event and spend the rest of the evening in a hotel room with my sexy boyfriend.

"I hope you have a lot of energy tonight, Evelyn. I've got big plans for you tonight."

My cheeks warmed as Leo whispered something naughty in my ear. I was relieved that tonight was the end of my business relationship with Stefano so I could give Leo all my attention.

Now that Nicoletta's portrait was complete and her memorial fundraiser was upon us, I could step back and let Leo and his team investigate the disappearance of Shay Adams and how it related to Nicoletta Vanzetti.

From this moment on, I was out of the investigation.

This was why I decided not to tell Leo about the naked selfie I had sent to Stefano. Things were going so well between us. I didn't want to start another argument. Unless the esteemed Mr. Vanzetti took the stage, announced my bad deed to the crowd, and flashed my nude photo on the presentation screen, I trusted Leo would never find out.

Since I had no memory of committing the relationship sin, I didn't want to hurt Leo over something I had no control over.

Then why do I still feel guilty about it?

"Bruschetta?" A server swooped in with a tray of savory appetizers. The young woman with bright red lipstick looked familiar, so I glanced at her name badge. "Chloe—from Sal's Family Restaurant."

"I know these are your favorite, Miss Sinclair."

"These are delicious," I said to Leo. "Stefano treated me to lunch at Sal's on Monday after our business meeting." Another thing I should've mentioned before he found out from someone else. I selected a hearty slice of crispy bread with marinated tomatoes and popped it into my mouth.

Leo lifted his brow and gave me a nod as we followed the crowd into the main ballroom for dinner. When I looked up at the stage, Nicoletta's portrait was on display next to the speaker's podium.

"Evelyn, your painting is incredible." Leo squeezed my hand supportively.

It was hard to believe, but this was Leo's first time seeing the portrait. Typically, he saw all my works-in-progress when he visited my studio, but this was a rush job, and he never had the chance.

Leo steered us toward the stage to get a closer look. I felt a sense of pride as he studied the fine details of the work. I had strategically placed some hidden pictures of her favorite things into the painting. There was a great blue heron in the fold of her skirt, the shape of her grandmother's brooch appeared in the grain of the wooden dock, and a—

"That was a bold move." Leo's gaze zoomed in on the lower corner of the painting—the exact same spot Dino had zeroed in on.

I pulled Leo closer so I could take another look. Finally, I spotted what the guys had already noticed—a ghostly hand reaching up from underneath the water. It was faint and hardly noticeable to the naked eye, but it was there and impossible to unsee.

"Shit," I said under my breath.

"You didn't do that on purpose?"

"What do you think?" I snapped.

The lights flashed, signaling it was time to take our seats for dinner. As we searched for our table number, it appeared Leo and I were seated at The Vanzetti Table of Honor. When we approached, Stefano greeted us with open arms as did Uncle Luca and their entourage of special guests.

I recognized the men. They had been at the bar the day Stefano and I had lunch at Sal's Restaurant. They must be a tight group of friends.

Just one more night. Tomorrow you will have your freedom.

SNITCH—LEO

My phone buzzed during the salad course.

It was a number I didn't recognize. As a detective, my cell phone number was available to the public. Witnesses, victims, informants...the call could be coming from someone who had information about one of my cases.

I excused myself and found a quiet place to take the call. I tapped the phone and answered, "Detective Ricci."

"I don't want to get in any trouble, but if I know something about the Shay Adams case, do I get some reward money or something?" the female caller asked.

My pulse quickened from the adrenaline rush of hearing Shay's name. "If you have information that leads to an arrest or helps us locate the victim, you will receive a cash reward. What do you know?"

The caller exhaled nervously. "I got that lady's purse. I found it. It's got her wallet with her ID, credit cards, some keys, a bunch of work papers and receipts—"

"What kind of work papers and receipts?" I asked. When the caller went quiet, I feared I was going to lose her. "You can remain anonymous and don't have to give details over the phone. I need to be certain what you have belongs to Shay Adams. Then we can arrange for an exchange. Cash for the purse. How does that sound?"

While I had the caller on the line, I listened to the background noise in an attempt to identify her location. Plates clinked, and people were talking in the background. Sounded like a restaurant.

"How much will you pay me?"

"Five hundred bucks."

"Okay. What do you want to know?"

"What kind of purse is it?"

"No name brand. Black with a gold buckle."

"What's the address on the ID?"

When she read it to me, I knew that information was correct.

"Read me something off the work papers."

Papers shuffled in the background. "Uh, it's a bunch of spreadsheets. The top of one of the pages says *expenses*."

It sounds like something a bookkeeper would have in her purse. I was convinced the caller was credible, and I had to get my hands on the only significant evidence we had so far in the investigation. "Where do you want to meet?"

"Wait," the caller said. "How do I know you're not going to arrest me? I have to go to work. I got kids. I can't go to jail tonight. What if someone sees me talking to a cop? People will think I'm a snitch or something."

Don't fuck this up, Ricci.

"I don't want you to get in any trouble. All I want from you is the purse and the details of where you found it. That's it. You're doing the right thing. I won't arrest you because you haven't done anything wrong."

"Okay. I guess you're right. But you have to come alone, and you can't wear a uniform or drive up in a cop car."

"No problem. Where do you want to meet?"

"Downtown. Go to High Street. I'll give you my work address when you get closer."

I rushed back to the table, told Evelyn I had to leave for an hour or so, then headed back to our hotel room to get out of this tux.

BARGAINING CHIP—LEO

I changed into athletic clothes, concealed my weapon under my jacket, and grabbed the emergency cash I carried for situations like this. I had driven Evelyn's Audi to the event, so I had a civilian car to keep my end of the bargain.

Once on the road, I was only ten minutes away. I tried to call Parker, but it went straight to voice mail.

"I got a tip from a female informer who claims to have Shay's missing purse. Checks out. Going to make a cash exchange near High Street downtown. Will give you an update after I secure the evidence."

When I turned onto High Street, I called the woman back. "I'm here. Where do you want to meet?"

"Mack's Diner. Sit at the booth closest to the bathroom. My name tag says Danielle. Order a Coke, then say you want a hoagie with fries to go. It'll be me taking your order."

I liked the idea of being in a public place for my own safety, but I wanted to be sure I could get all the information I needed out of her before making the exchange. When I walked inside, I sat in the booth with my back facing the wall and opened the menu.

A moment later, a mousy brunette with wide eyes approached the table. "Do you know what you want?" Her hands trembled as she held her pen and waitress pad, ready to take my order.

"I'll start with a Coke. I'll place a carryout order when you get back."

The informant nodded and scurried off to set our plan into motion.

My cell buzzed. Parker was calling me back. My informant was already on edge, so I didn't want to spook her by answering my phone. A moment later, I received a text.

PARKER: Call me back. Urgent. I found the connection between Evelyn's ghosts. Shay worked as a bookkeeper for Nicoletta's charity. Also got a message back from my contact in the Organized Crime division. Your friend Vanzetti has financial ties to the Outfit.

What the hell?

The waitress returned with my drink before I could respond to Parker's text. I turned my phone face down then pretended to study the menu. "Where did you get the purse?"

Her eyes skittered around the room. "I found it here in the parking lot. It was just sitting there on the ground, like someone had dropped it when they got out of their car."

"What did you do with it?"

"I hid it in my jacket and took it with me on the bus. I waited until I got home to see what was in it."

My phone buzzed with a string of incoming texts.

"Did you take anything from it?"

A fellow server delivered a couple plates to the table in front of mine. "Everything comes with fries, but if you want coleslaw, you have to make it a platter. It costs a dollar extra."

When the other waitress left, she continued. "I took the

cash. Three hundred and twenty dollars. That's it. I didn't try to use her cards or anything. I was going to sell the purse, but I got scared."

"Where did you stash it?"

The cook rang a bell in the kitchen and called out a number, indicating there was an order to pick up.

Now my phone beeped, indicating I had a new voicemail message. Parker must have some very important information to share.

"Look, I need to get back to work."

"Answer the question. Then I'll place my order." I pulled out my wallet and showed her the cash.

Her eyes widened at the sight of all that money. "I kept it in my closet. No one except me touched it."

"Great. I'll take a hoagie and fries to go."

She scribbled something on her order pad, tore the check out of her book, and placed it face down on the table. "You can pay for your order now."

I picked up the check and turned it over. The message read:

"Go to the men's room. I hid the purse in the back of the cabinet under the sink."

I slid Danielle a five-hundred-dollar tip and headed for the bathroom. On my way down the hallway, I glanced around to get a sense of who was in the room. There was a decent crowd for a late-night diner, but no one seemed out of place.

When I reached the bathroom, I stepped inside and checked under the stalls to make sure I was alone. Once I cleared the room, I crouched down and searched the cabinet, but the purse wasn't—

The door opened, and within a nanosecond, a gun clicked behind my ear. "Freeze, Ricci. If you make a move for that gun, I'll blow a hole in your fucking head."

I kept my hands still but shot a glance behind me to see who had gotten the jump on me. He was a middle-aged man I had never seen before, but I recognized his gun—it was the type used by professional hitmen.

While my instincts urged me to fight, two more men entered the bathroom and locked the door behind them. All three wore plain sweatsuits and ballcaps pulled down low to shield their faces. These guys were not amateurs—they were hired killers.

They wouldn't hesitate to take me out right here in this bathroom if I failed to follow their orders.

The handlers each grabbed an arm while the gunman removed my concealed weapon from the holster.

"What do you want?" I asked.

There were only three reasons why someone would hire a hitman. The first was to threaten my life or the lives of people I loved. This ambush might've been spawned to keep me from testifying in court or to steer me away from investigating someone who had everything to lose, but plenty of money to make their problems go away.

The gunman ignored me and spoke in Italian to his men, ordering them to search me for more weapons. They grabbed my wallet, phone, key fob, and the knife I carried when I went into a situation that required extra resources.

The second reason someone would hire a professional to attack a cop was to warn me to stay out of someone's business. In this case, they would likely take me to a second location, beat me half to death, then issue a warning detailing what would happen if I ever stuck my nose where it didn't belong again.

"You're asking the wrong question, Detective," the gunman said. "We already have what we want. You're just the bargaining chip."

My pulse quickened as I considered the third option in

this scenario—coercion. As I processed what was happening, I realized the exchange was a setup. There was no purse. They lured me into their trap, and I took the bait.

Not only had I been careless enough to get myself into trouble, but I had also left their prime target alone at the party—Evelyn.

As the worst-case scenarios spun in my head, my instincts took over and urged me to fight. If I didn't find a way to warn Evelyn, these dangerous men would grab her if they hadn't done so already. With two big guys holding me back, I tried to kick the gunman below the belt.

He must've expected I wouldn't go down easy, but instead of getting a bullet in my temple, I felt a sharp stab in my neck. *A needle—shit.* My vision blurred, and my body slumped forward from whatever drug was swimming through my bloodstream.

When I went limp, the men released me, and my body crumbled on the cold, dirty floor. As I clung to consciousness, the gunman knelt and stared into my eyes.

"Your girlfriend's talent is remarkable. But I don't think she's using her gift to its full potential."

The gunman laughed as his cohorts lifted me off the floor, shoved a gag in my mouth, and dragged me out the exit door into the alley. There was a getaway car waiting next to a line of dumpsters.

The last thing I remembered after they dumped me into the trunk was cursing myself for failing to protect Evelyn.

WARNING SIGNS—EVELYN

*L*eo missed dinner, and I was starting to worry.

He had left because of something work-related but couldn't give me details. His job was dangerous, and I constantly had to swallow back the horrifying what-if scenarios that raced through my mind whenever Leo and I were apart.

I was proud of my heroic boyfriend and was grateful for his service to our community. I would never want to change him, nor would I try, but dating a detective came with a gnawing dread that constantly had me on edge.

When our servers delivered desserts to our table, I stared at my cherry cheesecake and fidgeted with my fork, too nervous to eat. Leo was always worried about me, but he was the one who constantly put himself in harm's way to protect and serve the good citizens of Chicago.

I checked my phone for the billionth time to see if Leo had sent a message.

Nothing.

I looked up from my phone and noticed a man in a chef's

jacket from Sal's restaurant overseeing the staff. He looked oddly familiar—then I remembered where I had seen him. He was the man in the jeans and white sneakers who had been following me.

I had to find out who he was. "The food was delicious tonight, Stefano. Is that the chef?" I pointed to the man.

"Yes. That is Sal's son, Anthony. He runs the kitchen for the catering business."

I needed to tell Leo. Where was he? It was not like him to leave me worrying.

I had a horrible feeling in the pit of my stomach that something terrible had happened. If Leo had left the party because of work, then whatever the reason, it was urgent. I considered reaching out to Parker, but wouldn't he be with Leo? If I called, would I endanger one or both of them?

"Are you all right, Evelyn?" Stefano placed his hand on my shoulder.

When the warmth of his touch melted into my skin, a word popped into my head.

Fantasma.

I jumped, unnerved by simultaneous warning signs going off in my head. My sixth sense was telling me something was definitely wrong.

"I'm fine," I lied. "Dinner was wonderful. I don't have room for dessert." I tossed my napkin on the table and stood to excuse myself. "I'm going outside to get some air." I wanted to get away from the Italians for a moment to look up the meaning of my clairaudient message.

Since all the other words had been Italian, I assumed this one was, too. But I didn't know if this word was connected to my uneasy feelings about Leo. It could have something to do with Shay's case or be related to Nicoletta.

"I'll join you." Stefano offered his arm to escort me to the balcony.

"Great." I plastered on a smile, not wanting to appear suspicious. *Fantasma* could have something to do with Stefano as well. I had received the word when he touched my shoulder. But no matter the reason, I would keep it to myself and share it with Leo when he returned.

The five-star hotel overlooked the lake on one side and had an excellent view of the skyline on the other. I held my cell in my palm, waiting for my chance to search the word as soon as Stefano turned away.

As a gentle breeze blew across the balcony, Stefano focused all his energy on me. "Tonight was perfect because of *you*." His gaze traveled along my curves as he unapologetically checked me out and enjoyed the view.

So much for doubting my opinion of him. This was not a lonely man seeking friendship. This was a guy trying to move in on his buddy's girlfriend. He was standing too close for comfort, and my fight or flight instincts urged me to distance myself from him.

Where are you, Leo?

I needed to find out the meaning of the word *fantasma*. Now. I typed the word into my translation app and was shocked to find out the meaning. *Ghost.*

My heart bottomed out of my chest as my brain struggled to decipher the message. Who was the ghost? I sensed Leo was in danger and had a horrible feeling something had happened to him. Was Leo the ghost?

As my body trembled with panic, my cell buzzed with an incoming text:

LEO: Change in plans. Go with Stefano to the lake house. I will meet you there. Sorry I had to miss the party. Will explain when I get there. Love you.

While I was relieved Leo had contacted me, I still sensed something was horribly wrong.

I looked up from my phone and noticed Stefano also

checking his messages then realized it was a group text between the three of us.

Stefano grinned with devilish delight. "Looks like we'll be spending the night at the lake house tonight."

ONE LAST TIME—EVELYN

Flickering flames danced in the gas lamps as the limo rolled up to the lake house.

When I stepped out of the vehicle, I was greeted by a chorus of crickets, screeching bats, and night owls hooting their evening songs.

Once inside, Stefano dismissed Mira and Dino so the two of us could be alone. He opened a bottle of wine and poured it into the decanter. "While we wait for Leo, we can enjoy our drinks outside. There's something I want to discuss with you. Tonight was difficult honoring Nicoletta, and I would like your guidance on an important matter."

I checked my cell again. No messages. My battery's life was on its last breath, and I needed to find a phone charger. When we left the party, I didn't think to grab my overnight bag with my essentials from our hotel room. Leo and I had planned to stay the night after the fundraiser.

Perfect. I'm stuck here in my formal gown, a pinchy bra, and toe-crushing stilettos.

"Do you have a charger?"

Stefano placed my phone on a charging station and then led me down the stone-lined path to the seating area next to the water's edge. As the candles around us flickered, Stefano stood and stared into the darkness. A storm was on the horizon, and the air was still and humid. An eerie calm settled over the lake as Stefano prepared his thoughts.

As I waited for him to speak, all my frustrations bubbled to the surface. I was terrified that I hadn't heard from Leo, and I was done with Stefano calling all the shots and using me for his own selfish desires.

From the moment we met, he'd manipulated me into doing his bidding. I was tired of being nice to Leo's old friend and was done with Stefano trying to put a wedge between Leo and me. No more waiting submissively for Stefano to tell me what was next.

Stefano was cunning and manipulative and used his wife's death to get sympathy from Leo and me. But my eyes were open now, and I sensed there was a more sinister plan in play than him simply wanting me to paint his late wife's portrait.

He needed something from me and was willing to go to extremes to get what he wanted. I was done with Stefano's conniving ways and wanted the truth.

No more lies. No more deception. No more guessing games.

Stefano had worked his way into my life for a reason—now was the time to find out why. "What do you want from me, Stefano?"

He turned away from the water slowly and met my gaze. He studied my expression and regarded me like an innocent lamb about to be devoured by a ravenous wolf. "You haven't figured it out yet, Miss Sinclair?"

I clenched the fabric of my formal gown to release the

tension building inside me. "I know you are using me to make contact with Nicoletta."

Stefano lifted his hands and chuckled incredulously. "Miss Sinclair, I'm afraid you—"

"Don't you dare deny it, Stefano. I know you are desperate to make contact with your wife, but I don't know why. It's just the two of us now. Tell me, what do you want from Nicoletta?"

Stefano's expression darkened. "On the night of the accident, Nicoletta left me. We made love after the party and then fell asleep in bed together. We never argued. I had no reason to believe anything was wrong. But when I woke in the early morning hour, my wife was gone," Stefano said.

"Wait. Do you think she *left* you? As in, she wanted to end your marriage?" I knew from Leo that Nicoletta had left the hotel room in the middle of the night, but I hadn't taken that to mean she was leaving her husband.

"Yes, but that's only the beginning of my mental torture. Nicoletta is still here. My wife haunts this house and torments me through the night. She comes to me in the mist." He waved his hand over the lake.

"Her spirit lifts from the water in the dead of night and enters my bedroom. She bangs on the windows, slams the doors, and terrorizes me from beyond the grave."

He's right—Nicoletta is haunting this house.

The question was, why was she angry at him? There must be a reason why she escaped in the middle of the night. They seemed to live a perfect life, but no marriage was perfect. What happened that caused Nicoletta to leave her husband?

Is he a violent man? Did she leave him out of fear?

Nicoletta had a reason, and I was certain it had to do with the package she was so desperate to give me. What secret was she hiding?

"I need answers. You must help me, Evelyn. I can't go on living until I know the truth."

Now that I knew Nicoletta was tormenting her husband from beyond the grave, I feared Stefano may've been responsible for her death. He admitted that Nicoletta left him—a clear motive for murder.

Stefano had been lying to me all along, and if he believed I could communicate with Nicoletta through my gift, then she would be able to out her husband as the killer. I was in grave danger.

Fantasma. The same clairaudient message I'd heard earlier popped into my head. My blood ran cold, and I rubbed my arms to chase away the chills.

My body went rigid with fear. I needed to get away from Stefano, but I was too stunned and frightened to run. Stefano took off his tux jacket and wrapped it around my shoulders.

As he stood behind me, he whispered in my ear. "She's here. I know you can feel her." He dangled Nicoletta's charm bracelet in my face. "Put it on, Evelyn. I must speak to my wife one last time."

The charm bracelet. He knows I can channel Nicoletta's ghost through her personal item.

I shoved his hand aside and backed away from him in horror. I had to escape, contact Leo, and get the hell out of this house. I lifted my formal gown and clicked up the path in my stilettoes.

I wasn't safe here—I could feel it in my bones. It wasn't because the lake house was haunted. The uneasy feeling stemmed from the living monsters who resided here. As I hustled up the path, I checked over my shoulder. Stefano was close behind.

When I got to my phone, I would escape and hide in the woods until help arrived. I ran inside and surveyed the scene.

My blood ran cold when I realized something sinister had been set into motion.

Why are all these men here?

While I had no idea what was happening, there was one thing I knew for sure—I had fallen into a trap.

DECEPTION—LEO

I opened my eyes and found myself bound and gagged in the garage of Stefano's lake house. My head was spinning from the drugs, and my body felt like a herd of bison had trampled over me.

I struggled against my restraints to test their security. My wrists were bound to the arms of a chair with zip ties. My ankles secured to the chair legs. A rope pulled tight across my waist wrapped around the back of the chair.

These guys were professionals. Rescuing myself without a tool or an accomplice would be impossible, but neither of those resources were readily available.

The good news was, they hadn't killed me yet. The bad news was I was weak, injured, unarmed, and up against men whose job it was to make people like me disappear. But I had trained for situations like this and knew how to fight. There was a way out of this, I just couldn't think clearly enough to figure out a plan.

As I blinked away the shadows that clouded my mind, and the memory of the events leading up to my abduction became clearer, a new fear came crashing down on me—*Where is Evelyn?*

I remembered Parker's text message just before the guys got the jump on me:

"I found the connection between Evelyn's ghosts. Shay worked as a bookkeeper for Nicoletta's charity. Also got a message back from my contact in the Organized Crime division. Your friend Vanzetti has financial ties to the Outfit."

Mom was right—Stefano was connected to the mob.

Once I learned from Parker that my old pal Stefano Vanzetti was a member of organized crime, the unsettling realization settled over me that it wasn't me they were after. It was Evelyn. Stefano had figured out that Nicoletta had contacted Evelyn through her dreams.

There were three reasons why Stefano Vanzetti would stoop to this level of deviance to connect with the ghost of his dead wife.

The truth. He wanted an answer to the nagging question of why Nicoletta had snuck out of the hotel room after her charity event to sneak off to the lake house. Was she trying to leave her husband?

Love. Evelyn believed Nicoletta remained earthbound because she died suddenly and never had the chance to say goodbye to her husband. Stefano's desire to connect with her from the grave could be for the same reason. He needed closure.

Murder. Evelyn said Nicoletta was desperate to give her a package. Stefano was connected to the Chicago Mafia. What if it was evidence against her husband? Nicoletta may've witnessed a crime or otherwise been a threat to the organization. She had left her husband in the middle of the night. It seemed reasonable that she was trying to escape her marriage.

As I contemplated Stefano's motives, a sickening thought

crossed my mind. What if Stefano was responsible for Nicoletta's death? If he thought Nicoletta was ratting him out from the grave through Evelyn, the mob would go to any extremes necessary to silent the witness—Evelyn.

This is all my fault.

I played right into Stefano's plan. He'd always been a good liar since we were kids. A self-loathing dread drenched my body in a cold sweat. My job was dangerous. Being killed in the line of duty was a reality I faced every day I served my community. But Evelyn was an innocent victim in all of this.

Yes, she made it clear a hundred times over that she had an obligation to draw for the dead and use her gift to bring peace to the dearly departed. She had willingly put her life on the line to stop a serial killer, but that didn't make her a sworn officer of the law.

On top of everything, this time, it was personal. My old friend was behind the deception, and I'd helped him by giving Evelyn a reason to trust him.

My job was to protect her, and I failed.

No. I wouldn't accept that. I wasn't likely to walk out of this situation alive, but I would damn well save the woman I loved from suffering the same fate.

The lock clicked on the garage door that led into the house.

Someone was coming.

INSURANCE POLICY—EVELYN

The mood of the house had flipped. Dark energy polluted the air, filling my lungs with a heavy dread. A foul-tasting film covered my tongue, and the unholy aura of pure evil enveloped the room.

Luca, along with three men I had never seen before, gathered around the bar and conversed in Italian. The men were staring at something on the bar and were having a serious discussion about whatever it was.

The toxic energy from the group was palpable. As I moved into the room, my body felt heavy and bloated, like I had weights around my ankles while wading through a pool of putrid soup.

When I approached, the men snapped their attention toward me like a pack of coyotes sensing a wounded animal limping through the woods. Unnerved by their cold stares, I crossed my arms and dropped my gaze to the floor.

If I tried to run, they would tackle me. For now, I had to protect myself from physical harm and find out what was happening to Leo. Stefano breezed into the room and summoned me to the bar. "Evelyn, could you join us, please?"

Dino was behind me, preventing me from bolting out the back door. His hot breath beat down my neck as he shadowed me, ready to subdue me should Stefano require assistance.

Why do these men consider me a threat?

My heels clicked on the hardwood floor as I eased into the living room, cautious not to make any sudden movements. The three men stepped back, giving me space to join Luca and Stefano. As I approached, I stared at the bar in disbelief.

A chill shot through my veins when I realized what the guys were discussing.

A dozen photographs of me, painting the watercolor study of Nicoletta's corpse holding the package. The men had pictures of the nude painting of Nicoletta, displaying Shay's tattoos on her arms, and anchored to the bottom of the lake by the briefcase.

The art I had painted when I thought I was alone while Stefano and Leo were out boating.

Someone had been watching me from the window that day. *Dino.* He lied about leaving and spent the day spying on me from the house.

I held my breath as Stefano studied the morbid details of my art. Nicoletta's gory head wound. The charm bracelet tattooed on her hip. The briefcase that got her killed. "Tell me where the package is, Evelyn."

He tapped his finger over the photograph that showed a closeup of the briefcase.

I was speechless. The evidence against me was too damning to deny. The details were too precise. The godawful men in this room knew my secret: I have a paranormal gift that allows me to communicate with the dead through my art.

"The boss asked you a question, Miss Sinclair," Luca said.

Fear took hold, threatening my heart to explode. I couldn't admit the truth, and lying would only get me into more trouble.

Luca clicked his tongue, admonishing my silence. "There's an easy way to do this, and there's another way that you're not going to like so much." He motioned to his committee of vultures, ready to feast on my corpse. "I had a feeling you might not cooperate, so I bought myself an insurance policy."

I shifted my gaze nervously between Luca and Stefano. "What are you talking about?"

"Have you heard from your boyfriend lately?"

A rush of nausea washed over me as my gaze drifted to Luca's henchmen. Three male figures—the Trio of Shadows. I swallowed the lump in my throat as disturbing thoughts raced through my mind.

"Where's Leo? What have you done to him?"

A wicked smile crept across Luca's face. "Well, Detective Ricci has been real busy digging up *dirt* on our family business, but he was more than willing to drop by and pay us a visit this evening."

"Don't hurt him," I pleaded. "I'll do anything you say."

Luca rested his slimy hand on my shoulder. "I'm willing to make an exchange, Miss Sinclair. Tell me where the package is, and you and your boyfriend will walk out of here, deal?"

"I'm telling the truth. I don't know where it is."

Whap! Luca slammed my sketchbook on the bar. "Then draw one of your pretty pictures and show us where to find it. Hold a séance and conjure up Nico or whatever you witches do to summon the dead. I want that package in my hands before dawn, Evelyn. No more excuses."

He shoved a pencil into my hand and crossed his arms, daring me to deny him. I couldn't turn my gift on and off at will, but making excuses would only make things worse. If Leo and I had any hope of getting out of this situation with a pulse, we needed to band together.

Stefano had remained quiet while Luca ran the show. I had no clue why Luca was so desperate to get the package, but Stefano's motive was not a mystery—he wanted to make contact with his dead wife.

A séance is not a bad idea.

"I'll deliver the package—but I'll need resources to make it happen."

"What do you need?" Luca asked.

"Stefano, Nicoletta's charm bracelet, and Leo."

ITALIAN CURSE—LEO

A knife slid between my skin and the zip ties that secured my wrists and ankles to the chair. Once the bondage snapped, the goons yanked me out of the chair.

The gunman aimed his finger between my eyes and issued a warning. "If you make any attempt to fight or run, I'll break every bone in your body, *capisce?*"

I gave him a nod, accepting his terms. I needed my bones intact so I could save Evelyn.

The underlings lifted me to my feet and shoved me toward the door. If my goal was to escape, this would've been my time to fight. But my goal was to save Evelyn, and I reasoned that if Stefano had brought me here, she was on the property, too.

Memories of Evelyn bruised and battered from the last time she faced a killer triggered an adrenaline rush. I would fight, kill, or die to save the woman I loved.

Once inside, the gunman issued a final warning. "Forget all those ideas running through your head about how you're going to fight your way out of here and save your girl. If you make any move against me, my men, or the boss, your beautiful girlfriend will suffer greatly for your mistakes. Do I make myself clear?"

My jaw tensed as the warning pricked at the hairs at the back of my neck. "Understood."

While I heeded his warning, a storm brewed inside me. Threatening Evelyn would prove to be a fatal mistake for that monster and the man behind this—Stefano Vanzetti.

The men ushered me through the main house and led me to the guest suite where Evelyn and I stayed the weekend. The gunman shoved me inside. When the door closed behind me, Evelyn crashed into me and buried her head on my chest.

"Are you all right?" Evelyn pulled back and cupped her hand under my chin as she assessed my injuries.

Seeing Evelyn alive and unharmed gave me hope that I could still save her. "Did they hurt you?"

"No. But they know about the package. Luca has given me until dawn to deliver it to him.

"How many people are currently in this house?"

"Stefano, Luca, Dino, Mira, and three Italian men I've never seen before. I believe they are the shadows from my automatic drawing."

"Right. The Trio of Shadows. They're professional hitmen. They are the ones who grabbed me."

Evelyn's eyes welled with tears. "I'm so sorry, Leo. This is all my fault. I swear I'm going to get you out of this. I—"

"Listen to me, Evelyn. I need you to do exactly what I say. There's no time to argue or cry or do anything other than what I am about to tell you. Do you understand?"

"I'm listening."

"You need to escape. Do whatever you have to do to get away. Lie. Tell Stefano the only way to contact Nicoletta is to return to the graveyard. Once you're out in public, scream, yell for help, run—find a way to get attention and get someone to call the cops. The only way to survive is to get out of this house."

"What about you? How do I get you out of here?"

This was the question I didn't want to answer. "When I'm gone, I'm not going anywhere. I'll stay with you and do everything possible to save you from these monsters. I'll come to you in your dreams. I'll send messages to you through your drawings—"

"Wait. What do you mean? Are you saying you're going to help as a *ghost*?"

"There's no way out for me, Evelyn. They're going to kill me."

Evelyn's hands flew to her mouth, horrified by my words. "No, no way. I will never—"

"I love you more than anyone on this earth, sweetheart. I failed you. I should've steered you away from this instead of dragging you into their inner circle. I'm sorry we'll never get married and have kids—"

"Don't you dare give up on me, Leo." Evelyn grasped my shoulders and stared into my eyes. "You may be out of the game, but I will never let anyone tear us apart. I know the odds are against us, but I have something Stefano wants. Something money can't buy, and if he wants me to communicate with his dead wife, he'll have to agree to my condition —our freedom."

The bedroom door opened, and Luca appeared in the doorway. "Time is up, princess."

Evelyn kissed me tenderly on the lips then whispered in my ear. "*Fantasma.*"

This reminded me of the day she stormed into my interrogation room and tried to convince me that the ghost of her late friend was feeding her clues to track down her killer. I thought she was a nut job until she pulled that one-word clairaudient thing on me.

That clue led me to believe her gift was real.

The word *fantasma* translated to *ghost* in Italian, but it had a deeper and more sinister meaning in our culture—it was an Italian curse. A death threat. The person issuing the curse was literally saying, "*You* are a ghost because *I* am going to kill you."

Evelyn's fighting spirit and her clairaudient message gave me hope that we had a fighting chance. As long as my heart was still beating, I would keep fighting for Evelyn, myself, and our future.

As Luca and the crew walked us outside, I asked Evelyn what was happening.

"We're going to ask Nicoletta where she hid the brief-case," she said confidently so that the men could hear her.

"How are we going to do that?"

"You know, the way we *usually* contact the dead—through a séance."

I wouldn't call this a solid plan, but Evelyn had managed to get me out of my restraints and gave the men a reason to put us together. She was smart and resourceful. Now I had to do my part and figure out how to dodge a bullet and devise our escape plan.

SÉANCE—EVELYN

$\mathcal{I}$ spread a tablecloth that had belonged to Nicoletta over the outdoor bistro table while Leo lit the candles around the seating area by the water's edge. Once the atmospheric mood lighting was set, I arranged three white votive candles on the table and set out my drawing supplies.

Thunder rumbled in the distance. The storm was moving in. The setting was perfect for Nicoletta's séance. The problem was, I had no idea what I was doing. But I played my part as a confident medium who had done this type of summoning a hundred times.

I even took some liberties with my ritual to give it an authentic feel. I informed Dino that the color red was forbidden from my ritual. Anyone who broke this rule by having the color on a tie, the stitching on a sock, or even a red second hand on a watch would find themselves cursed for all of eternity.

He scoffed at my melodramatic declaration, but I caught him squinting at his Rolex as a precaution.

"Nice touch," Leo whispered.

"I'm just getting warmed up."

Stefano came out of the house carrying a bundle of Nicoletta's personal items and joined us at the table. Among the items were her wedding rings, a hairbrush, and a framed picture of her and Stefano at her charity event. The last photo taken of Nicoletta before her death.

"And, of course, the bracelet." When Stefano pulled Nicoletta's charm bracelet out of his pocket and clasped it around my wrist, Leo's eyes widened in horror. "Take that off. Now." He grabbed my arm and tried to remove it as if it held venom.

"Leo," I snapped. "I need this. It belonged to Nicoletta."

"I know. Have you worn this before? Were you wearing this the night we—"

"Leo, please. You're disturbing my concentration." I gave him a stern look, hoping he would get the message that now was not the time to have this conversation.

Leo took the hint. He lifted his hands apologetically and dropped the subject, but his expression was still laced with dread. It seemed strange that he recognized the bracelet, but I was certain he would explain later.

Thunder rumbled in the distance.

"We need to begin," I said.

Stefano dismissed all his men except for Dino. He stood guard a few feet behind his boss. For a tough guy, he seemed agitated even frightened by the idea of summoning Nicoletta's ghost. He tugged at his shirt sleeves nervously and loosened his tie as he studied the objects on the table and darted his gaze around the veranda expectantly.

I motioned to Leo and Stefano to take a seat around the small bistro table while I slipped on Nicoletta's robe over my clothes. I picked up her wedding rings and clutched them in my hand. I set the picture of Nicoletta on the table between a collection of votive candles.

Leo had seen me draw for the dead numerous times and

described the phenomena as *shocking*. For a homicide detective, that was a bold statement. Since Stefano was new to this, I explained what would happen and gave him some ground rules.

We all had a vested interest in finding the package, and I didn't want him to get spooked and break my concentration.

"Once I make contact with Nicoletta, I have no control over what I draw. What comes out on the page doesn't come from me. I'm channeling the energy of the dead."

Stefano's jaw clenched.

"I may draw for a few minutes or a couple of hours, but no matter how long it takes, don't wake me up, okay?"

Another round of thunder rumbled.

"Let's get started." Leo stared into the horizon as the storm clouds rolled in.

I inhaled a deep breath and moved my hands over the flickering flames. I focused my energy on Nicoletta's picture, reached out and held Stefano's hand, then closed my eyes as I meditated using the peaceful sounds of nature to calm my racing thoughts.

"Nicoletta, we need your help. Lead us to the briefcase. Show me the way." I didn't know if Nicoletta's ghost could hear me, but I promised the guys a séance and needed to pretend I knew what I was doing. I planned to draw, nothing else, and I hoped the universe would intervene and deliver the goods.

With my pencil in ready position, I tuned in to the chorus of nature. The calming sounds of frogs croaking, crickets chirping, and the gentle sound of Stefano's boat, bobbing on the water. A cool breeze blew back my hair as I drifted deeper into my meditation.

My hand began to move.

PREMONITIONS—LEO

Evelyn started speaking in Italian.

I knew without a shadow of a doubt she didn't know the language. The words coming out of her mouth were not her own—they were Nicoletta's.

The summoning worked.

Stefano's eyes widened with horror as Evelyn channeled his wife's ghost. What she was saying at first came out in a jumble of rambling thoughts as if there had been a paranormal glitch in the communication wires.

Evelyn's hand moved across the page as she started her first drawing. It was a sketch of a large tree that had fallen across a road. When she finished, she flipped the page and began the next drawing.

It was a woman, floating face down in the water, pointing toward the bottom of the lake. This time, a landmark identified her location—the dock. It was only a few feet away from where we were gathered.

As Evelyn filled in the details, the drawing showed a box the size of a briefcase tethered to a cinder block at the bottom of the lake. When the drawing was finished, Evelyn tapped her pencil over the dock image and counted aloud in Italian.

"Uno, due, tre..."

"Why is she counting?" Stefano asked.

"Quiet. Don't disturb her. We'll find out when she's finished."

Stefano's gaze was fixed on Evelyn as she flipped to a clean page to start another drawing. But as soon as she began, the sky opened up, and rain poured down. Stefano had anticipated the storm and popped open a golf umbrella.

"Keep the drawings dry." Stefano handed me the umbrella. Finding out where Nicoletta had stashed the briefcase was in our collective best interests, so I complied with his demand.

Evelyn kept drawing, undeterred by the storm.

Thunder rumbled, and lightning lit up the sky. The rain was blowing sideways, and Evelyn's back was getting wet, but my job was to keep the paper dry. We were too close to the truth to turn back now, and Evelyn would be angry if I stopped her because she was getting a little wet.

The next drawings came quicker, with a dire sense of urgency, as if time was of the essence. Evelyn's hand flew across each page as she completed a series of drawings that came together for a more horrifying scene than anything I'd witnessed during my entire career as a homicide detective.

Evelyn had drawn premonitions of death.

Stefano, Luca, Dino, and the Trio of Killers, all the men in the room except for me, were all present in Evelyn's art. But the men were no longer among the living—Evelyn had drawn each of them, very clearly, as corpses.

I didn't know how, when, where, or why the crime scene was going to play out, but if Evelyn's premonitions came true, a bloodbath was on the horizon.

MURKY WATER—LEO

Evelyn's hand stopped moving, signaling she had finished her drawings. One of a tree, then another of a woman, possibly Nicoletta, with the briefcase. The other six premonitions gave me hope that our situation with the mob might be survivable.

But then Evelyn did something strange—well, strange for her. Instead of falling asleep from exhaustion, she got up from her chair and headed toward the dock. Rain was coming down in sheets as lightning lit up the sky.

I practically threw the umbrella at Stefano, telling him to protect the drawings, then rushed after Evelyn. But before I could reach her, Stefano's bodyguard tackled me from behind, jammed his knee into my back, and twisted my arm to hold me in place.

"Hey! You need to stop her. She's not conscious. If she falls into the water, she'll drown!"

"She's going after the briefcase," Stefano yelled over the pouring rain. "I must have that package."

I watched in horror as Evelyn padded down the walkway

toward the water. I struggled against the brute, but he had about thirty extra pounds of muscle on me and was baring down on me like an anchor.

When Evelyn reached the water's edge, she walked down the dock, pointing to each post as she passed as if counting them.

Is Nicoletta showing her where she hid the briefcase?

"Evelyn! Wake up! Evelyn!"

Dino kicked me in the ribs to silence me. Stefano had caught up with her, eager to find out where she was leading him. Fluorescent lights illuminated the dock, and I could see their figures through the storm.

As I watched, helpless to stop her, Evelyn jumped off the dock straight into the murky water.

"Go after her!" With a burst of adrenaline, I flipped my body over, grabbed Dino's thick leg, and knocked him off his feet. I sprang up and bolted down the path. When I reached the dock, I scanned the water, but there was no sign of her.

I dove in and used my hands to feel around for her. I came up for air just as Stefano tossed a lifesaver into the water and jumped in to join the search. "The current is strong. She might've gotten pulled under the dock. I'm going to the other side to see if she went through," he said.

A moment later, I heard Evelyn gasp for air. She popped up out of the water a few feet away. When I reached her, she was tugging on a chain, trying to haul something out of the water.

I didn't care if she had unearthed a treasure chest of pirate's gold down there. All I cared about was getting her out of the lake.

"Evelyn, wake up. I need to get you out of the water." I reached up and held on to the lip of the dock while I kept us both afloat.

Footsteps thundered down the dock, and then Dino hoisted Evelyn out of the water. She was still in a daze but clutched the chain in her fist, desperate not to let it go.

Evelyn had found the briefcase.

THE RULES—EVELYN

Thunder rumbled and woke me from a deep sleep.

I blinked to reorient myself and lifted my throbbing head to check my surroundings. I was in the guest suite, tucked into bed.

I tried to get up, but my wrists and ankles were bound with duct tape. My hair was soaking wet, but my clothes were dry. Someone had wrapped me up in a warm blanket.

The last thing I remembered was conducting the séance as the storm rolled in. I tried to remember how I'd gotten inside or what had transpired during the summoning.

Oh, God. Where is Leo?

My chest ached, and I fell into a coughing fit. Foul-tasting water came up my throat, and I felt as if I had been submerged underwater. I was dizzy, confused, and horrified by all the what-if scenarios banging around in my head.

Had one of the hitmen tried to drown me? If so, why am I still alive?

"Leo?" I called out into the empty room.

No answer.

"Leo?" I called again louder.

Maybe the Italians were holding him captive in the adjoining room. I wiggled underneath the blanket and tried to get myself into a sitting position. If I managed to roll off the bed, I could inch my way into the other room.

Footsteps sounded in the hallway.

They're coming for me.

A lock clicked. The door opened. Stefano entered the room and closed the door behind him.

As he approached the bed, I folded my legs to my chest to kick him when he got closer. "Stay the fuck away from me." I was in no position to give orders, but clearly, someone had felt it necessary to immobilize me.

If Stefano was there to harm me, I would do everything I could to protect myself.

When he moved into striking range, I delivered a kick he easily blocked. My muscles were shredded, and I was so weak I couldn't squirm my way out from under the blanket. As if my situation could get any worse, the sudden movement sent me back into a coughing fit.

Stefano reprimanded me for trying to fight him. He eased me into a sitting position and patted my back to help clear my lungs. I coughed and spit up water on his pristine carpet. I had no idea why Stefano was treating me compassionately, but I considered it was better than the alternative.

If he was concerned for my well-being, why was he treating me like a prisoner?

"What happened? Where's Leo?"

Stefano studied my expression as if to gauge my sincerity. "What's the last thing you remember?"

"The séance. You and Leo were there, and Dino. You put Nicoletta's charm bracelet around my wrist. The storm rolled in..." I thought momentarily, trying to come up with what happened next, but I drew a blank.

"The next thing I remember is waking up here—like this." I lifted my bound hands to illustrate the point.

Stefano regarded my restraints, but his expression held no remorse. Whatever I had done that led to me being treated like a hostage must've been deemed a necessary evil. I was no physical threat to these men. The only weapon I could use against them was my gift.

"You have no memory of jumping into the lake?"

"I did *what?*"

"What about your sketches?"

"I don't remember."

"Don't tell me you have no memory of your drawings." Stefano seethed with revulsion as he stared into my eyes, daring me to defy him.

Terror pulsed through my veins as I realized he would never let me go. Whatever had happened, whatever I had done, turned out to be a fatal mistake. We were being held captive at a secluded lake house with a crew of killers and a family of mobsters who had already killed to protect their secrets.

There was no going back from here. Our fate had already been decided. Leo may already be dead, and I was next.

My mood darkened as I faced the man responsible for our murders.

"I will haunt you for the rest of your miserable life, Stefano Vanzetti. I don't care which one of your blood-suckers pulls the trigger. I'm coming for you. You will never escape my torture. My blood is on your hands. Leo's blood is on your hands. And I'll be damned to hell before I let you—"

Stefano flung the blanket off my body and lifted a knife from his pocket. He aimed the blade at my heart and narrowed his eyes as if deliberating my fate. "Your thirst for revenge is delicious, Evelyn. I would love to hear about your plans to destroy my life from beyond the grave, but right now, we have work to do."

He grasped my bound ankles, plunged the knife into the tape, and cut me loose. Then he tugged on my arm to help me stand and steadied me as I got my bearings. "Can you walk?"

I eyed him skeptically. My brain was running on low-power mode, but being free versus being helpless in bed was a more survivable option. "Yes."

As Stefano steered me into the hallway, I noticed I was wearing one of Nicoletta's dresses. Since Stefano had confirmed I had *jumped into the lake*, someone had removed my wet clothing and redressed me while I was unconscious.

"Who took off my clothes?"

Stefano scoffed. "That is the least of your problems, Miss Sinclair."

A fair sentiment considering my dire situation.

"Where's Leo?"

Stefano stopped and ran his hands through his thick hair. He seemed to be trying to control his temper. It wasn't work-ing. He wrapped his hands around my upper arms and pulled me an inch from his face. "You need to understand the rules before we join the others."

I pulled back to put distance between us, but he had a death grip on me, and I couldn't move.

"One: You speak only if you are asked a question. Two: You will choke back your insufferable attitude and show respect to the men in this house. Three: You will obey my orders without hesitation from this moment on."

My chest heaved as Stefano issued his warning.

"If you fail to follow the rules, there will be swift conse-quences, Miss Sinclair. Do I make myself clear?"

The right thing to do was nod submissively and bow to my captor's demands. I was already on my last strike with the

Italians, but Stefano could bark his orders to my cold dead body if Leo was already dead.

"Evelyn?" Stefano hissed.

"I will follow your rules *if* Leo is still alive."

My disobedience was a drug to him. He savored my resistance as a devilish grin curled on his lips. "Your loyalty to Leo is admirable, but it will be your downfall. You have made your choice, Miss Sinclair."

Stefano relinquished his grip, straightened his suit, and led me into the living room to face my future killers.

INTO THE GRAVE—EVELYN

The storm raged as Stefano led me to the living room. I had expected to see the death squad gathered around the bar and Stefano's lowlife uncle stirring up trouble, but Dino was the only monster in the room waiting to feast on my corpse.

When he saw me, he watched me cautiously as if my head might start spinning. He stood tall and unbuttoned his jacket to give him quicker access to his weapon.

I must've put on quite a show for the boys.

The guys conversed momentarily, then Stefano snapped and pointed into the kitchen. Dino responded by pouring a glass of water then delivering it to Stefano.

"Drink." Stefano lifted the glass to my lips.

My throat was raw from all the coughing, and the icy cold water burned as it trailed down my throat. Stefano blotted my wet lips on the back of his hand when I drained the glass.

Stefano's personality swings were making me dizzy.

Who is this man? A calculated mobster or a compassionate human?

Dino left the room under Stefano's direction, leaving me

alone with the boss. Without saying another word, Stefano led me to the bar where a series of my automatic drawings, eight total, were lined up for inspection.

"You have drawn yourself into the grave, Evelyn. The only person to blame for what happens next is you."

The first sketch was of a woman diving underwater. She was tugging a briefcase attached to a chain. Her long hair fanned out before her face, but I couldn't make out her features—Wait. The woman is wearing the dress I had on during the summoning. That's me.

I glanced up and noticed the case was on the bar beside my sketches. "Is that why I jumped in the lake?"

Stefano gave me a solemn nod. "It was chained to the dock. You almost drowned trying to retrieve it."

"What's inside?"

"It's locked. We haven't been able to open it."

I shifted my gaze to the next one. It was a downed tree that had fallen across a road. A street sign in the picture read, "Harbor Trail." I recognized the name of the road. It was a street just after the covered bridge.

It wasn't down a few hours ago. Otherwise, the road to Stefano's house would've been impassable.

It must be a premonition.

The front door burst open, and Luca stormed into the room with a crowbar. "There she is! The famous artist of Halsted. I hope you're well rested, sweetie. You've got a lot of explaining to do."

Stefano stepped between us to calm Luca down.

I returned my attention to the drawings to find out why Luca was so upset.

Oh. God. There's going to be a massacre tonight.

The following six drawings were all premonitions of murder.

The first drawing was of Stefano slumped on the ground

in a pool of blood. There was a gaping bullet wound in his chest. Two shadowy figures of a male and female form hovered beside his corpse.

The next three were of the Trio of Killers. The first guy was riddled with bullet holes. The next had been stabbed with a pair of scissors. The last guy's head was bashed in as if he'd been bludgeoned to death.

Dead. Dead. Dead.

Next, Dino's enormous corpse was stuffed inside a body bag. The zipper was open, and his lifeless eyes stared upward, horrified by the last image he had seen in this lifetime.

Lastly, Luca was sprawled out on the ground with a bullet hole between his eyes.

While I studied my sketches, the men had all assembled around me. The killers, Dino, Luca, and Stefano. Six men who would all be dead before the night was over—if my premonitions came true.

I had no way of knowing if what I had drawn was set in stone, or if the future could be changed. Only time would tell. I darted my attention back to Luca. Stefano had gotten him to lay down the crowbar.

Instead of physically assaulting me, Luca charged at me and backed me into a corner. My hands were still bound with duct tape, making it difficult to protect myself if he tried to hurt me. "You really are a crazy witch, you know that?"

Instead of defending my actions, I heeded Stefano's warning and shut my mouth.

"I don't know what your angle is, and I don't know what you're getting out of this, but I will tell you one thing I know for certain—the only bodies dropping tonight will belong to you and the detective."

I shot a pleading glance at Stefano, but he hung back passively, allowing his uncle to berate me.

"Your boyfriend will be the one with the bullet between his eyes. Not me. Not this guy right here." Luca flailed his arms as he raged, and I feared he was about to take his frustration out on me with his hands. "I'll give you one chance to explain."

He held up his finger an inch from my face. "Your boyfriend doesn't have a gun. You don't have a gun. None of my men are going to turn on me. So you tell me, Miss Sinclair. Who is coming to this house to put a bullet between my eyes?"

If I followed Stefano's rules of the household, I was expected to answer direct questions, shower the men with respect, and obey the orders given to me by a bunch of murderous thugs in expensive suits.

While staying alive was my objective, there was no way to explain, apologize, or make amends about the future bloodbath that would soon take place in this mansion.

If I tried to defend myself, I would piss off Luca.

If I stayed silent, I would piss off Luca.

My only option was to stay alive and hope whatever chain reaction led to the bad guys going down got set into motion before Leo and I became their latest victims.

Rain beat against the window as the storm appeared on top of us.

Luca laughed incredulously, perceiving my silence as defiance. "You haven't stopped running your mouth since you met my nephew. Now you want to give me the silent treatment?"

His eyes went cold. He raised his hand and was about to backhand me across the face.

I closed my eyes and turned my cheek to ready myself for the blow.

"Never put your hands on a woman."

I opened my eyes. Stefano had stepped in and blocked Luca from striking me. Luca glared at his bigger and stronger nephew and mockingly backed away with his hands up.

Lightning flashed outside the window, and thunder rumbled through the house.

"Your body is on the ground, too, Stefano," Luca said. "Your chest is blown wide open. Your little plaything won't save you when the bullets start flying."

Luca shifted his attention to me. "Beautiful women are like poison to him. If any of our enemies want to take him out, they don't send guys with guns. They send gorgeous women with knockout curves who have the power to drop a man to his knees with the bat of an eye."

Luca aimed his finger at Stefano. "If you want to die tonight, that's your choice. After we take care of Ricci, we're getting the hell—"

A sonic boom rattled the windows and shook the house like a bomb had exploded.

The jarring sound roused the room, and the men scattered to locate the source of the noise. Stefano clutched my arm protectively, ready to defend me from the unknown danger.

I was as confused as everyone else until I realized what it was. "The tree fell," I whispered to Stefano. "Look at my drawing. Check the street name. If this is a premonition, lightning just struck the tree, and it fell in front of the bridge."

While I was still confused by Stefano's night and day personality shifts, he had shown me mercy when his uncle had tried to hurt me. If the tree had come down, it was the first sign that my premonitions would come true.

As the images of my horrific sketches flashed through my

mind, I realized Leo and I were absent from the crime scenes —at least, our bodies were not there. I remembered the male and female shadows hovering beside Stefano's corpse.

Acid came up my throat when the realization hit me that I had drawn Leo and me as *ghosts*.

As long as Leo was still alive, I knew he was trying to find a way to save us. I was doing everything I could, too, but our situation seemed unsurvivable unless we got one of the Italians to switch teams.

My job was to turn Stefano against his family.

SHOT TO HELL—LEO

"*D*id you have a nice nap, Ricci?" The gunman grasped my chin and stared into my eyes to see if I was conscious. The last thing I remembered was Dino giving me a revenge beating for knocking him on his ass so I could save Evelyn.

I scanned the room to check my surroundings. I was no longer in the garage. I was inside a house. Not the mansion, but possibly another building on the property.

No sign of Evelyn.

Aside from the gunman, Mira was the only other person in the room. She stood dutifully by the door as the killer checked the security of my restraints. As I blinked away the stars flashing before my eyes, the gunman barked out orders to Stefano's chauffeur.

"If Detective Ricci attempts to escape or call for help, tell my men." He gestured out the window to his cohorts patrolling outside.

"I'm just the driver." Mira lifted her chin and stood proud, not wanting to get involved with the abduction of a Chicago P.D. detective.

"You work for the Vanzetti Family. You'll do whatever is asked of you." The gunman held his icy gaze on hers until she relented and gave him an obedient nod of understanding.

When the gunman left the house, Mira moved to the window and tracked him down the path toward the main house. Once out of sight, she gathered some first aid supplies and poured me a glass of juice.

She pressed a damp towel on my forehead to cool me down and gave me sips of orange juice through a straw. I was in pain and probably had a concussion and a set of cracked ribs. I was grateful she was showing me compassion.

"Where's Evelyn?"

Mira gave me a stern look and then pointed toward the mansion. "She's with Stefano. I don't know what's happening over there, except that she's in trouble. I overheard them talking about how to handle her after she explains her drawings."

"You need to cut me free."

Mira raised her eyebrows, wondering, it seemed, if I had lost my sense of reason. "I can't help you."

"Do you have a gun? Are there any weapons you can get your hands on?"

She paused as she considered my question, then pushed back her jacket to reveal a Glock. "It's all I have. The men outside are professionals. You will never get past them with a single weapon."

"I'm a professional, too." I was trained for situations like this and knew there was always a way out of any hostage situation. I had faith that I could take out three men, but I couldn't do it without at least one weapon. Or while tied to a fucking chair. To survive and save Evelyn, I had to follow a plan of attack.

Step one: Get Mira on my side.

Step two: Get free from my restraints.

Step three: Gather weapons.

Step four: Storm the castle.

"You're a liability to them, Mira." I didn't have the time to be delicate. The truth was brutal—and convincing. "You're a witness to the abduction and possible execution of a Chicago P.D. detective. Do you think those killers will let you walk away after seeing their faces?"

Mira's expression tanked. She was a civilian who worked for Stefano. While he regarded her as a trusted team member, the Sicilians considered her collateral damage. Even if she didn't care what happened to me, she would be a dead woman if we didn't join forces.

"Dino keeps a gun in my glovebox. We'll each have a weapon if I can get to the car."

I suppressed a winner's grin as Mira pulled a pair of scissors out of a desk drawer. "Before I cut you free, I need to know—"

The door opened.

The gunman returned.

Mira slid the scissors into her pocket.

"The boss would like to speak with you one last time, Ricci. Then I will finish the job. You've got an hour to live, tops. If you tell the boss what he wants to know, maybe he'll let you say goodbye to your girlfriend."

My entire plan just got shot to hell.

THE SMOKING GUN—LEO

The gunman and his cohorts escorted me to a carriage house on the far side of the property next to the old family graveyard.

The room had already been prepared for my arrival. I assessed the scene and had a sinking feeling this would be the last image I would see in my lifetime.

A large plastic tarp stretched across the floor, and a hard wooden chair with handcuffs attached to the arms had been placed at the center.

They are going to interrogate me before executing the hit.

Assassins used an efficient weapon that did the job without leaving a big mess behind. If my killer followed the playbook, he would put one bullet in my temple and two in my chest.

Three quick shots. No chance of survival.

I struggled against the men as they dragged me toward the chair, which resulted in the two of them kicking the hell out of me before they wrestled me into cuffs. Once subdued, the goons left to fetch the boss, leaving me alone with the gunman.

In my eleventh hour, I focused all my energy on Evelyn. How much I loved her. How I had failed to protect her. How I would ditch the tunnel with the bright white light and stay earthbound to help her.

"What's going to happen to Evelyn?" I asked the gunman. I had nothing to lose at this point, and he had nothing to hide.

The soulless bastard lit a cigarette as he contemplated my last request. "I haven't been given orders for her yet. The guys are arguing over it now." He took a drag off his smoke. "Stefano wants to keep her for himself. He believes he can turn her loyalty to him and make her forget all about you—with proper training."

A sickening smile spread across his face. "Luca's plans go even darker than that."

An adrenaline rush surged through my body as I considered what lay ahead for Evelyn. I knew her gift was dangerous, and I caved when she asked me to give her space to live and the freedom to expose her gift to people who wanted to train her to cater to their whims.

I wanted to chew my limbs off like an animal to free myself and stop these monsters from harming the woman I loved.

There was a knock on the door.

The gunman laughed at my struggle on his way to answer it. I expected Luca would be the one to supervise the hit, but when the door swung open, I was shocked to see Stefano had brought Evelyn here to witness my execution.

When she saw me in the chair with the tarp spread out underneath me, she tried to run to me, but Stefano clutched her arm and pinned her at his side. Her fucking wrists were bound with duct tape. Stefano was already trying to control her.

"Do you want me to restrain her, too?" The gunman

spoke in Italian and motioned to a second chair in the corner of the room.

Stefano gave him a nod of approval.

Evelyn resisted as he cut off the tape around her wrists and cuffed her to the chair, but she was no match against the ruthless killer. He secured her to the chair six feet from me, giving her a front-row seat to my murder. All the while, Stefano stood back and allowed it to happen.

It was one thing for Evelyn to know I had been killed, but it was sadistic beyond my comprehension why Stefano wanted her to witness it. What had happened in his life that turned him into a ruthless mobster?

This was the guy I used to ride bikes with down to the corner market and blow our allowance money on soft-serve ice cream cones and junk food. The kid who used to sleep over at my house and stay up late to watch superhero movies with me all night.

Me and Santoni stood up for Stefano when bullies made fun of him because of his accent or tried to push him around because he was smaller and weaker than his tormentors. My father taught him how to shave. My sisters helped him with his homework.

My mother baked him birthday cakes and never let that skinny kid leave her house without giving him a couple of sandwiches to take home in case his fucking prick of an uncle failed to provide his basic needs.

I prayed to God my mother would never find out Stefano Vanzetti was responsible for my murder. She would never get over losing me, but if she knew that little boy she nurtured and cared for like he was one of her own children turned out to be my killer, the truth would put her in an early grave.

Once we were all in place, the gunman stood at ease as Stefano led the interrogation.

"You have betrayed me, old friend. A credible source informed me that you have been investigating my business practices with the F.B.I. What have you uncovered about Vanzetti Investments that warrants an investigation?"

Screw him. I was a dead man already. "Fuck off. Be a man and let Evelyn go."

"Don't stay for me, Leo," Evelyn whimpered. "Follow the light and go into the tunnel. I'll meet you on the other side. Please, I won't be able to handle it if you stay as a ghost." Evelyn's body trembled as the realization settled over her that I wasn't going to survive.

"I can't leave you, Evelyn. You need me."

She shook her head. "I'm begging you, Leo. I won't be able to live with myself. This is all my fault. Look what I've done to you."

"What the fuck is wrong with you, Vanzetti? Get Evelyn out of here!" Her soul-crushing pleas were more deadly to me than the bullet about to go in my brain. I couldn't bear the thought of Evelyn blaming herself for this and reliving the horror of watching it play out in her mind for the rest of her life.

The gunman cursed at Stefano. "Let's get on with this. I need time to dispose of the body. We need to get out of here." He pulled his gun out of his holster and aimed it at my head.

"Close your eyes, Evelyn. I love you."

"No!" Evelyn screamed and squeezed her eyes shut.

I had shut my eyes, too, bracing for the blow.

Bang! A shot fired—then a body thumped to the ground.

Was it my body? Had I not felt the fatal blow to my head?

Two more shots were fired.

I opened my eyes.

The gunman was dead on the floor.

And Stefano Vanzetti was holding the smoking gun.

REVENGE—LEO

Stefano lifted the handcuff keys off the dead guy. He unlocked me first so I could help Evelyn. She was screaming so violently, she wasn't aware I was still alive and trying to console her.

"Evelyn. Sweetheart, it's me." I dropped to my knees, caressed her arms, and tried to get her attention while Stefano unlocked her cuffs.

It wasn't working. Evelyn couldn't focus and was rambling on about haunting Stefano for all eternity and how she would make his life a living hell. I hated seeing her experience trauma, but I was honored by her determination to avenge my death.

"Evelyn," I snapped. "Open your eyes. It's Leo."

Her baby blues softened when she realized I was still among the living. She touched my face to ensure she wasn't dreaming, dove into my arms, and squeezed me so hard I groaned from having a set of cracked ribs.

But pain had never hurt so good.

When the initial shock wore off, she checked around the room as she processed what had happened. Her gaze bounced between the hitman's corpse and the gun in Stefano's hand.

"You killed the hitman to save Leo?" she asked. "Why are you helping us?"

"Despite what you may think, I'm not one of them. Yes, I wanted something from you, Evelyn—the truth about what really happened to Nicoletta. But I would never allow any harm to come to you or Detective Ricci. What happened this evening did not come from me."

Stefano looked out the window and stared up at the house. "You two need to get out of here. The others will be back soon. Go to Mira, and she will drive you back to Chicago." Stefano moved back the chair, gathered the ends of the tarp, and rolled up the hitman's body.

"We can't leave by car," Evelyn said. "The tree fell across the road. There's no way around it." She explained her premonition to get me up to speed.

"Right." Stefano pointed to the door. "Then you will escape by foot. Follow the path along the water to the next house. It's three miles away."

"What about you?" I asked.

"I have unfinished business to take care of at the house. I'm not leaving until I get my hands on that briefcase. Nicoletta died because of whatever is inside the package. I will scorch the earth to find out the truth."

"No. There's a better way," I said. "Give me your phone. I'll call for backup. We can hole up at Mira's place until help arrives."

Stefano scoffed. "I may not have wanted to see you dead, my friend, but I will not invite the feds to raid my compound. I have not forgotten about your betrayal, Leo. I'm not going to turn myself in. Once I find out who killed my wife, the men responsible will meet my wrath. After that, I will disappear."

"You saved my life, Stefano. That counts for something. Cooperate with the investigation, and you'll do a couple of years in federal prison. You'll be free in no time and can rebuild your empire and go legit."

Stefano cracked a smile. "You want me to be a rat?" He clicked his tongue and pointed the gun at the door. "Get Evelyn out of here and take your time making that call."

I was a law enforcement officer and would do what I could to prevent a crime, but I understood Stefano's thirst for revenge. I could see myself doing the same thing if our roles were reversed. But it was time I learned from my mistakes.

Nothing was more important to me than keeping Evelyn safe. If Vanzetti wanted revenge, I was in no position to stop him. "Come on, Evelyn."

I tugged on her arm, but she was staring intently at the carriage house window—as if she had seen a ghost.

CLOUDY IMAGE—EVELYN

rip...Drip...Drip...
    I followed a trail of watery footprints to the window.

The storm raged as rain pelted the windows and condensation fogged up the glass. My feet sloshed through a puddle as I moved closer to the window until I could see my reflection in the glass.

Lightning lit up the sky, revealing two ghostly figures staring back at me—Nicoletta and Shay. Seeing them together validated Leo's suspicion that their deaths were somehow related. I was awake, but I could see them. After experiencing the trauma of almost losing Leo, my gift was stronger than ever.

"They're here," I said.

"Who?" Leo asked.

"Nicoletta and Shay. They're trying to tell me something."

Nicoletta tapped on the window while Shay stretched out her tattooed arm and pointed to the main house.

"Something bad is happening up at the house. I need to draw."

Nicoletta tapped on the glass again, giving me a brilliant idea. I didn't have my sketchpad or a pencil, but I did have condensation. I closed my eyes and placed the tip of my finger on the window.

While I used the storm's energy to clear my mind, my finger glided across the foggy glass. When I opened my eyes, I saw a cloudy image of a woman with glasses holding her hands up. It had to be Mira. She was in trouble, and Nicoletta and Shay were desperate to save her.

I turned to the guys. "Something bad is going to happen to Mira. We have to help her."

Leo and Stefano may not have agreed on much, but neither of these valiant Italian men would stand by and let another innocent woman die.

"Mira was trying to help me escape," Leo said. "I won't leave her behind."

"She is like a sister to me," Stefano said. "I'll die before I let anyone hurt her."

While I swiped away the evidence from the window, Stefano and Leo faced off.

"Give me a gun," Leo said.

Stefano stared him down as he considered his options. He had at least two weapons—his own gun and the long, heavy one he'd lifted off the dead guy.

"Before I do that, we must come to a mutual understanding. This compound is Switzerland. You are not an officer of the law, and I am not a member of organized crime. We are calling a truce to save Mira."

Stefano straightened his jacket. "Once we rescue her, you and Evelyn will leave my property, and you will take your time calling for backup. From that moment on, all bets are off. May the best man win." Stefano held out his hand to offer a binding handshake.

As my gaze bounced between them, I was getting a

contact high from all the testosterone fumes polluting the air.

After leaving Stefano hanging uncomfortably long, Leo grasped his hand and sealed the deal.

Stefano handed over the hitman's gun, and Leo laid out our plan of attack.

HEADSTRONG—LEO

The element of surprise was crucial to our plan. According to Stefano, the remaining two hitmen were charged with guarding the parameter while Dino was stationed inside to guard Luca.

Our first task was to get past the guards. It was pitch black and still storming. The men were likely split up, with one covering the front of the house and the other the back. I ordered Stefano to stay with Evelyn while I ran a recon mission.

I hugged the curve of the mansion, then dropped to the ground and commando crawled through the bushes to survey the front of the house. Lightning flashed intermittently, giving me a chance to see through the darkness.

The area behind the gate and around the front of the house was clear.

I repeated my pattern and searched the back.

The pool area—clear.

The seating area by the lake—clear.

The veranda—holy shit.

The night was full of surprises. I moved in closer to get a

better look. The green-eyed goon who had taken great pleasure in beating me, was lying on his back with scissors stabbed through his heart.

I recognized the murder weapon. Mira's scissors had been in her hands no more than an hour ago. She was about to free me from my bondage when the Trio of Killers showed up and thwarted my escape plan.

According to Evelyn's ghostly sources, Mira was at the house in mortal danger. As I stared at the hitman's corpse, it appeared the driver might be the more significant threat.

Good for you, Mira.

I reported back to Stefano and Evelyn. One man down. Mira and the third hitman were M.I.A. I needed Stefano to get inside and find out what was happening to plan our next move.

So far, Evelyn's premonitions had all come true. We had no way of knowing whether the future could be altered. For Stefano's sake, I hoped we had the power to change the outcome.

"What about me?" Evelyn asked.

"You're going to stay hidden."

"Stefano can't go back there without me. Everyone will be suspicious."

"You're not going back into that house, Evelyn. Have you forgotten—"

"Luca and the guys need to believe everything is going according to plan. We don't want to tip our hand that you're still alive and the hitman is dead. Trust me, I got this."

She wrapped her arm around Stefano's shoulder. "Pick me up."

He lifted her into his arms then she rested her head on his shoulder and pretended to sob.

Stefano shook his head, commiserating with me about Evelyn's headstrong attitude—a quality I loved and loathed about my girlfriend. "I'll take her straight to the bedroom to rest. No one will suspect anything."

Evelyn lifted her head. "Once I get there, I'll open the window, and Leo, you can sneak inside. I can give you an update on what's happening. The plan is perfect."

I would've loved to argue, but we were running out of time.

SURPRISE—EVELYN

$\mathcal{M}$y first objective was to stay calm. Luca was undoubtedly the one who ordered Leo's execution, and it would take all the self-control I could conjure up to stop myself from going primal on that bastard.

When Stefano entered the room, carrying me like a baby, Luca and Dino were working hard to open the locked brief-case. They had cleared off the bar and tried to pry it open with a crowbar.

Luca snapped his head up and asked, "Is it done? Ricci's dead?"

"Leo will no longer be investigating Vanzetti Investments."

"Good. I always hated that self-riotous prick. His mother, though." Luca whistled a catcall. "I've always had a thing for Silvia Ricci. Maybe she'll need some consoling when she finds out her only son is dead."

I clamped my mouth shut, clenched the fabric of Stefano's suit jacket, and pretended it was Luca's tongue. Silvia Ricci was the most loving and giving soul I had ever met. I should've trusted her insight when she warned us about the Vanzettis.

The guys switched over to Italian and conversed for a few moments. I hoped Stefano was getting an update on Mira, so we could save her and evacuate Stefano's haunted mansion.

"Hey, Evelyn." Luca snapped his fingers to get my attention. "Now that you're single again, you can pick between me and my nephew. Cry your eyes out tonight, pretty girl, but you better shape up in the morning and show some respect. We got big plans for you."

Stefano carried me off to the safety of the bedroom and immediately updated me on Mira's situation. "She escaped. The last remaining hitman is tracking her, but he hasn't found her yet. They don't seem to know Mira killed the other—"

When Stefano locked the door behind us, I jumped out of his arms and shoved him as hard as I could. He was bigger and stronger than I was, but my anger-fueled adrenaline rush made him stumble back a few steps.

"What is wrong with you?" I tried to keep my voice low, but I was furious and couldn't stop myself from lashing out at him.

"Evelyn, I understand you're angry, but remember our objective—"

"Luca is toxic. Why do you let him control you? He's a bully and uses you to get what he wants. Why can't you stand up to him?"

"He's the only blood relative I have left. In my culture, we are loyal to our family. I can't simply cut my uncle out of my life." Stefano moved to the window and unlocked it for Leo.

In my blind rage, I had lost sight of the plan. I took a deep breath to cool my temper, but the vile things Luca said about Silvia needled at my own sense of loyalty. I had to defend the woman who was like a mother to me.

"Why are you loyal to Luca over Silvia? Leo's family took you in as a child while your vile uncle abused you. You've grown into a man, but you're still that scared little boy who refuses to stand up to—"

The bedroom door burst open. Luca and Dino stormed into the room.

"You got some nerve, witch." Luca aimed his finger between my eyes as Dino wrestled me into a stronghold.

"You've got some explaining to do, nephew. I went to the carriage house to see Leo's dead body, but you can imagine my surprise when I found out who was under that tarp."

Luca gave the nod to Dino, prompting him to pull out his gun and press it against my temple.

Stefano held out his hands to try to diffuse the situation, but Luca cut him off.

"I don't want to hear your excuses," he said. "You're my nephew. I forgive you. What you will do now is listen, answer my questions, and do exactly what I say. *Capisce?*"

Stefano glanced sideways at me, then gave his uncle a nod.

"Good," Luca said. "Where's Leo?"

JUDGMENT DAY—LEO

All the lights were off in the bedroom. The window was open. Quietly, I crawled inside the room. "Evelyn?" I whispered.

No answer.

I moved to the side table and clicked on the lamp.

"Hands up, Ricci." Luca had one hand over Evelyn's mouth and a gun pressed to her temple.

I had my weapon drawn but didn't have a clean shot. I couldn't risk Evelyn becoming collateral damage. Slowly, I placed my gun on the bed and stepped away to signal my surrender.

Dino grabbed the weapon, aimed it at my chest, and ordered me into the hallway.

The men escorted me through the mansion and then into the ballroom. Hundreds of candles flickered as I entered the dimly lit room. There was no electricity in this wing, and the shadows from the flames danced on the walls and gave our macabre assembly a chilling vibe.

Four tufted chairs were lined up across from each other,

with Nicoletta's briefcase on a table in the center of the gathering spot.

Stefano stood behind one of the chairs with his hand resting on the back, waiting for our arrival.

That bastard double-crossed me. What the hell is he up to?

"Now that we're all here, let's take our seats. The show is about to begin." Luca was drunk with power, and whatever was going on in his twisted mind, Evelyn and I had no choice but to play his game.

Luca released Evelyn and shoved her toward one of the chairs. Dino flicked his gun at me, prompting me to do the same. We were seated across from each other, and Stefano chose to sit next to Evelyn instead of me.

"If either of those two gets their butts out of the chair, shoot their kneecaps off. No one is leaving until I'm finished with them."

Once we were assembled, Dino took a few steps back and stood guard. All the men had guns, so it would be pointless for me to overpower three guys and try to escape. For now, I would find out what Luca was up to, then trust my instincts to act when the moment was right.

"Ladies and gentlemen, welcome to Judgment Hour." He lifted his arms like a showman and grinned like a madman. "Before the main event—the opening of Nicoletta's treasure chest—I thought we would begin with a warmup act."

He circled our seating area as he brayed his monologue. "Since everyone here has a lot of opinions about my character, I thought we would have a family sit-down and talk about all of your secrets and lies."

He pointed an accusatory finger at each of us.

"Everyone here believes I'm the bad guy in all of this, but I know from first-hand knowledge that the three of you have been keeping your share of dirty little secrets from each other, too. While you guys are riding on your moral high horses, I'm sitting back, not saying a word, and watching the three of you play each other like a bunch of con artists."

Evelyn gave Stefano a wary glance. Were they keeping a secret from me? I was trained to detect lies and deceit, and as I sat there reading the room, the two of them were choking on guilty knowledge.

"Wait. I stand corrected. The four of you have been playing each other. It's unfair because Nico is not here to defend herself, but she is just as guilty as the rest of you—she might even be the worst of the lot—but I'll let you make your own judgment calls."

"Don't you dare speak ill of my wife." Stefano stood and widened his stance.

Luca held his hands out apologetically. "I'm sorry, kid. You need to hear the truth. I know I've always been hard on you, but look at the world we live in, eh? You grew up to be a strong, successful man. I guess I did something right. Trust me, I'm doing this for your own good."

Evelyn pursed her lips shut. She was as appalled by the sentiment as I was.

"And since we're all gathered here, I will be a good sport and toss my hat in the ring." He paused and took a deep breath. "I already know what's in that briefcase. No, I haven't peeked, but we'll come back to this point after we go around the room and everybody confesses to his and her sins. Starting with…"

While Luca tapped his chin and studied our expressions, I glanced at Dino to gauge his reaction to the impromptu Judgment Day. Sweat beads cropped up on his forehead, and he wiped his palms on his slick black pants.

Luca had not included him in his moral assessment, but Dino was nervous. Maybe he knows what's in Nicoletta's briefcase, too.

"Detective Ricci, we'll start with you," Luca said. "You

have two secrets—one you're keeping from Evelyn and the other from Stefano. Which one of them do you want to disappoint first?"

Evelyn focused her attention on me, desperate to hear the truth.

"Start with Evelyn. You've got three seconds to confess, Leo. Otherwise, she's going to hear it from me. You know what I'm talking about, right? This charm bracelet here with the 'L' engraved on the heart." He produced the evidence from his pocket and dangled the infamous bracelet from his fingertips.

Busted.

DECEPTION—EVELYN

I could tell by Leo's expression that he was guilty.

Given his history with beautiful women, I knew where his confession was headed before he even choked out the words: "Nicoletta and I dated a few years back. Before she met Stefano."

If it hadn't been for the threat of getting my kneecaps blown off, I would've bolted from the room to avoid Leo's story of how and when he had given Nicoletta the charm bracelet.

"She was new in town and wanted to check out the Navy Pier. We were hanging out, sharing some caramel and cheddar cheese popcorn, when we walked by a vendor selling t-shirts and trinkets. Nicoletta wanted a souvenir, so I told her to pick something out. She chose *that*." He pointed to the bracelet in Luca's hand.

The same bracelet she had attached herself to in the afterlife. The one that allowed her restless spirit to take over my body when I wore it. The same bracelet that carried the first initial of my boyfriend's name.

How could Leo have kept this from me? I wouldn't have

been angry if he had told me right away. We never talked about his past lovers, but since Nicoletta's ghost had come to me for help, Leo was responsible for telling me the truth.

I fumed as I recalled our conversations about Nicoletta and how he pretended not to have known anything about her. "I asked you point blank if you had ever met her, and you changed the subject and avoided my question."

"I'm sorry, Evelyn. I should've told you."

"Did you know about this?" I asked Stefano.

"Nicoletta told me before we were married," he said.

I was angry at Leo for keeping this from me, but I wouldn't let Luca tear us apart. "I forgive you, Leo."

"Now, it's time to rattle Stefano's cage," Luca said. "You know what? I'm going to help you out with this one. While you were here as our guest, you got a phone call from your partner. You haven't heard it yet, Detective, but you and Stefano can listen to this enlightening information straight from the source—The FBI."

Luca tapped the phone then Parker's voice came through the speaker.

"Leo, call me back immediately. The team made a major breakthrough in Shay's case that leads to Nicoletta Vanzetti. Shay was the bookkeeper for Nicoletta's charity. I found evidence in her work files that shows months' worth of fraudulent expenses on the books from Sal's Family Restaurant. Looks like it could lead to a money laundering case."

Parker took a deep breath.

"And I heard back from my contact in Organized Crime. The Outfit has done some reorganizing to fit the times. The Chicago mob has entered the financial markets. They split the family in half and added a second boss to their org chart —Stefano Vanzetti."

He paused to let his message sink in. "The traditional side of the family uses coercion tactics to get insider information on the stock market. Then, the financial side uses the information to make illegal investments and grow the family's fortune. Your buddy Stefano is known as—The Money Don."

When Luca ended the message, no one spoke.

Stefano's role in organized crime answered a lot of questions, but it was hard to believe that Leo's old friend had followed such a dark path. The neighborhood gossip was correct. We should've listened to Silvia from the start.

Stefano glared at Leo, vexing him for his betrayal. I did not know if he was angrier about the investigation into his family business or that he had linked Nicoletta to a financial crime that led to murder. Now, we were one step closer to discovering the truth about Nicoletta's past.

"Ding, ding, ding!" Luca chimed in. "That's the end of round one. While you two lovebirds stew over that, it's your turn to confess, Stefano. Does your buddy know how obsessed you are with his girlfriend?"

Instead of being pissed, Leo grinned arrogantly. "That's not a secret. He's been gunning for Evelyn since he laid eyes on her."

Luca laughed as he eyed his nephew, seemingly waiting for him to drop a bombshell. When Stefano failed to deliver, Luca prodded him along. "Good point, Detective, but I'm afraid your timeline is a little off. When exactly was the first time you laid eyes on Evelyn?"

Stefano glared at Luca.

"I'll give you guys a little hint. It wasn't the day he *accidentally* bumped into her at the cemetery. My nephew has gone to a lot of trouble to insert himself into your life, princess, and it sure as hell wasn't a coincidence."

Stefano's expression held no hint of remorse as he confessed. "I know everything about you, *Lauren Murphy*. I hired a team of private investigators to find out every detail of your life—*and death*. I know how long you were underwater, when you came back to life, and how your family rejected you because of your phenomenal gift. Becoming Evelyn was your sweet revenge."

I held my breath as Stefano detailed the timeline of my life.

"You go out with your friend Tess every Tuesday. You and Leo go to the same coffee shop every morning. You have a sweet tooth and favor cinnamon pastries. You paint by the window in your studio. You often get lost in your work and forget to eat lunch."

His accuracy about my habits was surreal.

"It hasn't been easy to make your acquaintance. You never walk anywhere alone—except for last Friday when you told your boyfriend you needed your freedom."

"How did you know about our conversation? Did you hire people to spy on us at the coffee shop?"

"I've been keeping tabs on you for months, waiting for my time to meet you without Leo around. It took a lot of patience, but it was worth it when I finally got my chance."

The idea that Stefano had hired people to stalk me and dig into my past sickened me. "You followed me to the cemetery the one day I decided to go out without Leo?"

Stefano shook his head, dumbfounded by his luck. "That was a beautiful surprise. Imagine the rush of seeing you, sketching Nicoletta at her graveside. I knew then meeting you was fate. I finally had the means to communicate with my wife and find out from Nicoletta herself what truly happened on the night she died."

"Why didn't you come to me?" Leo said. "All you had to do was ask, and I would've helped you. I'm a detective. I could've used my sources at the FBI to investigate the accident report and uncovered the truth."

"But you have already used your sources and uncovered the *truth* about my business, haven't you?" Stefano snapped.

"I looked up to you when we were kids. You stayed as a guest in my home. You sat at my dinner table. And in return, you betrayed my trust by investigating *me*—the Money Don of the Chicago Mafia."

The guys got sidetracked and started arguing about the definition of trust, but Luca stepped in to get them back on track.

"Whoa, guys." He signaled a timeout. "You can duke it out later, but while we're stuck on trust, it's Miss Perfect's turn to confess her sexy little sin. Remember that late-night selfie you sent to the boss, Evelyn? I'm sure a good girl like you already told your boyfriend about your little peep show, right?"

He lifted a photograph from his pocket but shielded the image ahead of the big reveal.

Leo snapped his attention back to center and zeroed in on my guilty expression. I had the nerve to judge him about keeping his secret but failed to acknowledge my own deception.

I sank down in my chair and prepared to face Leo's judgment.

BURNED—EVELYN

"Uhat the hell is he talking about, Evelyn?" Leo seethed as Luca lifted his eyebrows and studied my naked selfie that he apparently had cupped in his hand.

"I'm sorry. I never meant for it to happen."

"Meant for *what* to happen?"

"Last Monday night, while I was wearing Nicoletta's charm bracelet for the first time, she took over my body. That was the night I blacked out. I know now that we'd made love that night, but I have no memory of what happened between when I went to bed and when I woke up early in the morning."

Leo crossed his arms in anticipation of the bomb that was about to drop.

"In the morning, I checked my phone. That's when I realized I had sent Stefano *that*." I pointed to the picture in Luca's hand.

"Show it to me," Leo growled.

Luca was happy to oblige and handed over the photo.

Leo studied the photo and then shot me an accusatory

glare. "If Nicoletta took over your body and you had no knowledge of sending this, why didn't you tell me?"

"She was afraid," Stefano said. "Evelyn came to me for help, and as a gentleman, I gave her my word I would never breathe a word of it to you."

"You lied," I said. "You gave the photo to Luca."

Stefano clicked his tongue. "Not true. I never shared the photo. Luca would've found out about it only from my loyal and trusted associate, Dino."

All eyes drifted to the big guy.

Dino was sweating profusely, and his expression oozed with guilt.

"I guess that means it's my turn," Luca said. "Unless you want to do the honors, Dino?"

He shook his head and remained stoic, wanting nothing to do with Judgment Hour.

"Fine. I'll let you in on a little surprise, guys. Dino reports to me. He's always reported to me—even when you thought he was working for Nicoletta."

Stefano's expression burned with rage as he processed his bodyguard's betrayal.

"Dino has been updating me on your and Nico's meetings, activities, and transactions since I hired him after you and Nicoletta were married. At first, I did it to protect you. I wanted to make sure your new bride could be trusted with our family business, but it turned out she had plenty of secrets of her own."

Luca pointed to the briefcase. "Time for the main event. Now it's Nico's turn to confess."

FATAL MISTAKE—LEO

Luca tasked Evelyn with opening the briefcase and sharing the contents.

He seemed excited to find out the big surprise Nicoletta had left after her death. My gut was telling me whatever she went to so much trouble to protect had gotten her killed. If that were true, I would do everything possible to bring her killer or killers to justice.

Luca rearranged our chairs so that each of us had a front-row seat for the big reveal. Evelyn stood at the head of the class like a schoolteacher, ready to deliver her presentation.

"Okay, guys, here are the rules," Luca said. "None of us, not even our resident psychic, knows exactly what's inside the case. I have a good idea of what's in there, but I'll have to wait to find out with the rest of you. I need everyone to stay calm until all the contents are revealed."

My adrenaline was pumping as the mystery of Nicoletta's final message was nearing the end. Everyone would be focused on the contents and hopefully distracted enough to give me my moment to strike.

I planned to attack Dino first, as he was the biggest threat.

Stefano had shown me mercy, so I reasoned he wouldn't shoot an unarmed man in cold blood. Luca was a coward and never handled his own dirty work. If I disarmed Dino quickly, Luca would be afraid to challenge me once I had a weapon.

Unlike the others, I didn't care what was in that briefcase —not as long as there were still lives on the line. My objective was to save Evelyn and Mira and escape Stefano's haunted mansion.

Thinking of hauntings made we wonder...*where are Evelyn's ghosts?*

If Nicoletta had hung back to seek revenge, her ghost must've been pumping her fist as the contents of her secret were about to be spilled.

Had she known she was going to die? Was there evidence stashed inside that would reveal her killer? Or was there some other bombshell of a revelation we had failed to consider?

"Evelyn, whenever you're ready." Luca turned the stage over to her and folded his arms, basking in his deviant glory.

Evelyn placed her hands on the briefcase, but before she opened it, she shot her gaze to mine. "I'm sorry I didn't tell you about the selfie, Leo. I was so ashamed of what I'd done I couldn't face you. Can you forgive me?"

I was doing everything I could to stay focused, but seeing my girl wallowing in self-hatred shattered my focus. I wanted to tell her she was the most important person in my life, and I would spend the rest of my days showing her how much I loved her.

But there would be no "rest of our lives" if I got distracted. So instead, I committed to my mission of saving her life and gave her a simple nod.

Stay focused, Evelyn. I swear we'll fix this later, sweetheart.

She gave me a bittersweet smile and opened the case.

Pretending to lean forward for a better view of the brief-case contents, I uncrossed my legs and got myself into a ready position. I was a tackle on the offensive line of my high school football team. As soon as Dino lost his focus for a split second, I would burst forward, hit him low and hard, and knock that wall of muscle flat on his back.

Evelyn reached into the briefcase and pulled out a thick yellow envelope. She held it up and read the message:

"For Detective Leo Ricci, Chicago P.D."

Now I was the center of attention and would have to wait for my next shot. Damn.

I wasn't surprised my name was on that package. Nicoletta and I hadn't spoken for years, but there was no bad blood between us. We had a good thing for a while, but true to my character back then, I wasn't looking for a serious relationship.

If she had gotten tangled up in some sort of trouble, she could've come to me. Apparently, that had been her plan. She'd tried to share something important before her death but never had the chance to deliver the message.

Sorry, Nicoletta. I wish I could've helped you.

Luca stepped in and lifted the envelope from Evelyn's hands. "Interesting, but I'm not surprised. I have a good idea of what's in here, but I'll put this aside now. I give you my word. We'll come back to this."

He motioned for Evelyn to continue. Next, she pulled out a package wrapped in brown paper and stuffed inside a plastic bag.

"Open it," Luca said.

Evelyn used her fingernail to lift the tape. As she tore the paper, she stared at the floor and shifted her feet as she had down at the carriage house when she "saw" a puddle on the floor.

It seems the ghosts are in the house.

When Evelyn opened the package, she pulled out four passport books and spread them out on the table for all of us to see. Then she flipped the first one open and read the name. "Roman Santiago."

"Who the fuck is Roman Santiago?" Luca snapped.

Evelyn turned the book around and showed us the photo inside.

Roman Santiago was Stefano Vanzetti.

"Now we're getting to the good part." Luca took the book from Evelyn's hand and studied the information. "It seems your wife wanted to give you a brand-new identity, Stefano. Open the other ones," he said to Evelyn.

She opened each one, read the name, and turned it around for all of us to see.

There was one with a new identity for Nicoletta, Mira, and—*Dino*.

"Nico planned to ditch her perfect life here in Chicago, and she was going to leave me behind?" Luca chortled as he shook his head in disbelief. "Now that stings."

Stefano remained quiet, but his complexion had gone pale.

Evelyn went through the other items in the case and set them on the table for inspection: A stack of cash, credit cards with their new names, fake birth certificates, and social security cards.

It wasn't easy to get these illegal documents, and the big picture was starting to take shape in my detective brain. Nicoletta wanted out of the Chicago Mob, but instead of leaving her family behind, she made the fatal mistake of trying to take Stefano and her friends with her.

The penalty for deserting the mafia was death. What wasn't clear yet was who had ratted her out and who had her killed. Had the orders come from the top, or was it an internal decision made by Luca to protect his own family interests?

"Did you know about any of that?" Luca asked Stefano.

"Of course not." Stefano's face burned with rage. My gut told me he was telling the truth.

Evelyn pulled one more item out of the briefcase and turned the case around so we could see it was now empty.

She held a red envelope in her hand and read the name scrolled across the card:

"For Stefano."

FANTASMA—EVELYN

Water pooled at my feet as a paranormal presence chilled me to the bone. Nicoletta had been killed over the contents of this case. I believed whatever message Nicoletta wanted to deliver was monumental.

As I had at the carriage house, I could see her ghostly form now, and all her energy was focused on Stefano. She had taken extreme measures from beyond the grave to lead him to her final message. Hopefully, once she had accomplished her goal, she would find peace and move on to the other side.

My hands trembled as I handed the card to Stefano.

When he snatched the letter away, he didn't wait for Luca's permission before tearing open the envelope and pulling out the card. While he read the message, I slid my gaze to Leo. He was perched at the edge of his seat with one eye on Luca and the other on Dino.

Leo would never sit idly during a crisis. He was planning our exit strategy.

While I wasn't a match for any of the guys physically, I

scanned the room in search of weapons. If it came down to Leo engaging in hand-to-hand combat, I could help by knocking one of them unconscious with a heavy candlestick, picture frame, or glass vase.

"Come on, man. Read it out loud for the rest of us," Luca said.

I shifted my attention back to Stefano, who was reading the card silently. His emotions ranged from endearment to surprise. Then, as his gaze moved down the page, his eyes darkened with rage.

When Stefano finally read his late wife's final message, he lifted his eyes and zeroed in on Luca. His expression turned murderous, then as quick as a cobra, Stefano reached into his jacket, pulled out his gun, and aimed it at his uncle.

"You killed my wife, you fucking traitor!"

Simultaneously, as if Luca had anticipated Stefano's response, he pulled out his weapon, leaving the men in a homicidal standoff. "Easy, kid. You don't have the full story yet. Don't blame me for something I didn't do."

I froze as my heart raced with fear. In my peripheral vision, I noticed Leo hadn't moved either. Any sudden movements could send the guys into a gunfight, which wouldn't end well for any of us.

"On your mother's life, I didn't kill Nico. I'm guilty of many things, but I'm not responsible for her accident."

As the men argued, a swarm of shadowy figures circled us like they were trying to prevent our escape. Nicoletta appeared and her ghostly image carried the marking of the mortal wound on the center of her forehead.

She hovered beside Stefano as if waiting for him to join her. The situation was dire, and I feared Nicoletta's assumption was correct—Stefano was about to die.

We have to do something that will alter his fate.

My premonitions had been coming true. The fallen tree,

the gunman, the killer stabbed through the heart with a pair of scissors...The rest of us were still breathing, but I had little faith this battle would end without casualties.

Help me, Nicoletta. Show me what needs to be done to prevent our murders.

As I studied the rest of the shadowy figures, I recognized the gathering of spirits that had banded together with Nicoletta—they were the Hillcrest family, the estate's original owners. They had stayed together as was their wish nearly a hundred years ago.

The family of ghosts seemed to be there to bear witness or support Nicoletta in her quest for justice. As I darted my gaze around the circle, one ghost was absent from the bunch—Shay. I scanned the room until I noticed a water trail leading in from the window.

I tracked the watery footsteps until I found her.

Shay Adams was hovering beside Dino with her arm outstretched, aiming her ghostly finger at his chest—as if outing him as her killer. Water spewed violently from her mouth. As she struggled to say the words, Nicoletta followed her lead and pointed at her killer. She opened her mouth and moaned, *"Fantasma."*

Then as a show of unity, the Hillcrest family followed the lead of the freshly dead, pointed at Dino, and repeated the damning word:

Fantasma...Fantasma...Fantasma...

The sound of their ghostly chants sent shivers down my spine. It was clear to me now who the killer was, but what could I do to prevent the bloodbath on the horizon?

"Put the gun down, Stefano," Luca said. "Let's talk this out. I admit I found out about the passports and confronted Nicoletta about it. She begged me to keep it between us, and in return, we arranged to launder a couple hundred thousand dollars in hush money through her charity."

"You blackmailed my *wife?*"

"Hey, all I asked her to do was kick a couple large catering bills from Sal's onto the books. She rakes in so much money for those kids, no one would've noticed an uptick in the foundation's expenses on the books."

As soon as Luca said books, Shay unleashed a bloodcurdling scream and pounded her ghostly fists on Dino's chest. Even though I was the only one in the room who could see her, Dino flinched uncomfortably, and the flames from the candles waved violently as the force of her energy swirled around the room.

While Shay's restless spirit raged, I put together the clues. Shay was a bookkeeper for Nicoletta's charity. She must've noticed the fraudulent catering charges and had brought it to Nicoletta's attention.

I glanced down at the manila envelope with Leo's name scrolled across the front.

My junior detective instincts alerted me that the contents of that envelope held Shay's expense report, along with evidence that Luca was blackmailing her. Nicoletta wanted justice and freedom—a dangerous combination since her husband was involved with organized crime.

That was why she wanted to disappear and only intended to reveal her secret to Stefano once she had everything in place and was ready to run.

Nicoletta wanted out of organized crime and wanted to take the people she loved and cared about with her. She used the night of her charity event as a distraction to set her plan into motion.

You were so close, Nicoletta.

While I was mesmerized by the paranormal activity, Leo had been trying to get my attention. He held his hand level at his side and lowered it, signaling me to get down.

Good idea. Slowly, I lowered myself to the floor.

Stefano never flinched as he pointed his weapon at Luca's head, ready to fire his gun and make the next premonition come true. On the other side, Luca aimed his weapon at Stefano's heart, ready to blow open his chest as I'd predicted in my drawing.

Luca would kill to protect his despicable life, and Stefano had reached the tipping point now that Luca had tossed all his cards on the table. "Then tell me, Uncle. If you didn't kill Nicoletta, who did?"

"I don't know!" Luca shouted.

"He's telling the truth," I said.

Leo fired a death ray at me. The right thing to do was shut my mouth and stand by, but I feared Stefano and Luca were about to kill each other, and I needed to intervene. Leo's job was to protect and serve, but mine was to help restless spirits find peace so they could move on from this life to the next.

"Tell me, Evelyn," Stefano hissed. "Who killed Nicoletta?"

I banded together with Nicoletta, Shay, and the family of ghosts. I aimed my finger at Dino and said, *"Fantasma."*

The murderer was sweating profusely as, at last, his secret had been exposed.

Stefano's expression turned venomous, and he barked out, "You killed my wife over money?" As he aimed his gun at his former trusted employee, I squeezed my eyes shut and covered my ears in anticipation of the fatal shot.

"Wait!" Dino yelled. He held his gun at his side, but Stefano was poised to kill, so he wisely stood still to avoid provoking Stefano further. "I met Shay through Nicoletta. We were dating."

Dino is the elusive boyfriend. Now the pieces of our investigation were coming together.

"Shay was upset one day and told me she was worried about Nicoletta. She saw her crying and wondered if it had to do with the suspicious charges appearing on her expense reports," Dino explained.

"Shay knew too much. She had given the information to Nicoletta but told me she would have to report the fraud to the charity board if Nicoletta didn't handle it. Shay had to be stopped. I reported her to the Outfit. I turned her into the mob to protect Nicoletta."

"Then why did you kill her?" Stefano's nostrils flared as he prodded Dino. "Nicoletta trusted you, and you betrayed her."

"*She* betrayed *me*," Dino said. "After Shay went missing,

Nicoletta was distraught. She wanted out of the family, and I told her I would help her. We planned to run away together —just the two of us."

Damn. Dino wasn't saving his life with this confession.

Dino pointed to the passports. "I arranged a meeting between her and my contact to get the passports. There were only supposed to be two. One for me and one for her. She loved me. We were going to escape together and start a new life. When I found out from my contact that Nicoletta had deceived me…" Dino's face reddened with rage.

"She had a passport made for *you*, Stefano—she wanted you to come with us. I loved her. She *had* to die for her betrayal."

Stefano's expression turned murderous. A sickening sensation of dread fell over the ballroom.

They're here—the dead.

I didn't have Evelyn's gift, but I felt the pulse of negative energy reverberating off the walls.

"Nicoletta did love you, Dino—like a brother, no more."

It's now or never, Ricci.

While I prepared to make my move, I glanced at Luca. Would he side with Stefano or Dino? Luca had his weapon drawn, but he had it aimed between them as if he had yet to decide where his loyalty would land.

My instincts urged me to fight. I sprung out of the chair like a crouching lion and lunged at Dino. As I crashed into him, he raised his weapon at Stefano on his way down. The element of surprise had worked. I had caught Dino off guard, but as he stumbled, my sneak attack caused a chain reaction.

I could see it coming as if it was playing out in slow motion.

"Evelyn, get down!" I yelled.

Dino raised his arm and aimed his weapon at Stefano.

Stefano was ready to squeeze the trigger but hesitated because I was now in his line of fire.

Dino delivered a punch to the side of my head that dropped me to the ground. While I blinked away the stars flashing before my eyes, a single gunshot echoed through the ballroom.

KILLER INSTINCTS—EVELYN

*E*verything happened so fast.

I was under the table and lifted my head to assess the situation.

Leo was down, but he was conscious. No blood, which meant he hadn't been shot.

Dino was still on his feet, panting as he recovered from Leo's attack. He stared at the ground and sneered. I crawled out from under the table and peeked under the chair to see what had happened.

A thick pool of blood oozed out from under Stefano's body.

I covered my mouth to stifle a scream.

Stefano's shirt was soaked with blood, and I feared my premonition had come true. As I stared in disbelief, I noticed two things: He was still breathing, and the gunshot wound was higher than in my drawing.

My premonition had been altered. Stefano was still alive —for now.

Leo's intervention had apparently thrown off the gunman, and Stefano's wound had missed his heart.

Footsteps pounded on the hardwood floor. The room was dark, so I stayed low to avoid bringing attention to myself. Luca ran to the table and grabbed the envelope with Leo's name on it and ran away from the scene as his nephew lay helpless in a pool of his own blood.

I would've hoped he was running off to get help, but I doubted he would risk losing his chance to flee the scene to help anyone except himself.

As Dino watched Stefano fight to breathe, he leaned over, stole his gun, and lifted his phone from his pocket. Then, he rifled through the passports until he found his own, grabbed the cash envelope, and ran toward the rear exit closest to the cemetery.

On his way out, he turned back and shifted his gaze between me, Leo, and Stefano.

Before he ran out the door, he knocked over a row of candelabras into the velvet curtains. He aimed his gun at me as the material caught fire and spread quickly across the room. "You won't have time to save them both. Now you must live with your bad decisions."

He smiled with a sickening sense of self-satisfaction as he raced out the door.

But he wasn't alone—Shay and the Hillcrest brood chased after him.

Shay's motive for remaining earthbound was revenge, and she had recruited some loyal ghosts to help her seek justice.

The same was not true for Nicoletta. As Stefano lay bleeding, her ghost knelt beside him, cupped his head in her hands, and whispered in Italian. It seemed Stefano's time on this earth was about to expire, and Nicoletta wanted to be with him until the end.

Leo stirred as he regained consciousness.

The room was filling with smoke, and I needed to get him

out fast. Dino's devious plot to ruin my life by giving me the impossible task of saving two men from a fire didn't deter me. Saving Leo was my first priority. Then I would find a way to save Stefano's life.

Leo was barely conscious, and as I crouched beside him, readying myself to pull him out of there, I called out to Stefano. "Hang on. I'm coming back for you. Nicoletta is with you now. If there is anything you want to say to her, now is the time."

Stefano lifted his head and stared directly into Nicoletta's eyes. I had no idea if he could see her, but he undoubtedly felt her presence. The bloodstain on his shirt was spreading. The bullet must've nicked an artery for Stefano to have lost so much blood.

"Leo." I tapped on his cheeks. "I need you to focus, babe. We have to get out of here. The ballroom is going up in flames.

He opened his eyes and blinked as he came back to consciousness. "Are you okay? Who got shot?"

I gave him a quick update as I helped him to his feet. He was woozy and probably suffering from a concussion, but I was thankful he could walk out of there without me dragging him.

Once I got Leo outside, I left him in the rain and darted back inside after Stefano. The air was thick with smoke. I stayed as low as possible to avoid breathing in the noxious fumes and got down on my hands and knees when I got closer to Stefano.

When I reached the spot where I'd last seen him—he was gone. There were bloody footsteps and drag marks across the hardwood leading away from the scene of the crime and toward the rear exit door.

No one had passed me on the way in. Dino and Luca were long gone. The only other person in this room was not alive and had no strength or power to drag a grown man out of a burning building.

There was one person who remained unaccounted for, Mira. Had she been watching and waiting while the chaos had played out? We could unravel the clues later, but we needed to find a phone and call for help.

"Mira?" I shouted. It had to be her. No one else was here.

No response.

Even if Mira had helped Stefano out of the building, he was moments away from certain death. Hopefully, she had a phone because, with the tree down, she couldn't escape with him by car.

"Evelyn!" Leo shouted. "I'm coming. Is Stefano still breathing?"

"I'm on my way out. Don't come any closer. The smoke is too thick." I crawled out on my hands and knees and got out of there fast. Leo met me halfway and put his arm around me protectively as we rushed out of the ballroom and into the rainstorm.

"Is Stefano still alive?" He stared at the door as he calculated his rescue plan.

"He's gone."

"Dammit." Leo's expression tanked. Even though there had been a rift between them, Leo would never wish harm on anyone—especially not after Stefano had saved his life.

"I mean *gone* as in missing." I patted Leo's arm. "Sorry to scare you. He's not in the building. When I went back inside, there were bloody footprints and draglines. He was alive, and someone got him out of the building before I could."

"Luca?"

"Not likely. Uncle Dirtbag slithered off to save his own skin. I think it was Mira."

"Agreed. I found another surprise when you went back inside." Leo motioned for me to follow him around the corner under the shelter. He pointed to a lump on the back patio.

At first, I didn't realize what it was, but then I zeroed in on a face. "Oh, shit. That's the third hitman." His death pose was the same as I predicted: Blunt force trauma. The crowbar Luca used to open the briefcase was lying beside his body, covered in blood.

I hardly knew Mira, but for a slim, thirty-something-year-old who claimed to be just a driver, she had some serious combat training and a set of red-hot killer instincts.

Good for you, Mira. I hope your survivor skills are just as sharp.

Leo rolled over the hitman's body and searched his pockets. "No phone and no gun, but I'll take this crowbar. Seemed to work for Mira. We'll need to escape on foot, find a neighbor, and—"

The sound of two men arguing stopped Leo mid-sentence. The commotion was coming from the dock. Leo and I stood still and listened. It was Luca and Dino, arguing in Italian. I had no idea what they were saying, but Dino was on a jet ski and was about to make his getaway.

Luca apparently wanted to go with him.

"Why don't they take the speedboat?" I whispered to Leo.

"They must not have the key."

The argument escalated into a shouting match, then gunshots fired.

Leo pulled me around the corner to avoid getting hit by a stray bullet, then took a quick glance to see what had gone down. "Dino shot Luca."

"Between the eyes?"

"No. He's holding his arm and pacing. Probably just a flesh wound."

Leo shielded me with his body and steered me toward the house. "I know where Stefano keeps the key. It's in the main house in the mudroom. If we get there before Luca, we can track down Mira and Stefano and get out of here."

Leo seemed to have shaken off his injury enough to think clearly. The first stop when we got out of there was a hospital, but for now, Leo and I needed to survive the night.

As the high-pitched hum of the jet ski sounded, I spotted Dino riding solo as he sped off in the choppy water.

A wave of blue shadows followed in his wake. Shay and the Hillcrest family created a tsunami-like effect as they chased behind the killer.

The ghosts were doing everything in their otherworldly power to prevent Dino from escaping.

BLUE—LEO

Dino fled the scene. All three hitmen were dead. Stefano and Mira were M.I.A. Luca was out there somewhere, bleeding and scheming.

Evelyn and I entered the mansion through the garage. I didn't have a gun, but I had the crowbar Mira used to bludgeon the hitman to death. Luca was my only threat left unless Mira considered me dangerous.

I had no way of knowing her intentions, but it seemed she was the only person who remained loyal to Stefano. How I would handle her if our paths crossed would be a game-time decision.

"Keep an eye out for Luca," I said to Evelyn as I pointed to the dock. "He might have the same idea about getting the key."

I held my breath as I opened the drawer. The key was exactly where Stefano put it when we went boating last weekend. I slid it into my pocket, led Evelyn to the door, and was about to leave when—

"Detective Ricci," a voice behind me, to my left.

I spun around and found Mira there. Stefano was on the

floor on a plastic tarp that Mira had turned into an emergency mode of transport. I held my hand out to block Evelyn from rushing to his side. I needed to know Mira's intentions before we jumped in to help.

"Please," Mira said. "I must get him to a hospital. The tree is blocking the road, so we have to leave by boat. He's not going to last much longer."

"Are you armed?" I asked.

"No. The hitmen took my gun before they tried to kill me." She eyed the bloody crowbar in my hand. "As you can see, I had to improvise."

Mira's suit was soaked with blood, mud, and rain. I had no idea what training she had, but her bravery in taking out those murderers ranked among the highest-level first responders and military heroes.

"Are we on the same team, Mira?"

"If you plan to save his life, then yes. Tell me what you want me to do," she said.

I tossed her the boat key and handed her the crowbar. "Luca is still out there. Cover me while I load Stefano on the boat."

Evelyn pushed past me and dropped to her knees next to Stefano. She brushed his hair out of his eyes and cupped his cheeks. "Can you hear me?"

"Silvia," Stefano whispered. "Tell her I'm sorry."

Tears welled in Evelyn's eyes as she promised to deliver the message to my mother.

I squatted down next to Stefano and lifted him into my arms. My old friend was drenched with rainwater and soaked in his own blood. His complexion was ashen, and his lips were blue. "Hang on, buddy. It's my turn to save your life."

Mira led the way while I carried Stefano to the boat. Evelyn grabbed a fire poker from the outdoor firepit and held it like a spear as she covered my back. With no gun, we were at a disadvantage if Luca decided to snipe us as we escaped.

Luca's only way out was on that boat, and now that he was wounded, he would resort to desperate measures to save his skin. Strategically, he would try to eliminate me first. Luckily, I was being guarded by two brave, battle-tested women who would do everything possible to get us on that boat.

Bring it on, Luca.

WATERY GRAVE—EVELYN

The thunderstorm never let up as Mira served as captain of Stefano's boat.

The last place I wanted to be was on a boat in the middle of a storm with an armed and desperate killer on the loose. But I pushed my terror aside and focused all my energy on Stefano. We had tossed some cushions on the deck and made a makeshift bed to help stabilize him.

I tucked a pillow under his head and held his hand as the boat cut through the choppy water. It was a rough ride, but Stefano's condition was critical, and we had no time to waste. Stefano was no angel, but he had suffered an unimaginable tragedy at the hands of the people he trusted.

If fate had dealt me a similar blow, I could understand the need for answers. I forgave him for his injustices against Leo and me. When Stefano was called upon to do the right thing, he saved Leo's life and did everything he could to protect me.

For that reason, I was eternally grateful.

Stefano groaned in agony as the boat skipped over the waves. He lifted his eyes and tried to focus on me. "She's with me now."

I shivered when a chilly breeze circled around me. Nicoletta placed her ghostly blue hands on Stefano's cheeks and stared into his eyes. He was right about Nicoletta being with him, but he was fading fast, and I feared he was about to go into shock.

"You're right, Stefano. Nicoletta is here. She wants you to hang on. It's not your time to go. Stay with me."

"I'm going to be with my wife." Stefano closed his eyes and dropped his head on the pillow. He was still breathing, but his condition was deteriorating.

"How much longer?" I shouted to Leo.

He was looking through a pair of binoculars as he shined a flashlight at the water. I stood and peered over the railing to see what had caught his attention.

A capsized jet ski.

I searched the water and found Dino waving his arms to get our attention as he struggled to stay afloat. The rough waters made it difficult for him to tread water, and as I focused on his surroundings, I understood why.

The ghost of Shay Adams was circling him like a shark, creating a cyclone effect around him that threatened to drag him under. Dino screamed for help but was choking on the water crashing across his face.

The same way Shay had come to me in my dreams.

It seemed the vengeful spirit wanted Dino to suffer as she had done at the hands of her hired killers. He may not have taken her life with his own hands, but Dino was the rat who outed her to the men up the chain of command and stood by as the hitmen drowned her in a watery grave.

Dino's evil deeds had led to his dire situation, but it wasn't in Leo's nature to stand by and let a man drown. Protect and serve was his creed, and he would never dishonor his oath by standing down while a man struggled for his life.

"Cut the engine!" Leo yelled to Mira. "I'm going to reel him in."

Leo handed me the flashlight and told me to keep track of Dino while he rushed to get the lifesaver. As I aimed the light at him, I watched in horror as the current dragged him under. I held the light steady, waiting for him to resurface.

As the seconds ticked away, Dino's chances of survival diminished.

"Let him die in a watery grave," Mira said. Instead of following Leo's orders, Mira sped up to get back on course. "I won't risk Stefano's life to save a killer. I have a medical crew waiting at the dock."

Mira was right, and we both knew it. Leo flung the lifesaver into the water in a Hail Mary attempt to give Dino a fighting chance. As I shined my flashlight in the water, Dino appeared. His nose and mouth were still underwater, but his eyes were fixated on mine.

While the boat sped off, Dino's big body lifted out of the water. He hovered above the surface and aimed his finger at me, blaming me for his demise. He wasn't struggling to breathe or keep his head above water anymore.

He was a ghost.

UPWARD—LEO

*A*s promised, medics were at the dock to greet us.

I tossed out the rope, and a crew member helped us tie up the boat. The team wasn't wearing uniforms and had no identifiable markings on their rain gear. Mira must've called a private service to transport Stefano to the nearest hospital.

The crew stormed the boat, strapped Stefano onto a stretcher, and carried him toward an evac helicopter that had landed in the empty parking lot of the marina. Mira trotted alongside the crew and answered the barrage of questions from the medical staff.

I interrupted with a question of my own. "Where are you taking him?"

"Wisconsin General," Mira answered. "They are expecting him. Thank you for honoring our deal, Detective."

"Take us with you!" Evelyn called out. "Leo needs a doctor, too."

"Sorry, miss. There's no room in the helicopter," one of the medics said. "We'll call for an ambulance. Stay here until help arrives."

I was fine, but Evelyn appeared to be in shock. Something had stolen her attention. Her blue eyes shined as she stared at the sky above the helicopter. Tears streamed down her cheeks as she pointed upward.

"Evelyn, are you all right? What do you see?"

"Stefano."

HER PATH—EVELYN

A bright tunnel swirled above the helicopter, and the sky glowed with the golden aura of eternal peace as Stefano's spirit ascended into the heavens.

His body was whole again, and he was no longer suffering from his mortal gunshot wound. He was oblivious to the medics on the ground, pounding on his chest and performing CPR. He didn't see Mira valiantly clutching her cross pendant and praying over his lifeless body.

Stefano was only aware that his beautiful wife was there to greet him.

Nicoletta hovered before the entrance to the other side, waiting for her husband to join her. Her skin no longer radiated a ghastly shade of blue, and the morbid gash in her head had disappeared. Her natural beauty had been restored as she basked in her eternal glory.

When Stefano finally reunited with Nicoletta, the energy of their embrace lit up the sky in a rush of colors more intense and spectacular than this world had ever known. My heart swelled with joy as I witnessed Nicoletta and Stefano's undying love in this world transcend to the next.

As I watched Nicoletta pass through the tunnel to the other side, I remembered her message to Stefano. *"Our love will never die."*

When Nicoletta's spirit disappeared into eternity, the swirling tunnel of light closed before Stefano could follow her path. He waved his hand to find the opening, but it disappeared.

The light was meant for Nicoletta only—*not Stefano.*

He was dead but not gone.

Stefano's spirit was locked out of heaven.

THE PACKAGE—LEO

$\mathcal{D}$ear Leo,

By the time you read this letter, I will likely be dead.

The events in my life have spiraled out of control, and there is no way out other than the grave. I accept responsibility for my mistakes, but please understand that I had no control over my family's actions.

This package serves as my confession and desire to seek revenge against the men who destroyed my life. You are the only person I can trust, Leo. I know you will use the evidence within to seek justice for Shay Adams and take down the monsters who murdered her.

The penalty for leaving my family is death. I have a plan to escape, and if I make it out by some miracle, you will never find me or hear from me again.

Thank you for your service, Detective Ricci. For your help, I am eternally grateful.

Nicoletta Vanzetti

. . .

THE PACKAGE WAS a goldmine of information and evidence against Luca Vanzetti and other key players in the family business. When Luca found out Nicoletta had a fake passport made and planned to leave the family, he blackmailed her in exchange for his silence.

Luca submitted fraudulent catering bills to Nicoletta from Sal's Family Restaurant as a means of payment for the hush money. Shay Adams, the bookkeeper, noticed the discrepancy and brought it to Nicoletta's attention, not knowing Nicoletta was in on the fraud.

Shay had also confided in her boyfriend, Dino, about her concerns. He's the one that led the mob to silence her.

Nicoletta supported her claim with expense reports and stated that Sal and his family were not involved. The mob had muscled in on their business and took control after Luca did Sal a *favor* and loaned him money to expand his catering business.

As for Stefano's chauffeur, Mira, she was not *just a driver* as she had claimed. She was a highly trained executive protection agent who served as Stefano's personal bodyguard. While Dino appeared to be the boss's number one guard in public, Mira's incognito role as a driver kept her close to the boss while working undercover as his true protector.

Mira had not been charged with any crimes and had not been seen since Evelyn and I had watched her leave in the helicopter.

The best witness in our case turned out to be the man accused of the crime that led to murder—Luca Vanzetti.

He sustained a minor gunshot wound to the arm, and once he was arrested, he confessed to more than a dozen crimes in exchange for the promise of lesser charges. His wealth of information against the mob would take years to sort out, so the case got kicked over to the FBI.

I had never seen a suspect turn more quickly against his accomplices. Luca pointed his crooked finger at every key player on the org chart and blamed most of his bad deeds on the family's bodyguard, Dino—a dead man who could not say otherwise.

Unfortunately for Dino, Evelyn's premonition had played out. His body was discovered floating in the lake after his jet ski accident. And not far from there, the remains of Shay Adams were discovered wrapped in a tarp and weighed down by a cinder block by a dive team.

While Nicoletta had no way of knowing what her fate would be, the package she so desperately wanted us to discover led to justice for Shay, Sal's family, and ultimately for herself.

Despite all that information, Nicoletta had not mentioned a single word about her husband. No evidence pointing to Stefano's financial crimes. No explanation of why she left him. No indication she was happy or unhappy or frightened or madly in love with the guy.

It was like Stefano Vanzetti never existed.

GLITCH—EVELYN

Stefano was dead.

Leo and I were the last to see him before he disappeared with Mira in the helicopter. In my witness statement, I recounted his final moments and how I witnessed the medical staff performing CPR in a desperate attempt to save his life.

I described his gaping chest wound, his delirium, and how Mira had gone to extremes to save her boss—but her efforts were in vain.

While I had seen Stefano's ghost and knew he was no longer alive, I didn't mention that detail in my statement. Leo, however, backed up my claim and confirmed he had witnessed the same life-saving procedure and believed Stefano had not survived the gunshot wound.

Based on our testimony, Stefano Vanzetti was classified as dead.

Leo had healed from his injuries, and I had thrown myself into my work. I was reeling from what I had witnessed when Stefano and Nicoletta had been reunited.

Seeing them together was pure bliss. The love they shared

in this life had carried over into the next. It was beautiful, awe-inspiring, and euphoric—until the reunion turned tragic.

Nicoletta had moved on to the other side without Stefano.

I waited for Stefano's ghost to visit my dreams. Every night I'd light a candle and ask him to visit me so I could help him. If anyone on this earth could figure out how to contact me, it was him.

But Stefano never came. The idea that he was a restless spirit filled me with dread. All I wanted was for him to contact me so I could help him find peace.

While I was grateful that Leo and I had survived the ordeal, Nicoletta and Shay had found justice from beyond the grave, and Mira had escaped the mob's wrath, I was angry Stefano hadn't survived.

I channeled my rage and funneled it through my art.

THREE MONTHS LATER...

The gallery buzzed with excitement as our charity auction was about to begin. Leo and I held hands as we mingled with our guests and sipped champagne.

"This is your best collection to date. You're going to raise a fortune for Nicoletta's charity tonight." Leo squeezed my hand supportively.

"I hope you're right. The auction pieces are a tad edgy for the masses, but hopefully my rebellious subjects will find the perfect buyer."

"Evelyn, are you ready to begin?" my gallery manager, Gibson, asked. She was rocking a black leather suit, mile-high red stilettoes, and a string of black pearls. After a thumbs up, the house lights dimmed, and Gibson stepped into the spotlight.

"Welcome friends and patrons. Tonight's charity auction will be donated to the Nicoletta Vanzetti Foundation. One hundred percent of the money raised will benefit hospitalized children and their families while they receive life-saving medical care."

Gibson thanked our sponsors and explained the rules of the auction. "All bidding takes place through the app and will close in one hour. Bidders are present here in the gallery and internationally via the online auction site. We have a monitor to the right of the stage so you can watch the bids rolling in."

Gibson directed her attention to me. "Please welcome our gallery owner and resident artist, Miss Evelyn Sinclair."

I stepped onto the stage and smiled at my supportive boyfriend and all our family and friends gathered around the stage. Silvia, Parker, Santoni, Tess, and the rest of our friends and family were there to support me. I lifted the microphone and addressed the crowd.

"A thin blue veil separates this life from the next. For some, the transition to eternal bliss comes easy. While others have unfinished business that holds them back from crossing over. It is my pleasure to introduce my latest collection, *Locked Out of Heaven.*"

The crowd applauded as I stepped off the stage. Leo greeted me with a bittersweet hug. "I know you feel bad for Stefano, sweetheart. If his ghost is still out there, he'll find you when he's ready."

Tears welled in my eyes as a fresh round of frustration overcame me. *Dammit, Stefano. Why won't you let me help you?"*

Our guests oohed and aahed at the disturbing yet thought-provoking paintings that shared a common theme: A recently departed soul standing before the tunnel, and an army of beautiful angels, blocking the entrance.

"The bidding has now begun!" Gibson announced. The monitor displayed the bids, while our guests enjoyed their drinks and periodically cheered as the numbers increased over the next hour. While I had a moment before the auction closed, I took Leo's hand and led him upstairs to my studio.

I guided him to my lounge area and lit a white candle on my coffee table. "It ends tonight," I said. "I've done everything in my power to help Stefano, but I have to let go and focus on the most important person in my life—*you*."

Leo pulled me into his embrace and kissed my lips. "I love you, Evelyn. You know I'll always support you. I got a couple of personal days coming up, and I want to take you somewhere nice—just the two of us. I'm thinking somewhere *dry* without a lot of water around."

I cracked up at Leo's sense of humor. "Sounds romantic. Let's find a cozy patch of desert somewhere and hole up in a hot tent for a few days."

I returned my attention to the flickering flame as I prepared to say goodbye to Stefano and close that chapter of our lives. After Leo and I had survived our ordeal with the mob, we were closer than ever.

Our relationship was the most important part of my life, and I needed to refocus my energy to find happiness instead of focusing on things I had no control over.

Someone knocked on my studio door. "Hey, Evelyn," Gibson called out. "The auction ends in two minutes!"

I thanked Gibson and told her we were on our way.

"Let's do it together." I held Leo's hand and pointed to the candle.

We leaned over and blew out the flame.

Goodbye, Stefano.

Leo and I hustled downstairs just as the timer ticked down. Our friends gathered around as we watched the monitor as the last bids came rolling in. Each painting was in the upward five-figure range as I had hoped for.

A few seconds left.

Three...two...one...

When the final numbers on all three paintings locked on the screen, I was sure the app had experienced a glitch.

SOLD: $1,000,000

SOLD: $1,000,000

SOLD: $1,000,000

There was no way each piece had sold for the maximum bid amount. While Gibson scrambled to find out what happened, the answer became clear when I noticed the winning bidder's username: Fantasma_001

I jabbed Leo in the ribs to get his attention. "Look at the username," I whispered.

Leo and I exchanged knowing glances as we came to the same conclusion—Stefano Vanzetti was alive.

EPILOGUE

My toes sank into the white sandy beach as I carried my supplies to the boat. I packed a cooler for two with a selection of meats, cheeses, fruits, and coconut shrimp—a Cayman Islands delicacy.

I loaded the boat, rubbed sunscreen over my body, and set out my "Open for Business" sign on the dock. Now all I had to do was wait for my first customer. I turned on some upbeat music and popped the top off a couple of Caybrews and passed one to my dear friend. "To you, Mira."

"It's *Monica*," she corrected.

I lifted my bottle in salute then took a long swig of the local beer as I soaked in the sun. Mira—*Monica*—insisted I keep a low profile and always wear a shirt to cover the scar on my chest. If I wanted a fresh start, I needed to remain dead to the world.

My loyal friend had gone to great lengths to save my life and get me out of the country. It was the least I could do to ease her mind.

The boat rocked as a warm breeze blew through my hair. I was grateful to have my second chance at life, and this time around, I would find a way to make up for the sins of my past.

A reminder alert buzzed on my phone.

I pulled out my cell and created an account for the online bidding system.

I scanned the list of auction items, and once again, my dear friend had taken my breath away.

Locked Out of Heaven by Evelyn Sinclair

Three paintings.

Three opportunities to support Nicoletta's charity.

One chance to send a message to Evelyn.

"What are you up to, Stefano?" Monica checked over my shoulder to see what I was doing.

"Sorry, I don't know anybody by that name." I focused on my task and watched the numbers increase as buyers world-wide hoped to earn the coveted spot as the highest bidder. I waited to enter my bid so as not to ruin the surprise.

As the hour passed, seagulls circled the boat, hoping to snatch a bite of our lunch if we let our guard down. The island life was laid-back, and it was never the wrong time to have a drink, nap, or lay around and do absolutely nothing.

This was a dramatic change from my previous life, and I hadn't yet become accustomed to becoming Mr. Roman Santiago. In time, I would settle into my new world. I had an unlimited supply of money—thanks to my offshore accounts where I had strategically hidden my fortune.

The Money Don planned ahead.

I had my bodyguard and loyal friend *Monica* with me to help keep me safe, and I wanted to use my wealth for good in my new world. My reign as the Don of the financial side of the Chicago mob was over. One day, the opportunity to make amends would find me.

For now, I was the humble captain of my own charter boat. Available for sightseeing tours and day trips to the island's best snorkeling spots and the world-famous Stingray City.

If I learned anything from my dear friend Evelyn, it was that the universe works in mysterious ways. All I had to do was open myself up to the possibilities.

The timer on the auction ticked down to two minutes—*almost time*. I set my bids on all three paintings and held my breath as the seconds ticked away.

Ten, nine, eight...

I tapped the button and placed my bids.

"Congratulations! You are the high bidder." The message flashed three times across the screen.

I laughed as I imagined Evelyn and Leo's surprise when they saw my username. Monica would lose her mind if she knew my plan, but I owed it to Evelyn to let her know she was right—it wasn't my time to go.

I pulled Nicoletta's charm bracelet from my pocket and held it in the sunlight. The cheap metal trinket sparkled in the sun like diamonds. I leaned over the side of the boat and dropped the bracelet into the clear blue water.

Now that Nicoletta and I had moved on to new adventures, it was time to say goodbye.

Until we were reunited on the other side—*again*.

READY FOR ANOTHER CASE?

Evelyn & Leo face their most dangerous threat yet in Drawn to the Past.

Secrets. Lies. And a past he can't remember.
Read Drawn to the Past Now

PREVIEW OF DRAWN
TO THE PAST

Sloane Mathews

No one will miss me if I slip away for an hour.

All my friends were at the bonfire tonight for the annual Halloween bash, and I was dressed up in my Little Red Riding Hood costume for the occasion.

I lived for the spooky season and embraced the pumpkin-spiced lattes, ghostly goodies, witchy black cats, and all the fall fetishes celebrated this time of year.

The perfect excuse to cosplay with my fairytale-obsessed boyfriend.

He wanted to keep our relationship a secret, so we made plans to meet in a remote location not far from the party. I took a few sips of warm beer from my plastic cup to appear social, but butterflies of excitement fluttered in my stomach in anticipation of seeing him—Professor Bradford.

"Hey, Sloane," my roommate Lindsey hollered from the other side of the fire. "Cute costume!"

I twirled around in my red cloak and thanked her with a thumbs-up and a smile.

While my friends were rocking out to "Monster Mash," snuggling to keep warm next to the bonfire, and swapping horror stories about the fall semester, my thoughts kept circling back to my sexy and brilliant literature professor—the man I was madly in love with.

I made my rounds and chatted with my friends before heading to the nature path that would lead me to Mr. Nolan Bradford—the tenured professor. The crisp fall leaves crunched under my patent black shoes as I strolled through the woods to our secret meeting spot.

I smiled at the memory of our first meeting. We had an appointment to go over a critical essay on Romeo and Juliet that I'd bombed, and from the moment I walked into his office and sat on the edge of his desk, I knew by the way he focused all his attention on me that the attraction was mutual.

His intelligent brown eyes lit up when I complimented him on his whimsical socks. I noticed everything about my handsome professor, including the alligator design peeking out from under the hem of his dress pants.

"I love golf. My wife got these for me after a trip to Florida last summer."

So, the only bad thing about my boyfriend—he was married.

Once I trekked down the path and the bonfire was out of sight, I used the flashlight on my phone to guide me to our secret location. Nolan wanted to meet me on a deserted back road where no one from the party would find out about our affair.

As the music from the party and the collective buzz of people talking died down, I felt nervous about being alone in the middle of the woods on the outskirts of the city. I was, after all, from a small town where we never worried about locking our doors in the evening.

Chicago, however, was a dangerous place to roam around alone at night. I worried I might cross paths with a meth head or a psycho maniac just waiting for a dumbass freshman to trek through the freaking wilderness by herself to hook up with her married boyfriend.

But he won't be married for much longer.

Nolan and I were in love—no more secrets and lies. I was tired of sharing with another woman and wanted him all to myself. A few nights ago, after we made love in his car, I gave Nolan an ultimatum—her or me.

Tonight, I would find out his answer.

I gave him my virginity, my love, all my attention and adoration, but in the past, he'd refused to leave his wife, Cora. Nolan said he'd tried to divorce her for years, but their marriage was complicated.

I was almost at the end of the trail when I spotted Nolan's car on the side of the road. I knew it was him because I could see the fuzzy dice dangling from the rearview mirror.

I knew that Nolan would make up his mind—he'd choose me.

I smoothed my hair back, applied a fresh layer of cherry-flavored Chapstick to my lips, and inhaled a deep breath to calm the butterflies.

From that night on, I could tell the world that I, Sloane Matthews, was Professor Nolan Bradford's girlfriend. I would take him back to my hometown to meet my family over Thanksgiving break and introduce him to all my friends.

All the boys who never looked at me twice in high school would regret it when they saw me snuggled in the arms of my brilliant and handsome professor. And the prissy girls who treated me like a nobody would see—

Snap! Snap! Snap!

There was a shuffling sound in the woods a few feet away from the path. I used the light on my phone to search for signs of life.

"Nolan?"

I held my breath and listened for a reply.

Nothing.

Maybe it was a squirrel or a nocturnal animal scurrying around in the woods. I stayed on the path and aimed the light on the trail as I walked, careful not to trip over the slick rocks along the way.

I stopped when I noticed something shiny on the trail ahead. *Oh, my God.* I cracked up when I spotted a handful of condoms glistening like golden foil breadcrumbs leading me to our rendezvous point. It was the same brand Nolan used, so I knew it was him playing a game.

"Hilarious, Nolan. You can come out now. I'm getting a little spooked out here." I waited a moment, but he never responded. "Nolan?"

No response.

I kept walking and came across a pair of lacy black panties—they were mine. Nolan had removed them with his teeth the last time we'd made love. The professor had his share of kinks and fetishes and loved to explore the Dom side of his otherwise meek personality.

He liked to play rough and seduced me with a combination of pleasure and pain. I wanted to please him, but I was more into cuddling in a soft bed with pillows over bondage and spanking.

As I continued down the trail, I spotted a black carnation on the path, along with a photograph attached to the stem with a red ribbon. The picture was of Nolan and me having sex in his car.

What the hell? We were alone then, which meant Nolan

had planted a camera in his Volvo and had taken pictures without my consent. Maybe this was his strange way of apologizing to me.

Nolan and I had a lovers' quarrel on the night I'd given him the ultimatum. I was tired of sneaking around and wanted our relationship to go public, so I told Nolan he had to make a choice. If he was only interested in smutty sex, then I was out.

We argued about it, but I stood my ground. I hoped a few days apart would smooth things over. The thing that bothered me, though, was that right after our fight, someone sent a weird package to me.

It had about twenty photos of me at various locations on campus. A picture of me at the library, one at the dining hall, and another of me hanging out with friends in the common area.

Inside the package, there was also a receipt from a restaurant I had tossed in the garbage, a ticket stub from a football game I had attended, and a scrunchy I had misplaced after Nolan and I hooked up in his office after hours.

It didn't come with a note or anything, so I figured someone was playing a prank on me, but now that I found this random stuff here, in the woods where Nolan had said to meet him, I wondered if this was Nolan's kinky way of apologizing to me after our fight.

Where are you, Nolan?

I checked my phone for a message from him.

Nothing.

Nolan probably had his phone off. He was like that. The geeky guy who preferred to live in the moment and absorb his surroundings over clicking and scrolling mindlessly on his phone.

Snap! Snap! Snap!

Footsteps pounded toward me.

"Who's there?" I searched the woods to see who was charging toward me, but I became disoriented in the darkness. Instead of waiting for someone to ambush me, I hoofed it toward Nolan's car.

As I fled, I tripped over a branch and landed hard on my knee, ripping my white tights. I shined the light on my injury and felt nauseous when I saw a deep gash and blood oozing down my leg.

Mud and bits of leaves stuck to my skin, and I worried it would get infected with all that dirt caked in the wound. I could go to the campus clinic later. My bigger problem was limping out of the woods and reaching Nolan's car.

Pull yourself together, Sloane. This place was crawling with woodland creatures. The noise came from a squirrel or an opossum or a raccoon—

"Wither away so early, Little Red Riding Hood?" A voice called through the darkness.

I was frightened at first, but sighed in relief, knowing my boyfriend was the only nerd in the woods quoting the Brothers Grimm tonight. "Nolan, where are you? I need your help. I tripped over a branch. I'm bleeding."

I aimed my phone at the sound of his voice. "Honey? Is that you?" I shined the light into the darkness. Someone was there, standing in the woods, wearing a wolf mask. As I stared at the figure, neither one of us moved.

It had to be Nolan dressed as my counterpart, the Big Bad Wolf, but why then did I feel a deep sense of dread?

This felt wrong. I knew I made a mistake and needed to get back to the party. Slowly, I backed away, but as I retreated, the wolf pursued me.

I quickened my pace, but my leg was stiff and sore from the injury, and I couldn't break into a run. As I limped down the path, footsteps pounded behind me on the trail.

"Get away from me! Help!"

Wham!

A heavy body slammed into me with the force of a truck and knocked me off my feet. When my head hit the ground, the force of the blow nearly knocked me unconscious.

As I lay there, stunned, my attacker grabbed my ankles and dragged me through the woods off the beaten path. My Little Red Riding Hood costume rode up my back, and my bare skin scraped against the rocks and leaves and sticks that covered the earth.

I struggled against my attacker, but I was disoriented from my head injury and couldn't find the strength to free myself. I cried out for my friends, hoping someone could hear me back at the bonfire, but in the recesses of my mind, I knew I had strayed too far from the path.

Under the moonlit sky, I stared in horror as light reflected off the blade of an axe. Overcome with fear, I clawed at the dirt and kicked to slow my attacker down, but I was too weak from my injury to struggle free from my captor.

"Who are you? What do you want from me?"

My attacker answered my question by sliding off the mask.

Oh, God. No, no, no... A rush of fear and anger overcame me when I knew beyond doubt the identity of my attacker.

The wolf raised the axe above my head.

As the blade came down, I cursed my killer's name and vowed that my spirit would not leave this earth until I had my revenge.

Continue reading *Drawn to the Past* Now.

ABOUT THE AUTHOR

Kat Shehata is a New York Times bestselling author—with the help of a psychic.

After teaming up with world-renowned psychic Sylvia Browne, Kat co-wrote and published *Animals on the Other Side*, which became a New York Times bestseller.

Kat's writing career took a romantic turn when a story about a homicide detective and a woman who knows too much refused to let go. That story became the *Drawn to Death* series—gripping romantic suspense novels that blend murder investigations with high-stakes emotional tension.

Her work has earned two Benjamin Franklin Awards and the Killer Nashville Claymore Award for Best Suspense.

Kat holds a bachelor's degree in theatre from Wilmington College, a professional writing certificate from the University of Cincinnati, and an MFA in Writing from Spalding University. She splits her time between Cincinnati, Ohio, and Boca Raton, Florida, where she is always working on her next story.

ACKNOWLEDGMENTS

As with any book, there are so many people to thank. The first round of book love goes to my incredibly supportive husband. Working out the world and characters for this story has consumed my thoughts and energy while writing.He has read many drafts and versions of this story and always delivered constructive feedback to help me work through the process.

We have taken weekend trips to Chicago so I could live in Evelyn and Leo's world and absorb the energy of the Windy City. He even ordered a healthy green smoothie at the coffee shop while I had my usual cappuccino so I could have an authentic Evelyn and Leo experience. I am blessed to have this wonderful man in my life.

High-fives to my kids for always believing in me and supporting my dreams. Fist-bumps to my friends who are especially eager to read the steamy scenes of my books and grill me about all the delicious details. *There's a lot to talk about in this book, right?* Thanks to my editor Deborah for helping my story reach its greatest potential as well as the behind-the-scenes experts crucial to my team.

Most of all, I want to thank the readers! I have an artist's soul, and the most important part of my career is delivering books readers will love. Bloggers, reviewers, and readers, I appreciate your support more than words can express—group hugs to all the book lovers who support my writer's journey.

Being an author is the best job in the world, and I enjoy interacting with readers on social media. Let's connect! www.katshehata.com

ALSO BY KAT SHEHATA

Drawn to Death

Drawn to the Mafia

Drawn to the Past